THE SHELTER OF EACH OTHER

The Shelter *of* Each Other

MILREE LATIMER

LUMINARE PRESS

WWW.LUMINAREPRESS.COM

The Shelter of Each Other
Copyright © 2023 by Milree Latimer

Printed in the United States of America

Luminare Press
442 Charnelton St.
Eugene, OR 97401
www.luminarepress.com

LCCN: 2023906922
ISBN: 979-8-88679-259-1

For my sister Isabelle
and her gift of family…1933–2016

ALSO BY MILREE LATIMER
Those We Left Behind
Out of Place

"There are only two ways to live your life.
One is as though nothing is a miracle.
The other is as though everything is a miracle."

—Albert Einstein

Chapter One

June 3, 1944

MARGARET GRACE PACED THE TOTAL PERIMETER OF HER front porch, gaining speed at each corner. She knew that Bill wouldn't arrive any sooner if she galloped. Patience was not one of Meg's virtues.

Here, on this new front porch of her old house at Broadview Farm, she paced along from front to back, never letting up her step. Old dusty boxes hauled from the subbasement under the kitchen sat on the back porch. She rushed by them, trying to shut her eyes to what she'd discovered this morning: letters, papers stuffed in piles, some tied together with string, a few still in their opened envelopes, each piece shattering her past and shutting down the joy of seeing her old home gradually transforming into a new place.

The old farmhouse was becoming a shining new house, by virtue of her doggedness, from shingled roof to concrete basement. Having taken on a monumental endeavor in wartime when many civilians were hunkering down, she'd decided to create a home for herself from the shell of the farmhouse in which she'd grown up and to make this renovation part of her war effort. She'd organized a salvage committee among her neighbors and loaded her pickup truck with scrap from the old farmhouse, then taken it to a local war services collection area. This was who the self-possessed woman Meg was or had been. She was an independent, forward-thinking woman, who seemed not to understand the meaning of "I can't," or "Some things won't be changed." Until the day the workmen, when finishing the kitchen floor, found boxes under the old planks.

Meg's life changed the moment those boxes were unearthed.

Renovating her childhood home had brought her moments of delight and hours of frustration. A new shingled roof, up-to-date yellow clapboard siding, a red door, an Old House becoming New. Done. Finished. Rebuilding the old house held a sense of moving into a new place in her life. Here, on the cusp of her thirtieth year.

Meg's yearnings for home, her own home, had been realized throughout the last few months, when she'd visited almost every day to watch the carpenters, the painters, the plumbers work their magic. So she'd tell them, urging them on.

But now, pacing around the porch, she felt bewildered and betrayed by what she'd found in the old, dusty, bent boxes.

Oh, yes. Meg needed her detective friend, Bill McBride, to come and help her understand the bombshell that had just landed on the doorstep of her life.

BILL MCBRIDE, SPEWING GRAVEL UNDER HIS CAR WHEELS, was on his way. He'd hung up the phone after she'd called, gotten into his Ford, and headed out to Rural Route Number Two, Murphy Road. He was familiar with the relentless Margaret Grace Blackwell, the woman who could annoy some people, inspire others, and who energized him. He believed he'd never have joined the town police force were it not for her constant urging, sometimes bordering on pestering. Margaret Grace, known as Meg to most people, was as proud of him as if he were her own son. But today he'd detected something in her voice on the phone that he hadn't heard often from her. Confusion. Humiliation.

Turning into her driveway, he remained perplexed by her insistence that he come out right away. "I need your help, Bill," she'd said on the phone. Was that break in her voice a sob?

The times were difficult, and Bill wondered if she'd had bad news about some of her one-time students. Many of the seniors in the class to whom she'd taught English at the local high school had signed up to serve in the armed forces. Three of Bill's friends were in Italy, one who'd lied about his age. If one of "her boys" had died overseas he knew it'd break her heart. Those students were her life, her family, just as Bill was.

Meg watched the dust rise at the far end of the lane, an announcement that Bill was arriving.

Meg, approaching her thirtieth birthday in a year, had decided there might be more to life than husband and children. The young men who might have courted her at one time were possibly threatened by her keen intellect, which she chose not to disguise. And her desire to challenge herself drove the last suitor out the door. She was building a desk for her new office in her renovated home. When Bill had asked if he could help her, she'd looked him in the eye and said, "Why would you?"

But what she'd loved most was teaching young students, watching them become who they could be in the world. Meg's passion was central in her classroom, instilling the love of story, the beauty of words, and opening students' minds to what lay beyond the walls of a school.

This was particularly true for young men like Bill McBride, who'd come from the village north of town where he'd only known poverty and, Meg suspected, abuse. Bill McBride was one of Meg's success stories. His prompt answer to her call on this day was not surprising.

Meg represented to him what family might feel like; Bill represented to her what it meant to care for someone.

Today, Bill pulled around the circular drive and stopped by the porch. Meg waved a welcome hello and stepped out to greet him. Bill's new red-and-white Ford coupe displayed the same dash and confidence that its owner showed as he skipped up the steps.

"Hello, Meg. Stay there. I'm coming to you."

She pulled up a chair and patted the cushion of the rocker beside her. "Here you go, Bill."

"Place is looking great. You've really given the old house a brand-new look." He waved his arms over his head like a real estate salesman in the middle of a spiel. "Love the yellow paint."

Meg's smile in return was brief, soon replaced with a flicker of sadness that dimmed her eyes to gray-blue.

"You okay, Meg?" He sat on the rocker and turned to her, reaching out a hand. She took it. This was a gesture unlike her usual tentative self when emotion was in the air, particularly one that might project neediness on her part.

"Not really, Bill. In fact, my life as I know it has just been turned on its head. Come on in the house. I want to show you something."

"Meg, what's going on?" Bill stopped her at the door. "You're pale. Did somebody die?" Bill knew that Meg was worried about her dad who'd been diagnosed with heart trouble, one of the reasons George and Edna had decided to move into town and give the farm over to Meg.

"Don't start asking me questions yet. Wait till you see what's inside."

Bill hadn't heard that sharpness in her tone for a long time. When Meg opened the screen door into the front hall, she stopped, and her head dropped. For a moment Bill thought she might be dizzy and reached for her arm.

"Do you need to sit down?"

"Bill, I don't need to sit down, but I want you to come with me out to the back veranda, so stop fussing over me." She stopped, folded her arms, and turned to him. Meg's mouth pulled into a tight grimace, she inhaled a long sigh through her teeth, and let her arms drop with a slap against her sides.

"Okay. I'm stopping right here. What the hell is going on?" Bill stalled in midstep as they approached the kitchen and ran his hand through his hair. "Tell me before we go any further. Is there someone out there, have you caught another vagrant on your property, should I go back to the car and get my gun?" A wry grin emphasized the line between his eyes. But Meg's eyes were blurred with tears.

"Oh. Oh, my gosh. What … oh I didn't mean, come, come sit." Bill pulled a chair from the kitchen table and, with his hands on Meg's shoulders, guided her onto the old armchair that had been her father's. Bill grabbed for the handkerchief that he'd earlier stuffed into his suit-jacket's breast pocket. When he handed it to her, she waved him away, wiped her cheek on the arm of her sweater, straightened her shoulders, and shook her head.

"No, I do appreciate your concern, Bill. I may not appear to, but I do." She beckoned to the chair opposite her. "Just sit down here for a moment."

Bill sat down and leaned over to her, elbows on his knees,

his chin resting on folded hands. "Okay, Meg? I'm here and I'm listening. Shoot."

A snow-white cat wandered across the kitchen floor, seemingly appearing from the air. With a proprietary nonchalance she jumped onto Meg's lap. She nuzzled her head into Meg's hand, a signal for a pat. Almost absent-mindedly, Meg began to scratch her head and looked over to Bill.

"You'll need to call on your best training to help me with what I'm about to show you, Bill. And no, it's not a body, but … I guess in a way you could say … it's several bodies."

They sat in the aftermath of her words, both letting the silence surround them. Only Scrabbles's purring cut the air.

She looked down at Scrabbles, and for a moment held her hand against the cat's sturdy back.

"I'm just saying, Bill, that I've discovered some things that are probably … no, definitely life-changing for me. Things that've left me wondering who the hell I am." She let a protesting Scrabbles drop from her lap and head for the door. Meg stood up, opened the back door to let her out, and beckoned to Bill.

"Come, come with me. You'll see what I mean."

Meg had been a woman who pushed away confusion. Her determination to live life "straight out," to override stumbling blocks, had gained her the reputation of that woman with the "spine of steel." She'd worked alongside her father, George, as a small girl, planting and harvesting, taking care of cows, milking them. The vegetable garden near the steps of the back porch flourished with her care and tending. Nothing seemed to daunt her. Almost nothing.

"That girl can do anything she puts her mind to," George told his neighbor Andy. "Sometimes I think she knows what to do before I even tell her."

She learned to drive the new tractor when George could no longer abide her pestering; Meg was ten years old when she set out across the field, driving as though she'd done it all her short life.

But early in her teens she knew being a farmer was not her life's purpose. Unlike some other girls in her high school class, she avoided what she considered a waste of time. Boys. Dances. Anything that deterred her from learning and observing the world. The problem for Meg was she saw beneath the world as it presented itself; she sensed there was more. What she intended to show Bill on this late afternoon was the evidence of how much more there might be beyond the real world. Packed in dust-covered boxes on the back-porch bench were letters that proved to Meg that her world was not and never had been true.

She picked up one of the letters and handed it to Bill.

He stood reading, then paused and looked over at her, his face a mask of puzzlement. "I don't understand. What is this?"

"Just keep on reading."

"It feels unreal to me, Bill, it feels like I'm Alice in Wonderland and I've just fallen down the rabbit hole. Everything—my whole life—is no longer what I thought it was."

"How can I help?" he asked and led her back into the house.

As Bill left, Meg stood on the steps of her front porch, her hand clamped on the rail, watching as the taillights of his Ford disappeared and he turned onto the main road. She lifted her hand in her familiar see-you-soon wave.

The sky to the west cast a golden hue across the horizon.

The golden hour, her mother, Edna, liked to call this time of day. The colors and the memory of sitting on the old porch with her mom caught a place in her chest like a half breath, a whisper of a lament. Rather than go back into the house, or worse, return to the back porch, Meg called to Scrabbles, that green-eyed, snow-white furball cat. She'd refused to call her Snowy or Snowflake or, God forbid, Whitely, as one of her students had suggested. Scrabbles suited her scrappy nature and her vagabond appearance.

"Scrab? Scrab? Scrabbles Blackwell, get your ass out from under that tree and come keep me company." With a rustle of long grass, a willow branch moved aside like a parting curtain, and a pure white, lanky, long, old Scrabbles emerged from her napping nest.

Meg sat on the porch and listened to the cows lowing in the back pasture and the crackling sound of the aspens in the breeze. Scrabbles climbed onto her lap and rested, curling into her welcome arms, and Meg felt the solid comfort of the house around her, just as Scrabbles nestled into the assurance of her lady's closeness.

The renovation of the old house was a rebirth of a collection of memories. Board by board, shingle by shingle, door by door, linoleum strip by linoleum strip, she'd watched her childhood home break into pieces, each taking a place in her body that recalled a day, an hour, a moment.

Coming down from her room in the loft to find a shining Heinzman piano sitting by the window in the parlor.

Playing Pachelbel's Canon in D.

Standing on the old ramshackle porch watching her mother and father climb into their Chrysler packed to the roof and follow the moving truck away and into town.

Her felt remembrances now were like broken mirrors,

shattered by the boxes of letters found under the kitchen floor when the carpenters had ripped it up.

On this summer morning, feeling an unusual sense of well-being, Meg had gone into the closet where she'd stowed three of the cardboard boxes, each labeled with George's scrawled printing: Letters, articles, photos. They were bent but sturdy, which told Meg someone cared about the contents. She had carried them to the back porch and had begun to slice at the tape. The first box she opened did not hold old family pictures. Oh, yes, there were pictures of strange and unfamiliar people, some in old First World War uniforms, but it was the letters that destroyed any lingering peace of mind. Fingering the paper, now fragile with age, Meg felt the life she'd known fading away like the vanishing ink on the page.

BILL HAD TAKEN TWO BOXES OF LETTERS WHEN HE'D left, saying, "I want to have a closer look, if that's okay with you, Meg." His businesslike manner brought some release from the shock that'd torn through her body and cut her breath off at the inhale.

Meg closed her eyes. "Who am I now?" she whispered into Scrabbles's ear, the one partially bitten by some unknown predator.

"Do you know?"

Scrabbles lifted her head as if she understood and stared up at Meg.

Meg reached down beside her and opened the box she'd kept when Bill left. An earlier first glance in this one had offered up revelations that Meg was not sure she wanted to share just yet, even with her trusted Bill.

Margaret Grace Blackwell discovered that her traditional restlessness and the hollowness she often felt were more than random reactions. A truth lay in this restlessness and her hesitation to trust.

She'd conveyed a sense of remoteness, as though her soul lived behind a glass wall. Finding these letters, seeing herself as possibly related to a past about which she knew nothing, she began to understand the distance she'd felt sometimes within her family—a distance that could be a self-fashioned solitude. A curtain of protection fashioned for reasons beyond her knowing. Her mother, Edna, had often said to George: "Our girl is a bit of a solitary soul. Maybe we should move into town, where she might have friends close by." Today, though, Meg did need someone to help sort through the maze she was experiencing, which was why she'd walked to the phone and called Bill McBride.

"I need your help," she'd said, no thought of calling anyone else occurring to her. In another time, only a short while ago, she'd have gone to her mother or her father with her painful news, but now they'd become parties to the rawness of her wound.

LIGHT FADED FROM THE SKY, LEAVING A DIM AFTERGLOW. Meg became a shadow there on the porch, the only sound the motion of the rocker. She folded her hands, calling forth a plea ... "Let this be just a bad dream. Or someone's imagination."

Later that evening, Meg sat in the living room under the standing lamp, its shade and light reaching down to her as though to comfort or illuminate the words on the page: words written by a woman she didn't know but who'd known her.

Meg folded her wool sweater across her shoulders. For a moment she paused.

The letter was written in now-faded ink, penmanship carefully fashioned as though the writer had taken pains to let her thoughts be seen. It was signed "Your loving sister, Bridget," and dated early September 1915.

Warren Hall, Gerald St.
City of Toronto

Dear George,

It seems sitting down to write to you is the wisest and the clearest way to explain what's happened. Jack had a serious fall down the stairs—he tripped and fell headlong. Why he didn't break his neck I'll never know.

I was packed, ready to leave, for good, before he had his fall. He couldn't be left on his own because it really shook him up. Dr. Winslow came over when I called him. Nothing was broken, he's a tough old bird, but he was bruised. His body and his ego. For which now I care little.

I'm in a predicament. Well, actually, it's more than a predicament. There's more to this story to explain but I'd rather do that face-to-face with you.

I've left home. Some of my reasons I believe you'll already know, but the final straw, the shattering moments, I'll save to tell another time.

Jack and I reached the end of our relationship the night he had the fall. I want nothing more to do with him.

I've a job at a munitions factory outside the city

on the east side—that's why I was packed and ready to go that night. Something's happened that's pushed me and, yes, Jack into the abyss.

Mrs. Lowell, remember the neighbor across the street, the widow who knows everything about everyone? She's going to watch out for Jack for a while, take him meals, and the doctor will check in on him. That's all I can or am willing to do.

If my words somehow don't make sense, forgive me. Luckily, I've discovered friends here who are willing to help me as I work through what I need to do next.

I tried several times to convince him I needed to be out and away and on my own, but he'd have none of it. He convinced himself I'd never survive, I believe for his own warped purposes. Over the past year he's become more possessive and possessed about knowing my whereabouts, who I'm seeing, even questioning why I need to leave the house. My decision to leave has been coming for a while, maybe even years. He even locked me in my room once, can you believe?

He's never said aloud that I'm the one who's helped increase his business, never said thank you for the furniture designs I created, or acknowledged me at all. I've written all the copy for the descriptions in the catalog and he takes the credit and the money. He's caught up in becoming wealthy and only sees me through his accumulation of money. This is a man whose view of the world is about how large his bank account is and who helps him do that, without being beholden to anyone, particularly me. I'm someone he must control in any way he can. There's more to that

Milree Latimer

story which you probably know better than I because you were there all those years watching how he broke Mom's spirit.

My resentment is hatred of who he is—an angry, dangerous man.

Our mother gave up a promising career as an artist. I don't know the whole story; but I do know he crushed her spirit.

I wish I'd had a chance to talk with her about why she let him do that, but I was too young to understand. I will always blame him for her death.

I ask nothing from him. Nor do I want anything. With my planning, putting away the pittance of what he paid me over the years, I have a bank account.

When you receive this letter, I'm hoping you'll write back to me. I'm going to need your help.

I may be asking you to take me in for a while.

With my fondest regards,
Bridget.

P.S. Remember, shortly after Mom died, we sat out on the porch one night, and we told each other if one of us needed the other, no matter the reason, we'd be there. This is one of those times, George.

Meg folded the worn letter, with slow and deliberate purpose. *Who was this woman, Bridget? Who was she? Why do I feel I know her? Who was Jack whom she hated so much?*

When she opened the envelope to replace the letter, she noticed a picture tucked in behind a small piece of paper. "August 1916, 7 mos." was written across the top of the paper in George's handwriting. *Margaret Grace is beautiful,*

Bridget, your daughter is beautiful. It was a picture of herself, a seven-month-old baby, possibly one George wanted to send to Bridget, but for some reason he hadn't. Meg realized she was staring down at a photo of herself, and the woman Bridget was her mother. Meg felt she was staring into a confusion of mirrors.

Part One

Chapter Two

1894

CLARA NICHOLSON HAD DREAMED OF BECOMING AN accomplished artist throughout her life. Left an orphan at twelve years old in England when her parents died of typhus, she was brought to Toronto in Canada by her Aunt Vivian, who took it upon herself to care for Clara as she might a daughter. Vivian encouraged her to flourish as a painter, finding teachers to mentor her growing talent. When Clara married her love, Steven, he too advanced her dream. Her world was then inhabited by people like her husband who believed in her talent, willing to support her and the two children he fathered.

Thus, Clara trusted in a benevolent world. She sought ways to open the door to her life's work where days could be devoted to the beauty she witnessed—the greens of new spring leaves, the warm blast of dazzling sunlight, the dark and the light blending like twilight as it moved across a sky.

Her dream was quashed when Steven died of a brain hemorrhage resulting from an accident while building a new Legislative Building in Toronto. As a builder, he was an artist in his own right and believed in Clara's genius, working extra hours at the site to be sure she could devote her days to her canvases. All that ended when falling stones struck his head as he climbed to walk a section of scaffolding. Clara's life disintegrated for a time at his death. Her heart broke in her losses, both her dear Steven and her art. She realized she'd have to give up her painting, as she was now a widow with two children and no apparent way to support them or herself.

Yet, life intervened in the person again of her Aunt Vivian, who rose to the moment, inviting Clara and her children to live in her spacious home on a tree-lined street in Toronto. "You and the children will stay with me until you get your feet under you, once again. You are a beautiful artist; the world is more beautiful seen through your eyes. You and I will find a way for you to keep painting."

Clara, who ached to be on her own, taking care of herself, her daughter, Bridget, and her son, George, knew she could only accept Aunt Vivian's generosity for a limited time. She needed to find other ways to support her family and to live the creative life crying out for light.

Two months after Steven's death, Aunt Vivian sat Clara down and said: "Just down the street from where we live is a Normal School for training teachers. Think about it, Clara. You could become a teacher, support yourself and your children, and continue your painting."

At first Clara was puzzled by her aunt's suggestion. "How could I continue my painting while I'm training to be a teacher?" It seemed that the two directions were miles apart.

Aunt Vivian smiled. "There are ways, Clara, to follow our passions. The building that houses the Normal School for teacher training also has a room for what is called the Society of Artists."

"Aunt Vivian, how do you know all this? Seems you have resources that I didn't know about."

"Just hang on. I'm well-known in this city for good works, particularly in the area of the arts. My husband, your Uncle Frank, when he died, left an endowment to the society to encourage young artists. The money provided funds for opening a small art school that was to be in the same building where teachers are trained. What I'm saying, Clara, is you could become a teacher and go to art school as well."

"Thank you, Aunt Vivian. Thank you, Uncle Frank!" With arms in the air, Clara flew to her aunt and encircled her in an embrace that could have crushed her. Aunt Vivian was the petite one in the family.

At this juncture in Clara's life, Aunt Vivian's offer shone light on her dreams to become an artist and on the future of her children.

"Clara, I took you and your children in as a gesture of kindness. My sister, your mother, would have expected no less of me. God bless her soul. You, Bridget, and George will stay while you attend school. Your children will be cared for and educated. And who knows what life has in store for you? Maybe someday I'll visit a showing of paintings by that famous Clara Nicholson."

"I hope you are right, Aunt Vivian. And I hope someday I'll be able to return such kindness to you."

Three weeks later, Clara enrolled in the city Normal School and signed in for classes at the Society for Artists.

CLARA STOOD AT THE DOOR OF THE ART CLASSROOM, her hand resting on the brass doorknob. Her painter's canvas carrier slung over her shoulder, she hesitated only a moment, then knocked.

A man flung open the door, his face at first tightened in irritation, but within seconds his eyes lit wide, and Clara felt an uneasy moment caught in his penetrating stare.

"Yes?" He stood hand on the edge of the door. He made no move to invite her in or to send her away. Only his stare remained constant.

Taking a breath, Clara shifted her carrier, extended her hand, and smiled.

"Mr. Blackwell, sir, would it be possible to speak with you?" Her voice, her being, expressed assurance. And for some reason that Clara did not understand, his demeanor shifted. The man standing before her became polite, almost courtly.

"Ah, yes, my dear, do come in." Clara wondered if he possibly knew about her connection with one of the benefactors of the society, her Uncle Frank, and saw her influence. And thus, the change in his welcome. But how would he know? He didn't know anything about her yet. Not even her name. Aunt Vivian had discovered that a man named Jack Blackwell taught this class.

Now, accepting his invitation, Clara walked into the studio where four women stood at easels, each engrossed in her canvas. Clara turned to Mr. Blackwell and looked directly at him, holding her gaze steady, her words flowing without hesitation.

"I'm attending teacher training, sir, just down the hall. I live with my aunt here in the city and she's encouraged me to come to this school for my training. I know that the Society of Artists and the art school are housed here. And, if I may be so bold, I've come, Mr. Blackwell, to ask if you will take me on as one of your art students. I've been told by some other artists that I'm a talented painter. Eventually

I hope to make it my life's work." Hands folded across her dress, she waited.

Poised and appearing confident, she walked toward him, reached out her hand once again. "My name is Clara Nicholson, Mr. Blackwell. I'm here because I wish to study with you and better my skills as an artist."

He held her hand for a moment longer than propriety allowed, but Clara let it rest there, a gesture worthy of note in this man's world, a woman signaling submission. For Jack Blackwell needed submission from women—a dark room in the deep places of his being.

Clara slowly withdrew her hand, still feeling she might be in charge of this moment. She knew that Mr. Blackwell was no longer a member of the Society of Artists, yet still mentored aspiring artists. His teaching methods continued to produce successful artists, which was one of the reasons the society kept him employed and a reason Aunt Vivian encouraged her to enroll in his class.

Breaking into the moment, Clara asserted her presence. "Mr. Blackwell, I have two canvases with me I'd like to show you, and if you see promise, and I believe you will, I'd like to begin tomorrow." Waiting for no further invitation, Clara drew two small canvases from her carrier and placed them on a table by Jack's side.

On this day as Clara presented her work to him, Jack Blackwell, who knew brilliance when he saw it, gazed at two paintings rendered by someone he knew immediately to be a natural artist. The simplicity of green field grasses moving in the wind created a sense of beauty in nature, the colors blending lush with life. He experienced a sense of immediacy, of being there standing knee-deep in the grasses, stillness portrayed on the canvas. Within minutes he knew that an extraordinary artist stood in his studio. His mind whirled with the possibilities of linking his fading reputation to her rising star. This woman's remarkable talent could be a path to the fame he craved. With a fawning flourish he led her across the room to a painter's stand where brushes and colors awaited her. Clara, not sure yet why she'd been so readily accepted, followed him.

"Come now, Miss Nicholson. Let me take your bag and shawl. I have a stand and a canvas by the window."

Throughout the next days, Jack Blackwell stood a seemly distance from Clara's left shoulder and watched her paint miracles, mesmerized by the lustrous color that flowed from her hand to her brush to the canvas. Unaware of his presence, Clara painted a scene, caught in a world of her own, creating images that emerged on the canvas from a place deep within herself. Color flowed from her brush fashioning a cerulean sky, under which waves of yellow grain moved in a summer breeze. A small child off in the distance, possibly the artist herself, was making her way through a wheat field, her long creamy skirt lifting and moving in wafts of air, with strokes of a brush. Jack wanted to place his hands on her shoulders, so he might feel the heat of inspiration, the energy of imagination.

Her brush paused and finished the stroke. When she stood back, away from the canvas, she appeared like someone awakening from a dream.

During the next few days, Jack became besotted by Clara's exotic beauty and dazed by her artistic gift, which seemed to flow from an ethereal place like a dream coming into view on the canvas. He, without conscience, saw within her a possible path to the acclaim he so sought.

The critics in the society had crushed him. "Your work is formulaic and pedantic," one critic had declared. "Our society encourages freshness and originality. Possibly another form of art might be more suitable to your craft. However, your teaching allows you to sustain your membership for now."

He wanted, no, *craved* a way to regain his reputation so stained by this society.

Clara was a woman not easily manipulated by Jack's charm, but she knew he could be someone from whom she might gain. She knew she was a much better artist than he was, and even though he'd lost his luster in the society, he still had ways and connections in the art world that might help her gain distinction. As Aunt Vivian had said, "You need to begin somewhere, Clara, and being there in the Ontario School of Art is a place to start."

He presented an opportunity, so Clara believed, to gain a foothold in the art world. Jack's bluster and his braggadocio about how one of his students outshone even the best of the other society members might give her the prestige she needed to break into their world. So she believed.

Jack began to work with Clara, encouraging and providing his best artistic knowledge to enhance her already rare gift. He wanted to be seen as her Svengali, taking credit for her possible meteoric rise in the art world in months to come. Clara in turn appreciated his business acumen and the connections he'd polished; however, Jack's need for domination held a shadow side.

Clara believed Jack inspired her, and he could become the path to recognition in the art world and beyond. Jack believed his control over her rise as an artist would guarantee his superior status in the art world.

Chapter Three

1895

CLARA THOUGHT JACK'S IDEA TO GO TO THE RIVER FOR A picnic was charming, although she wondered about spending time with him in such an informal manner. He'd asked if she might like to take a Sunday and make a picnic in his favorite countryside place, by a river. On the day he arrived to pick her up at Aunt Vivian's home, he was driving a horse and carriage that he'd hired. Clara felt rather splendid as they drove through the city, out into the landscape, one she hoped to capture with her paints during the afternoon.

They'd been working together for almost eight months, and with Jack's guidance sometimes a bit too controlling to her liking, her paintings were transcendent. He'd taken it upon himself to show them to three members of the society, one of whom was the woman who had described his work as "pedantic." Showing Clara's work had the effect he'd hoped for. Not only did they applaud her extraordinary talent, but they also lauded Jack for his discerning eye and fine mentoring. When they suggested she might join their group, of course in company with Jack, he'd taken great pleasure in saying, "Thank you, but Clara and I have decided to create our own artists' circle." Something about which Clara knew nothing.

Jack had other plans for himself. And for Clara.

On this afternoon, with the sun sparkling off the river, Clara took a cream-colored blanket from her picnic basket, leaned toward Jack, and beckoned, "Could you take an end please, Jack?" She'd begun to call him Jack since their work together took up most evenings. Her teaching practices filled her days, her painting the evenings. What Clara hoped for was to find a way she could support Bridget and George and spend her days painting. What Clara needed, she'd decided, was a patron.

"Jack, could you take the corner?" Clara said, once more. Jack seemed to drift into thoughts of his own.

"Jack?"

His shoulder brushed against the blouson sleeve of Clara's dress, and a sense, a warning signal, traced its way down her arm and into the palm of her hand. Not since Steve had her fingertips tingled. She felt nervous excitement mixed with an odd disquiet.

Moving away from him, she fluttered the blanket onto the grass.

Still, Jack remained standing. "Clara. Let's leave the lunch. For now. Come down by the river." For a moment a light breeze caught the tops of the grasses. The horse tethered to the log stirred and shook his mane.

With a slow movement, Jack took Clara's hand as they made their way down the grassy slope where a wooden bench sat under the overhang of the newly leafed branches of an elm, a place waiting for Clara's eye and brush. So she believed.

"Maybe we should bring our food down here, have our lunch," Clara said, stepping through the grasses, her hand still resting in Jack's.

"I was hoping we'd have a few moments to talk before we eat." He paused, brushed the twigs and dust from the bench, and offered a place to Clara. "I have something

I need to ask you, something that matters to me, a great deal." As they sat down on the bench, Jack looked out over the river and again seemed far away. Tucking her skirt under her, Clara sat, hands folded. A feeling of anticipation colored her cheeks…accompanied by an uneasy sense that Jack was looking quite serious…like a man who…Clara stopped her thought there and turned to him.

"Jack, before you ask your question of me, I need to say something. I'm afraid I've not been totally honest with you. As my teacher…I'm grateful for your guidance. As the friend you are becoming, I've not told you everything about myself." Looking down at her folded hands, she waited for what might be the end of their affiliation.

Jack shook his head from side to side, a smile forming at the corners of his mouth.

"Clara, I think I know what you are about to tell me. I've done some of my own sleuthing, as I'm sure you have about me. We both ultimately want the same thing — your successful art career." When he paused, Clara felt his eyes on her face, like a flashlight's beam searching out a dark space. She took a moment, swallowed, and returned his gaze. This was not a time to blink.

"How…how did you know? I gather you are talking about my children, Bridget and George."

"Yes, Clara, I am. And before we go further, I want you to know. I'm neither angry nor hurt. Well, possibly some hurt because you didn't trust to tell me everything."

"You haven't answered me."

"When we accept students, Clara, we are able to ask for their records. I've known for a while that you are a widow and that you have two children, Bridget and George."

Before Clara had any chance to respond or be affronted, Jack moved from the bench and kneeled before her.

"Whatever are you doing?"

"Clara Nicholson, will you marry me? Children and all."

She stared down at him. Her thoughts flashed—this could mean support for her children, it could mean she'd leave teaching and become the artist she yearned to be.... She hesitated. She'd witnessed Jack's temper with two of the other women in the class, a scene that caused the women to run from the room, one never returning. He'd not ever lose his temper with me, she thought, and looked down at him, still kneeling.

The new leaves of the elm began to sway with a sudden breeze announcing a coming storm.

Neither Clara nor Jack acknowledged the cooling air or the rising wind. Instead, Clara reached for Jack's hand. "Please, you look silly down there on your knee. Jack, you don't know me, nor do I know you. Yet I feel we have a bond, a creative bond. I need you to come to know my children. Bridget and George are the most important people in my life. George is seven years old— an active and single-minded boy who adored his father. Me remarrying could be hard for him. And Bridget. Oh, sweet little girl, only a baby when he died, never knew her father at all."

Clara looked out over the river, imagining the handsome young man she'd married. She'd been only seventeen when he'd courted her, and by her eighteenth birthday they'd married and she'd given birth to George. Memories of all that had been possible floated before her like the branches and twigs drifting in the river waters. "It all ended so soon," Clara whispered into the cooling air.

Jack, beside her on the bench, watched her eyes dimming, her arms folding across her body. He realized that he could be losing her to a memory, powerful as it was, and he needed to do something. His plan could die here under the elm.

But Jack knew what to do. With a soft touch, he cradled her chin and turned her face to him.

"Clara, if your children are anything like you, I will surely love them." He waited.

Clara whispered. "Oh, Jack. And they will love you."

Jack smiled.

Chapter Four

1902

THE BLACKWELL HOME STOOD WELL BACK FROM THE street. An imposing house. A place for Jack that symbolized success and for Clara, home. A grand house fashioned in gray stone, sheltered by a tall gabled roof; windows broad and long overlooked the gardens, front and back. A veranda welcomed visitors and important clients, might they choose to come to the Blackwell house for dinner, to be entertained in an understated yet splendid manner.

In the springtime, ceramic pots of hyacinths graced the steps, and in summer Clara brought out the hanging pots of red geraniums. She cared for the arrangement and the life of these flowers and her gardens as she might a landscape appearing on a canvas. She needed beauty around her to counter the melancholy that she felt at times, times that were becoming more frequent.

Inexplicably for Clara, Jack's attitude was shifting toward her growing success as an artist and the recognition she was receiving from the art world. He no longer commented on her paintings, except to criticize. "Your characters look very sad sometimes. Can you give them life, Clara? Maybe you need to try painting some happier people?"

Eventually, she gave up asking for his advice or his impression. And Jack's resentment heightened. His hope of becoming a noted painter and expert in the art world had been displaced in his eyes by Clara's increasingly shining reputation. The gall of rejection ached like a physical pain, one that felt years old, because, for Jack, rejection was a searing and ancient wound. He returned to hating the members of the society, who only saw him as a hanger-on to Clara's brilliance.

"I'll show those bastards." Resentment toward the society had become a poisonous bitterness, swirling like a whirlpool of acid in his stomach, and the public recognition of Clara's paintings only increased his rancor.

Jack had inherited his father's lumber and furniture design business, for which he had both shrewdness and craft. His skill as a craftsman, linked with his acute business mind, should have been enough for him to counter his jealousy at Clara's escalating distinction as an artist. It wasn't.

He knew in his depths that Clara's prominence was due not only to her skill and technique but her inborn artistry, and that she had long ago surpassed him as an artist. He'd grown to hate how naturally she placed color on a canvas, contrary to the delight he'd shown when he first watched her paint. He despised going to her showings and listening to people comment about how they saw and felt the vitality of life within her landscapes, how the stillness and clarity portrayed brought calm to their souls.

Initially, Jack had gloated over discovering Clara, and he gloried in the acclaim he felt standing in the reflected light of her gift. Students clamored to be part of the art classes she was teaching privately. But he was not a man able to sustain such admiration for a woman, particularly his own wife. Soon he stopped going to her showings, complaining about time spent "following her around."

Clara experienced the fallout of his rancor in quarrelsome ways, criticism of a detail in her work, arguments over her hours devoted to her painting.

"You spend more time working on your art than taking care of your family," Jack muttered one day when he arrived home to find Clara in the cabin-studio that he'd built for her; Bridget and George were in the kitchen frying eggs and bacon for supper.

"I have a showing at a local gallery in two weeks. I need to be ready because the owners of an art gallery in Toronto are coming. An artist friend has invited them." Clara was hesitant to tell Jack which gallery because the owners were members of the Society of Artists who had scorned him.

His eyes darkened and his mouth tightened. A showing at the Society of Artists was the undoing for this man battling the demons of jealousy, coveting the talents that had drawn Clara to him.

"This show will not take place." He spat the words at her. "This is wrong, just wrong. You are a mother and a wife—act like one." Jack threw the words over his shoulder, started to walk out but turned back. "And damn your friend. She has no right interfering in our lives." He left, slamming the door behind him.

Sophie Watson was this friend and a protector of Clara's. They'd met at the art school. Sophie, a known artist in the community and a mentor for young artists, had come into Jack's class one day, sent by the society to speak to the students about being mentored. Clara was enthralled and had gone after class to speak with her, a decision on Clara's part that would have dark ramifications for both women. Jack had stayed away that day.

After Jack's incomprehensible reaction to Clara's showing and his strange animosity toward Sophie, she decided to talk with the one person in the world who'd listen without judgment. She knew Aunt Vivian had willed her estate to her and to the children exclusive of Jack, a generous bequest that could ultimately give Clara and her children independence from his growing hostile behavior. Aunt Vivian had told Clara quite plainly, "This man will have no access to your heritage, nor the children's."

Three weeks after Jack's outburst Clara went to talk with her aunt.

"Aunt Vivian, Jack may be an angry, failed artist, but he's an extraordinary businessman. Why can't he be satisfied? He's increased his father's business tenfold; he's his own man. Yet his sense of failure is so bitter that he resents my successes—they're like a malicious poison to him."

Clara's words were like sparks flying haphazardly about the room.

As she sat grasping the teacup filled with soothing tea, she felt the heat of the sun's rays through the glass roof of her aunt's conservatory. The warm light played across her body, giving her moments of relief from an ongoing nagging pain in her belly.

Aunt Vivian watched and listened while Clara vented her frustrations. A discomforting thought occurred to her: Clara looked and sounded ill.

Clara had come to Toronto to visit one of the well-known galleries to discuss a possible showing. An extraordinary coup, precipitated by her aunt's contacts in the arts world and encouraged by Sophie Watson who'd become an art critic in Toronto. Both Aunt Vivian and Sophie believed Clara's talent to be extraordinary. Watching Clara gain distinction in her own town, Aunt Vivian and her friend Sophie had urged her to consider an exhibition at Toronto Art Gallery, owned and run by the Society of Artists. A distinguished salon that attracted international art critics and gallery owners. The very group that had denied Jack further membership.

The time had come, they believed, to show her work, work that some critics were describing as *impassioned and fresh*. But there was no joy in Clara today, only frustration. Aunt Vivian was perturbed by Clara's lack of joy in her paintings and, more than that, the dullness in her eyes and the gray pallor of her skin.

Vivian wondered if Jack might in fact be an abuser.

"Clara, you don't look at all well…are you working too hard? I know you are preparing for a show, and the possibility of an opening in the city is on the horizon. Maybe you could give yourself a few days' rest before we announce your dates. I'm sure Sophie would be fine with that."

"I think you're right, Aunt Vivian. I've begun having stomach pains almost every day. I went to see our neighbor Dr. Winslow. He thinks I might have an ulcer, a condition I don't understand, but he's given me a powder to take each night to calm my stomach."

"It's possible Sophie and I have placed too much pressure on you, asking you to consider having an exhibition here in Toronto. Maybe we need to ask the curator to move the date or postpone for a time."

Clara, alarmed by Aunt Vivian's suggestion, reacted with some heat. "Absolutely not. I will not postpone, if for no other reason than I'm sure Jack would be pleased if I had no showing at all."

A truer statement than Clara realized.

One week after her visit with Aunt Vivian, Clara prepared to leave her house for a final meeting with the owners of the gallery. Paintings were completed, ready to be transported. She'd dressed in her high-collared, starched blouse and her blue wool skirt, and, wanting to portray her artist's soul, sported a hat covered with yellow flowers. As she reached to open the door, the bell rang.

Opening the door, she was met by a messenger who smiled. "A message for you, ma'am, a letter from the City Gallery." In as long as it took to open the envelope and read the short note, Clara discovered that her exhibition due to open in a month had been canceled.

Sophie, Clara, and Aunt Vivian went to the gallery that day. Sophie exasperated, Vivian annoyed and ready to do battle, Clara still in pain, knowing in herself that Jack had something to do with this humiliation.

They pushed to inquire why she'd been canceled, but the young man only stammered and stumbled, never giving a reasonable answer.

But it was Sophie who asked the question, "Has Mr. Blackwell had a part in this?" Whereupon the young man asked the owner of the gallery to speak to them. The owner was the very woman who had given the final word on dismissing Jack from the Society of Artists.

"I'm very sorry, Mrs. Blackwell, but your husband came here threatening us if we didn't cancel your exhibition. Fearing what he might do, and fearing possibly for our own safety, we canceled. Mrs. Blackwell, your husband is a dangerous man."

Chapter Five

CLARA HAD BEEN LYING ON THE CHESTERFIELD BY THE fireplace in the kitchen most of the afternoon and into the evening, after coming home from the gallery—she couldn't decide which was more agonizing, the news that her opening had been canceled or the pain in her abdomen.

Jack, arriving home late as always, walked into the kitchen and seeing her there on the daybed, started to go by her with only a nod of his head.

Clara, who was seething, shouted, "Why are you doing this?" She sat up and thrust her arms toward Jack, her hands out, her eyes wide. "You canceled my showing. Why! And"—now, almost screaming—"you threatened them. Who are you? What kind of monster have you become?"

"Clara. Stop this, now. Calm yourself. You're hysterical. I just want the best for our family." Jack's voice was low, menacing. "You'll be disappointed and crushed when people begin to criticize you, and they will. I want to protect you from public censure."

He turned to walk up the back stairs to their bedroom. "I'll get your medicine. You need to calm down."

"No. You can't do this. You can't." Clara stood to confront him, but as she rose, her face contorted into a paroxysm of pain. She gasped and fell back to the sofa, sweat collecting on her forehead.

"There, you see, you're not well. I'm getting your medicine." His voice remained cold.

"Jack," she tried to stand but doubled over. "I need a doctor, get Dr. Winslow," she gasped. The pallor of Clara's skin had taken on a darker tint. Spittle and blood dribbled from her mouth. Leaning over, she grasped at her stomach and vomited. As she fell back onto the pillow a breath rattled deep in her throat. Her head dropped back. Her eyes stared out at nothing.

Expressionless, Jack looked down at her, walked to the phone, and called Dr. Winslow. He arrived within minutes of the call as if he'd been waiting for something sinister to happen in the Blackwell household.

"SHE WAS ALREADY GONE WHEN YOU CALLED ME, JACK. I'm sorry." Dr. Winslow stood looking down at Clara. "There was nothing we could have done. I think she'd begun to bleed internally."

George and Bridget stood frozen in the middle of the room. Brother and sister, pale with fright, clung to one another. Their stepfather, distancing himself, stood by the couch, staring down at the dead body of his wife.

"She must have been in terrible distress. Why didn't you come for me sooner, Jack? Do you know if she took the medication I prescribed for ulcers?"

He looked over to Jack, whose eyes were bright with unshed tears. Dr. Winslow walked to him and whispered, "Only an autopsy can tell what took her so swiftly."

Jack moved away from the children and raised his hand as though to stop the doctor's words. "There will be no autopsy. I will not have my wife's body violated."

"Jack, how can you not need to know what took Clara

so violently? What if it's some virulent germ, what about…"
He nodded his head toward George and Bridget.

"Dr. Winslow, this conversation in front of Bridget and George is inappropriate, please—follow through on whatever you need to do. Let this night be over."

A look of disbelief and horror crossed Fred Winslow's face. A man's wife had died less than an hour ago, and he, the doctor, was being dismissed. Jack stood at the open door, ushering him out. As he turned to leave, he looked back at George and Bridget, both sitting, silent. Still frozen in place.

"One more thing," he beckoned, wanting Jack to follow him away from George or Bridget's hearing.

Both men stood at the open door. "I'll need to send for the coroner." Jack started to shake his head. The final straw for the doctor. "No. You cannot refuse this. The coroner needs to pronounce." Irritation began to sharpen Fred Winslow's words. He leaned into Jack, turned his back to the children, and with scornful fury spat words at him, "Unless you need me to call the police."

Jack again raised his hand, and let it drop. "Dr. Winslow, I've just lost my wife, the children their mother, and you seem to be accusing me of some heinous act." In that moment, Fred Winslow saw something in Jack he'd not witnessed before. An icy coldness.

"All right, Jack, I'll leave you to your grief. I'll call the funeral home and the coroner. In the meantime, I'll see Mrs. Lowell and ask her to come. She knows…knew…Clara well and is a good neighbor." He pointed to Bridget and George. "They'll need comfort."

Dr. Winslow turned to George who was now holding his sister close, arms around her body. She'd begun to weep.

As the doctor left, he passed by Jack without a glance or a goodbye. He left like a man not yet finished with this.

Fifteen minutes later the front door opened, and a voice called from the hallway. Mrs. Lowell crept quietly toward the silence in the kitchen.

"Jack, George, Bridget, it's me, Mrs. Lowell. Dr. Fred just came to tell me. I came right over." As she came through the archway into the living room, she paused. Sadness, grief, pain, disbelief filled the room. Bridget left the sofa where she'd curled by George and ran to Mrs. Lowell, a neighbor who'd become like a second mother to her.

"Mama's gone. Mama's gone. She didn't even wait to say goodbye." Tears dripped from her chin, her tousled hair caught in the corner of her mouth.

Mrs. Lowell dropped to her knees, gathered Bridget into her arms, and wrapped her into her shawl. These were arms used to comforting her own grown family. Jack looked on, like someone watching strangers on a stage. George stood, walked to his sister, fell to the floor, and buried his face into her hair.

"I couldn't do anything Bridge. I'm so sorry. I couldn't do anything."

"Ah, sweet boy." Mrs. Lowell reached around Bridget and placed a hand on his back. "'Twasn't your fault. Turns out your mama was sicker than any of us knew. Maybe she didn't want us to know." She looked to Jack who was staring straight ahead, offering nothing.

Mrs. Lowell wondered at his appearance. Later she told her daughter, "I've never seen anyone so paralyzed; he was like a man in a daze."

Chapter Six

Sophie Watson wept.

Tears of frustration, tears wet with grief for the loss of her friend.

Sophie wept for the unrealized Clara Nicholson, the artist who brought grace and elegance into the art world. She wept for Clara's portrayals of life and nature, her feel on the canvas of what it is to be human, the joy and the pain. Now, she was gone.

Outside Sophie's window, her garden swept down to the river, a garden that Clara had captured in the painting hanging over the fireplace. Their friendship had blossomed in their mutual love of art and their care for one another, Clara entrusting her flourishing artistic talent to her mentor, Sophie, who'd taken Clara under her wing and had seen her decline over the past few months, both in body and in spirit.

Today, Sophie sat with Mrs. Lowell's letter spread out beside her. The day was fading: yellow, orange, and red painted a path across the sky over the lake. She imagined Clara laughing at the beauty and telling Sophie: "I'll hold those colors behind my eyes. When I go to my easel in the morning, those passionate reds and ruddy oranges will be at the end of my brushes." And Sophie knew with an assurance of the artist within herself that Clara would paint the sunset in glorious color.

Now the color was gone. From the sky, from the painting Clara might have created, and from a part of Sophie's life. She remembered the conversations she'd had with Clara, sitting here in the comfort of Sophie's back parlor. She'd known something was amiss. Sophie saw an aura of darkness surrounding Clara like a gray cloud. The tears were often just behind her eyes. On those days Sophie would reach for Clara's hand and lead her into the back parlor, her arm around her shoulders. Moments were silent, words left unsaid, only the comfort of human connection filled the room. Until, on one particular day, Clara had leaned over to Sophie and reached for her hand. They sat—two women, fingers entwined, one waiting, the other gathering her story to tell.

"Sophie, I've come to ask you for help." Clara sat, eyes gazing downward. Her hands, still gloved, now rested on the arms of the chair. Her back was straight, her feet together flat upon the floor.

Without pausing Sophie began to answer, "Oh, Clara, anything for you…"

"No, please. Wait. It's not for me. I need you to promise something that's more than about me and art shows or my painting. It's about Bridget."

Sophie leaned closer to her friend and took her hands. "I know what you are wanting to ask me, Clara, and the answer is absolutely yes."

"Wait. How can you know? I've only decided today. And all because of a quarrel with Jack. You and I haven't talked much over the past while except about my art and shows— how could you know something that I've only just come to recognize myself?"

"Do you mean what's happening between you and Jack? About your paintings?"

This friendship between Clara and Sophie had stayed constant throughout the years since art school, sometimes with very little personal contact between them, yet letters and Clara's occasional visits to the city to see her aunt and Sophie had kept their closeness alive. It was Sophie who set up an easel in her paint studio for Clara where she could paint freely without fear of interruption, or worse, critical comments from Jack.

It was Sophie who invited two friends who ran art galleries in the city to come see the oil portrait that Clara had created of her daughter, Bridget, sitting head down, a book in her lap. Some strands of hair fell across her face. The painting depicted a mother's love, so much so that even in her mind's eye Clara caught the essence of her young girl—the pensiveness, the absorption, and the pearl-like sheen of her skin.

It was Sophie who had brought Clara's talent to the attention and eyes of the Society of Artists—and it was Sophie who learned in horror that Jack Blackwell had dismantled Clara's future.

Clara, who knew her world was beginning to shatter, responded to Sophie's question about Jack with the passion of a protective mother. "Sophie, I need to ask you to watch over Bridget. Whatever may happen to me, I need to know she will be safe. I need to know you will find her when I'm no longer here." There it was for both to see and know. Clara, who was ill and afraid for her daughter, was looking to her friend Sophie to protect Bridget.

"And George?" Sophie asked.

"George is strong. He will leave, eventually. I can't ask him to take his sister with him. As his mother I know what he must do to save himself. He inherited the determined spirit of his father and has placed that energy into hating his stepfather."

THE FINAL CUT HAD BEEN JACK'S VINDICTIVENESS, dissolving her contract with the Society of Artists. Now, Sophie stood from the high-backed chair, the one where Clara had often sat, and walked to the desk that sat under the wide window overlooking the garden. There she opened the drop-down door and pulled out the drawer where she'd placed the envelope Clara had left in her care.

Dipping her pen into the ink bottle, she took two sheets of cream paper and, in her distinctive script, wrote to Mrs. Lowell. Her words flowed onto the page, just as her tears had coursed her cheeks only moments ago when she'd read the news of Clara's death. Moments passed. Sophie realized she'd stopped writing, the pen poised above the page.

A clear thought hung in the air. *I need to tell Mrs. Lowell my fears. I need her help. This time I won't let Clara down.* She would gather allies. Mrs. Lowell, Aunt Vivian.

Sophie wrote her letter, hoping against hope that her fears might be understood.

Dear Mrs. Lowell,

We've lost a dear and wonderful friend. You, her neighbor, I know have been a constant for Clara, someone she could rely on. She spoke of you often. Now I am writing to ask of you what she needed from me. Possibly you and I together could take on the mantle of protector. I'll explain.

I'm not sure how much you know about who Jack truly is...for reasons I'll tell you later, I'm fiercely afraid of him and of what he is capable. Without going into detail at this point, I know how relentless and vicious he can be.

Clara told me some of her experiences, and I feared for her—I'm sure he was abusive, more times than I knew, more times than she chose to tell me. She didn't use those words; however, the fact that he took away her passion for her art in such a brutal manner can only be seen as tyrannical. He is a man with no heart.

Why I'm writing to you today is all about a promise I made to Clara.

She asked me, shortly before she died, if I'd protect Bridget in any way I could—if I were able to get her out of that house now, I would—but she is under his guardianship, and I have no sound evidence to take him to the courts. And knowing how he manipulates and works the system, I'm sure he'd have the police on me, if not his goons, if I tried. Jack chose never to be involved in his own dirty work.

If you could just keep an eye on Bridget in any way you might, and I will try to stay in touch with you. George I know will leave as soon as he can. He's seventeen and I know from Clara how he despises his stepfather. I think he'll be gone...I'm sure there isn't a way I could persuade him to stay—in fact, it might be better if he goes. Clara intimated she thought he might try to kill Jack. I'll say no more now, except could you please let me know how Bridget is faring?

Sincerely,

Sophie Watson

With renewed resolve, she took the second sheet of writing paper, dipped her pen into the ink well, and wrote, each word a declaration.

Dear Vivian,

I can only imagine the depth of your sorrow at the loss of your beloved Clara. My heart is broken that my beautiful friend is gone. We share our shock and our despair.

The solace I have, and I hope it will be so for you, is as I look up from my desk, I see her astonishing, luminous painting of the night sky over the lake. I have Clara Nicholson in my study, in my living room, and in my kitchen. She laughed that I hung her brilliant colorful daffodils in my kitchen.

Now, Bridget and George have lost a loving mother. The world of art has lost a light.

Please know that Clara, when she visited the last time, gave me the information about your kindnesses, the resources she had available because of you, and a copy of her will, wise woman that she was.

When the time is right, I would like to visit with you and talk about Clara's wishes for both Bridget and George.

Yours in sympathy,
Sophie Watson

Chapter Seven

June 4, 1944

SLEEP WAS NOT POSSIBLE. MEG LAY WITH HER HEAD turned toward the window, where the moon illuminated the white hyacinths out in her garden. She lay like a child might, flannel blanket tucked under her chin.

Moments dragged by until she sat up, wrapped her mother's blue, knitted shawl around her shoulders, slipped on her fuzzy slippers, and padded down the stairs into the sitting room and over to the piano.

There on the bench lay the sheet music her dad always asked her to play for him when they'd sit together on the bench, Meg playing while George sang in his deep baritone voice. A song that was his favorite. And Edna's. Her dad and her mom, two people in a story that was no longer true.

Meg sat down, placed her fingers on the keys, and started to play. The words were on her lips for only a moment before tears blurred her vision.

"Oh, give me something to remember you by, when you are far away from me..." She lingered on the keys, letting the plaintive music wash over her.

Then.

Meg stopped playing.

The words *"something to remember you by"* now carried stinging thoughts of betrayal, disconnection. Her fingers slammed onto the keys, creating a cacophony of notes that mirrored the discord she felt. Margaret Grace Blackwell had learned, for reasons beyond her understanding, to quash anger, to put away grievances, but tonight her confusion boiled into an unfamiliar rage. She felt the room was closing in around her, tightening her chest.

"Why didn't you tell me?" she shouted at the picture of George and Edna that sat on the piano. In this moment she needed air, as though discovering that a woman named Bridget might be her mother...Bridget?..."I know that name," she whispered. A memory flashed: her bedroom, a woman...and it was gone.

Meg walked to the front coat closet, kicked off her slippers, and pulled on rubber boots, the ones she wore when she tromped out through the back fields, those very fields where her ten-year-old self drove the tractor and gathered in the sheep. A time that felt in this moment like a made-up story. Reaching for the knob, she opened the door and walked out into the night.

Hands shoved into the pockets of her jacket, she made her way around the house, through the gate, into the grassy field, a faint rustle behind her revealing Scrabbles taking up the rear.

To the east a murky pink edged the horizon. Meg felt the bitterness of George and Edna's dishonesty moving through and out of her body as she put one foot in front of the other.

Interesting, she thought, that as she walked through the grasses, she experienced what she might call—if Meg believed in such phenomenon—an epiphany. She remembered a conversation from several days ago, when the students in her senior English class began talking about disconnection, searching for a place of belonging. Shakespeare's play *As You Like It* had started the conversation. The war in Europe had heightened it.

Meg had stood still as they talked, giving them the space they needed to be courageous in their lives, there in that classroom, and to question aloud where they belonged in the midst of uncertainty.

Now, here she stood, in among the trees and the grasses, and she wondered—call it an epiphany if need be—if she could be on a path to discovering where she belonged, and someone called Bridget perhaps walking that same path, somewhere.

Part Two

"*I could stay, and search for what had been home,
or I could go, now, before the walls shifted
and the way out was shut.*"

—TARA WESTOVER, *Educated*

Chapter Eight

1908

Bridget lay across her bed, sobbing.

Angry words from the kitchen below pierced the floor like projectiles. Her stepfather's voice, charged with bitterness, sounded like a stranger who'd burst into the house. He shouted with a force that propelled words up the stairs and into her bedroom, loud enough that even burying her face into the pillow could not shut them out.

"You've been nothing but a disappointment. Your life is a failure. Your mother believed in you, and you broke her heart. I'm thankful she's not here to see how pitiful you are."

Another voice, tight with fury, rose above her stepfather's harangue. George, her brother, her hero, was on his way out the door. Leaving for good.

"Don't talk to me about failure. You have never, ever been my father nor a husband. I didn't break Mom's heart; you did that all on your own."

Bridget sat up from her bed and ran to the top of the back staircase, the stairs that she ran down each morning to make breakfast for Jack and her brother. This morning she stood at the top and screamed. Bridget Blackwell had never screamed with such fury in her life.

"Stop! Stop! Just stop!" Quiet like the eye of a hurricane rose from the kitchen. Someone scrambled to the bottom of the stairwell.

"Bridget. Come down. Your brother is packed and leaving us. See if you can talk some sense into him."

"Jack. Leave Bridget be, she's nothing to do with this or us." George moved from the outside door where he was standing, his hand clutching the doorknob. "Leave her be. Please."

For a moment all three stood anchored to their spots. Then Bridget moved.

Bridget started to walk down, step by careful step. She grasped the railing as she descended, placing each foot carefully on one step at a time. Still, no one spoke.

Reaching the bottom of the stairs her words burst into the air.

"Mama would be so unhappy if she heard the two of you. You know how she hated when people yelled at one another." Her words were a rasp, an attempt not to cry. When Jack walked to her, his hand outstretched, she waved him away. "No. I'm not the peacemaker. That was always Mama's job. I quit." Since Clara Blackwell's death, six years ago, a young Bridget had tried to take on the matriarch's role in the household. A swell of anger rose in her chest. Walking to George, her head down, she whispered between her teeth.

"Bridge, what'd you just say?" George watched while she came up to him.

"I said, damn the pair of you."

Bridget was right. Clara Blackwell, mother and wife, would have George and Jack sit down and stop their "nonsense." But Clara was no longer here, her presence only a crushed memory.

"Bridget Blackwell, where have you ever heard that kind of language?" Jack Blackwell needed to play "father" at this moment.

Bridget stood by her brother and slipped her hand into his. Without editing herself at all she lashed, "From Mama, Jack, from Mama, when she was angry with you. And with you, George."

"You would never hear your mother using that language. Never. She was a lady, unlike you right now, young woman." His tone was harsh, his eyes glittering. "I'll hear no more—I suggest you go straight back to your room."

George dropped Bridget's hand and spun on his heel away from the door toward Jack. For a moment Bridget believed he was about to strike the older man.

"Leave my sister alone. And! How dare you even talk about Ma…she was sick, sick and tired, and she died without telling any of us how ill she really was. And, Bridget," he turned toward her, "will have nightmares forever after seeing her mother in such pain. No child should ever witness that horror. So, don't you dare speak of her again. You didn't even care about her." His voice rose with rage.

"George." Bridget reached her hand to him, a hand that pleaded. But in that moment, with no warning, Jack raised an arm and struck George across the cheek. A sound that cut through the air like a gunshot.

"Jack, no!" Bridget ran to grab his arm. Any resemblance to family twisted into something none of them recognized. Jack in a fury thrust off Bridget's grasp, a jolt that sent her scudding across the tile floor to land with a thud against the wall where she lay fighting for breath.

Icy silence penetrated the room.

Bridget's brother stood at the door—an animal ready to lunge at his stepfather. George's eyes were coal black. A howl erupted from Jack as he sank to the floor, crawled to Bridget, and gathered her into his arms. He rocked her back and forth, fearful that he'd murdered her, witnessed by George.

"Bridget, Bridget, Bridget."

Her breath gradually slowed, her inhales deeper, her exhales stronger. She pushed him aside. By now, George was standing over the two of them, threatening to pull Jack to his feet and finish what he wanted to do. Beat the man into oblivion. Bridget raised her hand to stop him. She struggled out from under Jack, and with fire in her soul, stood up. Then, with unaccountable grace, she reached down to help Jack stand up.

No one spoke until Bridget. "I need to go tend to my arm. It's bleeding." Bridget moved toward the hallway leading down to the kitchen. She limped but gradually straightened her back. Jack started toward her, hand outstretched, his face filled with concern.

"No. George was right. I have no business here right now. Both of you. Deal with yourselves. I'm finished." Bridget's words were edged with finality.

George picked up his bag. Without a glance toward his stepfather, he walked to the front entrance and opened the door, where he paused, turned, and watched Bridget disappear into the kitchen. A shake of his head and he was gone.

Brother and sister, cut apart from one another, while Jack declared to anyone who'd listen that his stepson was dead to him forever.

Chapter Nine

May 1915

SEVEN YEARS SINCE GEORGE HAD DROPPED OUT OF SIGHT and Bridget had created a life here in her stepfather's house, a life where she'd locked away parts of herself. Oh, she could be polite. She listened to his stories of business conquests, his self-satisfaction about growing wealth.

Her heart ached whenever she thought of her mother and her beautiful paintings—scenes that once transported Bridget into magical worlds, all now gone, taken from the walls and stowed in the attic. Putting that pain away, she lived cut off from the deeper essence of herself, only rescued from despair by writing. Her years at school and then college became islands where she found her muse waiting, where stories became a connection with the world around her. She believed words were her paintings, gifts of grace received from her mother.

Writing and story were Bridget's escape from reality's wreckage. She found places—an old shed behind the house, where she'd manufactured a table from some broken furniture left there. It turned out that Bridget had discovered where her mother's desk had been left. Jack had disposed of most of Clara's belongings, including her worktables and her paint cupboards, but this table, broken as it was, gave Bridget a sense of connection to her mother and a place to be inspired. She kept notebooks out here, away from Jack's eyes. If he ever questioned her about where she'd gone after school, she was able to say, without misleading, that she was at home.

"You just didn't hear me, Jack," she'd say.

Stories came to Bridget like phantoms lodged in her brain. Some were fantastical, some were memories of a childhood that flashed in scenes—Clara running from their old house down the path to greet Bridget's father, home from a trip. Those scenes were the substance of stories that Bridget wrote, stories she kept locked away, to come back to maybe, she thought, someday to take out into the world.

Bridget saw elegance and beauty in words and in things of the world, just as Clara her mother had seen elegance and beauty in the green of a forest. Bridget's eye for beauty, which she'd inherited from Clara, saw possibility even in a piece of wood, probably far beyond anything that Jack could summon. Clara's ultimate trick on Jack was to have bequeathed her eye for natural beauty to her daughter. She'd have smiled upon her treasured girl's gifts.

On this day Bridget sat at a desk in the sitting room, one her stepfather had built and carved, the one on which he used the special screws he'd designed, special fasteners that he'd been selling to carpenters and builders—anyone interested in buying. These days his cabinet-making business was gaining repute throughout the area, so much so that he'd hired workers to take on the orders that were coming in faster than he could build. Yet the truth was that his growing success had much to do with Bridget, her eye for the unusual and the beautiful.

Jack Blackwell's profits were growing, and Bridget's designs were gaining repute among businessmen in the furniture world.

"Fine elegant furniture: Designed for Finer Homes and Businesses" was the sign on Jack's door in the office that overlooked the factory floor. He'd decided to teach Bridget the ways of business: how to sell an idea once it took form. As they worked together, he discovered her natural talents, a dexterity with her hands for building, an artistry with design, and her eloquence with written words. She'd become lead designer in Jack's business, a role she played willingly to carry on the memory of her mother, someone he wanted no part of remembering.

After Clara died, Jack had gone through the house and gathered up her paintings that graced the walls: the sunset she'd fashioned while she sat on the back porch; a sky whirling with clouds in the aftermath of a storm; the colors of the spring garden behind the house. He'd taken them all, wrapped them in brown paper, and carted each canvas up the narrow stairs to the attic, where they lay collecting dust on the wooden floor. He'd forbidden Bridget to go up, and he kept a lock on the door at the bottom of the stairs.

One painting lay wrapped in a blanket under Bridget's bed—one she'd rescued as her father strode around the house stripping the memory of his wife from the walls. The picture was an oil, thick with color and paint, a tall brave sunflower that was reaching up and beyond to the sky, one that stood on its own in the garden. Bridget loved that sunflower. It held for Bridget the essence of her mother's beauty and her struggle to reach toward the light.

Now she sat, a letter from George on the desk before her. One she had been hoping for. As she began to read, she felt a tightness in her throat.

Broadview Farm
May 1915

Dear Bridget,

This will be a short note. It's early morning and I have chores to get to very soon.

I wanted to be sure to tell you I've not ever stopped thinking about you. I'm giving you my address so you can write back to me, any time. I'm living here with a nice family who needed a farmhand to help run the place.

I'm sorry to have disappeared as I did. It took me a long time and many miles (I got as far as Newfoundland for a while) to come to terms with myself, feeling like a coward for leaving you, hating Jack so much, I had to get far away. Otherwise, I'd have come back to kill him.

Edna Murphy, and her sons, Harry and Edward, own the farm. John, her husband and their dad, contracted severe pneumonia last year, which took him very suddenly. It's a prosperous farm and needs an extra hand to help run it. Edna is a very able woman; however, there's a lot to be done every day. The boys help but they're still young.

I answered an ad in the Farmer's Almanac when I got back to Ontario for a man looking for a farm business opportunity. I hitchhiked on a wagon from the train station in Hamilton right to Milboro and from there, so I'd look respectable, I bought a horse and wagon and rode out to Broadview Farm. I bet you're smiling, because what do I know about farming? Well, I'm learning. Edna is a good teacher, as

are Harry and Edward. They have been taking care
of the farm since her husband died.
Right now, I need to go and help with the haying
and feed the pigs. Whole new life.
Bridge, if any time you're afraid of him, just go
over to Mrs. Lowell and call me on her phone. Here's
the number at the farm where I am, ML2-7708.
Don't think you have to stay there forever.

Always,
George

P.S. Don't be like me. Don't disappear on me.

Bridget went upstairs and tucked the letter into her bottom
dresser drawer under her slips and camisoles. The return
address on the envelope caused a smile to relax her face. It
was from *Miss Rachel Arnott, your pen pal. Broadview Farm,*
Wentworth County P.O. 42 Wentworth ON.

George hadn't wanted Bridget to have trouble with
Jack. So, he'd given a fictitious name and the address of the
farm. If perchance Jack discovered the letter and found
that her brother was writing to her, there'd be "hell to
pay." Bridget's words. There'd been other short letters from
George throughout the years, nothing that ever said what
he intended to do or where he was. At one time Bridget was
afraid she'd lost him forever. He'd been so angry when he
left—she wondered if he was cutting her out of his life. This
was the first letter where he seemed settled and willing to
tell her about his life. Bridget smiled to herself, so like her
brother to take all this time and finally confide in her. She
hoped he'd found a peaceful place in his life.

However, since he left, George's name had not crossed their stepfather's lips, nor was Bridget to speak of him. "He is no longer part of this family," Jack had pronounced the day after George left.

There, in the quiet of her room, George's letter resting in her hand, she made a promise.

"We will see one another again, George…he will never splinter us."

Chapter Ten

BRIDGET SAT WITH GEORGE'S LETTER AND TRACED HER fingers across the words she'd memorized: *Bridge, if any time you're afraid of him, just go over to Mrs. Lowell and call me on her phone. Here's the number at the farm where I am, ML2-7708.*

"Bridget. Bridget." Her stepfather's voice echoed up the stairwell. "The gentlemen are here from the city to look at the new designs. Need you to come and make tea and keep notes."

Her reply to George's letter would have to wait.

"These designs are quite original, Mr. Blackwell. Do you create your own?"

Out in the kitchen, Bridget poured the boiling water over the tea leaves in the blue and yellow pot, the one that had been her mother's favorite. While she poured, she listened to the conversation floating out from the parlor. "I did them for a time, Mr. Andrews, and when my wife was alive, she was the one who helped me." He paused. "My stepdaughter is my apprentice now."

Jack was astute at misleading others about how he and Clara had worked together. And, after she died he expanded his deceptions, continuing to accept congratulations for his designs when in fact Bridget's artistry and dexterity overshadowed anything he produced. Had it been George who proved to have such a talent, Jack might have, truth told, given credit where credit was due. Not so for Bridget. Not so for a girl, now a woman. Women had their place.

As she listened to him, Bridget waited to hear if he would acknowledge her, that the designs were hers, that the innovative artistry was hers. The curves and intricate lattice-backed chairs that shone to a mahogany patina were her creation and expressed her inner sense of beauty.

What she overheard was Jack's self-satisfaction. His words, "Bridget the apprentice," sat like gravel in her chest. She was tempted to walk into the room and spit out her truth: "I created those designs. I wrote those descriptions you read in the catalog. I'm no apprentice!"

Jack spoke of himself as a man ahead of his time, bringing a young woman into his business and teaching her everything he knew. He was her "Svengali," he'd say. Jack used the term, not knowing the nefarious nature of the word, but it was his practice to try to sound "worldly," only succeeding sometimes in making himself look ludicrous.

Listening to Jack fawning over these men, using her mother and herself as tokens of his success, Bridget felt a tight place in her back where resentment grasped at her, like a claw unsheathing its sharpness. Bridget felt invisible in his eyes, a tool for his own glorification.

She heard the gentlemen's puzzled tones when Jack mentioned that his stepdaughter was his apprentice. "Your stepdaughter, sir?" The voices carried tinges of disbelief. A woman? An apprentice in the furniture manufacturing business?

Irritation caught her breath while she piled the teacups onto the tray. Bridget rattled the cups as she pushed through the swinging door into the parlor. Making an entrance, she walked over to the side table holding herself erect, doing her utmost to project self-possession.

"Ah, let me introduce my stepdaughter, Bridget." Jack beckoned her to come by him.

Two men stood by the table with their backs to Bridget. As they turned to her, they stopped, cocked their heads, and nodded. Bridget felt she was a momentary distraction to them. Without pause she reached her hand to one of the gentlemen. "Sir. I'm Bridget." She grasped his hand in a firm, confident manner. "I helped Jack create those designs." A tense silence filled the room, until Jack responded, a tight smile creasing his face. "Well, I've been teaching Bridget some of my trade secrets and, uh, yes, uh…she is a fast learner."

A slight smile played along the corners of one of the gentleman's lips while he stood back and folded his arms. Both men stood silent. Bridget knew they were surveying her—dark hair curled up and pulled away from her face, a clear-eyed and steady return to their gaze, a generous mouth still pink with the natural essence of youth. Her height, unusually tall for a young woman, gave an aura of self-confidence. Of course, she thought, they're wondering, trying to understand if it might be possible these designs were hers.

Bridget knew this moment would irritate Jack. She was not to step beyond the boundaries he'd established for her. She was never to display her intellect nor outshine him. She already knew somewhere within herself that she possessed poise, assurance, and a good mind. A voice like an inner touchstone consistently murmured as Bridget grew into womanhood and experienced her creativity, her sense of knowing—a voice that seemed to come from another dimension, maybe her mother? Bridget had learned survival skills in this male domain, and these few minutes with the gentlemen were part of her quiet rebellion, a trespass on the life she'd lived until now.

"Sirs? Tea?" With a slight gesture she turned, picked up the pot, and poured, all the time realizing she'd become the center of attention in the room.

"Shall we look at these designs?" Jack moved quickly around the table turning the carefully drawn and inked furniture plans for the two gentlemen to view. Bridget could see he was anxious to regain control of this meeting. Each plan was numbered, each had dimensions and the name of Jack's company printed across the bottom, another Bridget touch. Beside each drawing were sketches of the fasteners and screws he'd created. He was a cabinetmaker and a businessman who knew instinctively what would intrigue these gentlemen. When they began to ask about the durability of his creations, he spoke with pride in his designs; however, he neglected to add that Bridget had begun to overtake his creative abilities as a designer. A fact that chafed his ego, most particularly because she was a woman.

He'd belittled his wife's artistry and ridiculed her noted talent, took opportunities to block her distinction in the art world, and now he intended to place the same strictures on Bridget's life. This moment with Jack and the businessmen was a defining one for Bridget. Seeds of resentment had grown like weeds. Soon she'd go, leave his house and his power over her.

With aplomb fueled by growing animosity, Bridget stepped up to the table, walked around, and stood by Jack. It was her way of saying, "I'll take charge here."

"Would you like to see Design Number One?" she asked. At this moment, the gentlemen witnessed an assured and composed woman. "You have a fine businessman here, Jack, or do we dare say businesswoman?" One gentleman smiled and walked over to the table. "Show us what you have here, Bridget? May I call you Bridget?"

Jack moved to allow the man room to stand beside her. A pink flush appeared on his neck above his collar. He knew that she was intelligent and resolute, characteristics in a woman that aggravated him, particularly in Bridget. Jack had decided that Bridget could be his road to wealth, in the same way he'd seen Clara, at one time. In Bridget he saw someone who would do his bidding and never, never outshine him.

He'd created a furniture factory from the lumber business he'd inherited and had become known for his designs, the sturdiness of desks, chairs, tables. He assumed the title of president, hired the best woodworkers and cabinetmakers he could find, sold his patent for the fasteners and screws he'd invented, and with it all, had accumulated some wealth.

Bridget became artist incognito. She drew the designs that he and his workers fashioned into beautiful objects of wood, but when she watched him take her original creations and place his name upon them, her resentment festered.

Over time, her antagonism toward him increased. She'd watched Jack dispose of her mother's paintings and witnessed how bitterly he turned against her memory. His dismissal of George warned her about how he could attack those around him with ruthless contempt.

Bridget knew too that he watched her every move and had since Clara died: who she talked to, where she went, questioned her at the end of every day. "Who did you see at that college today? You're like your mother, always wanting to be a little too highfalutin with all her art stuff. I can teach you everything you need to know to be in this world.

Together you and I can become wealthy, make names for ourselves. That's why you need to stay here with me."

His tone, threatening.

After the businessmen left, Bridget felt an urge, a feeling she'd not often experienced. She felt emboldened. The men's comments, and Jack's reluctant recognition of Bridget's capabilities, spurred her on to make a decision to leave.

Chapter Eleven

THROUGHOUT THE SEVEN YEARS SINCE GEORGE HAD LEFT home, Bridget had lived the life of a woman captive to Jack's wishes. She'd also become wily. Knowing she might someday need a plan to leave, she'd put away some of the money Jack gave her for household expenses, funds that lay under her slips and camisoles in a dresser drawer. Money she'd need to save her own life.

Bridget had a dream that night, one that felt like a declaration.

The dream invited her into a place that felt like home. Not the house where she'd lived all her life, but a home with walls that seemed to unfold as she walked through to a back garden. A tree, her tree that she'd climbed and hid in as a child. Yellow leaves and dark branches beckoned her. When she drew closer, a woman's face peered down at her from among the leaves, a face that resembled her own, yet older, much older.

The face spoke. "I'm here. We will go."

The trunk of the tree opened, and Bridget walked through.

On the eve of her twenty-third birthday, she put her plan into motion. A suitcase tucked under her bed held a rolled black cotton skirt, a white high-collared blouse, pins for her hair, and an extra pair of black, laced boots. Undergarments were folded into her skirt. Bundled under her clothes were stories she'd written and saved over the years.

Bridget had contemplated many stories and thoughts by candlelight far into the night, jotting them onto scraps of paper left over from those she'd used for furniture designs; her words often felt like they were coming from a spirit being who sat and spoke to her. These notes were soon tucked into and between the pages of a notebook, left there for the possibility of other eyes someday.

Words, designs, imagination were life's essence to Bridget. They kept her sound, steady, and unwavering. The shadow of Jack's control receded when the creative spirit took her to an ethereal place or allowed the delicious feeling of a story that lay beyond the walls and lawns of this place that was more prison than home. Bridget's life and hopes were hidden in a drawer under camisoles and undergarments. Everything there waited for the right moment.

She felt a clarity not experienced until now, and her decision became a staunch resolution. She welcomed the determination that flowed through her body like elixir. She planned to catch the train to Toronto the next morning. No longer did she feel trapped in his house. A way to escape was becoming clear, a way he couldn't possibly block.

The Great War in Europe offered an exit. Bridget, creative and resourceful, had devised a plan that would take her far from his control, possibly forever. For the first time she felt something like anticipation.

In her room, now packed in among her belongings, was a letter—one she'd received a week ago—from The Imperial Munitions Board confirming a meeting at her convenience and the possibility of work in one of the new factories outside Toronto. Her hope was to join the numbers of women helping to win the war. How could Jack stop her from leaving for a cause that mattered to everyone worldwide? A cause that held the future of the world. A war to end all wars.

She'd left the downstairs lights on for him to make his way through the house when he arrived home. She knew the businessmen who'd come to his office that day had invited him out for drinks, and that he'd come home inebriated. Other nights like this she'd helped him to get to bed. Not this night. He'd have to get used to taking care of himself from now on.

Later, close to midnight, Bridget awoke to the sounds of Jack's stumbling footsteps on the stairway. He was mumbling and groaning like a man might who'd been drinking most of the evening. Bridget knew those sounds, but tonight there seemed an edgy irritation to his grumbling.

When he arrived at her closed door, she heard him rattle the doorknob; a hint of fear crawled across her skin.

"Bridget." He seemed to be talking into the door, his voice muffled. "Bridget, g...gg...et uuuup."

Throughout many years she'd seen him drunk and she'd put him to bed, but never before had he approached her room. Bridget had been clear since George left that her room was her sanctuary. He'd honored her wish. But not on this night. He shook the doorknob again.

"I need to tell...you...tell you...something."

Bridget switched on the lamp and grabbed her robe hanging on the bedpost. Throwing it over her shoulders, she padded over to where she could hear him still mumbling.

"Just a minute." She spoke through the door. When she opened it, she tried to block his way in. Even drunk as he was, Jack pushed past her and stumbled into the room.

"Jack. Stop. No. Go to your own room." She grasped at his arm, but he pushed her away.

"No, no, no…no, no, no." Now in the middle of the room, he dropped and sat on the edge of her bed. "NO, NO, NO, we need to cele, cele…brate. I got us a huge…" He waved his arms over his head. "Huge…con…con…tract."

Bridget hadn't left the door. But now, realizing he might fall back onto her bed, she walked to him to pull him up. As she reached down to him, he swayed to gaze around the room, a man realizing something was amiss. "What'ssss the sssuitcase for?" He pointed to the luggage she'd packed and left on the floor. Dread twisted in her stomach; she could feel her palms sweating, her heart banging against her chest. Old reactions to his temper. It didn't matter in this moment that she was twenty-two, a woman with a plan to leave, or that soon he could no longer have control over her. But she'd wanted to tell him in the morning with the taxi waiting at the door.

"Bridget?" Jack seemed more quizzical than antagonistic; her heart slowed. Careful to stay out of his reach, she moved toward the door, ready to have him leave. "Jack, I have a job, or I will have one soon. It's in a munitions factory outside Toronto."

A slow, long lament escaped from his mouth, "No-oo-oo-oo. You can't leave. You're supposed to stay here, with me." An old demon entered the room. He reached and clutched at her arm, his fingers digging into her skin.

"Jack, that hurts!" Fearful of what he might be intending, Bridget tried to pry his fingers away. But his face contorted into someone unrecognizable. "We're meant to be here, together." His words were throaty, harsh, and threatening. A primal evil overtook him, black eyes shining, mouth straightening into a thin, tight line. He stood, a tall, muscular man, force fueled by fury, and grasping at Bridget's arm knocked her off balance and threw her to the floor. Her head thudded against the corner of the bed, and for moments, not knowing how long, Bridget lost all sense of what was happening to her. As she came around, he was leaning over her raising his hand; she pushed and pummeled at his shoulders, but she hadn't the strength to stop him. His hand came down and across her cheek, striking her with a fierce slap. "No one else leaves me. No one. You'll go nowhere! You'll…stay…here."

He growled like a crazed animal, spittle at the corners of his mouth. Bridget thought he'd gone mad. And possibly he had for those few moments—mad with rage—because another woman was leaving him. When he grabbed her neck, Bridget realized he was trying to strangle her. He was trying to kill her! She screamed, "Jack! It's Bridget!"

As though someone had thrown a switch in his brain, he stared at her. A puzzled crease crossed his forehead, and backing away, he dropped his hands at his sides and turned to the door. He walked like a man awakening from a bad dream. As he left, he looked back at Bridget, now sitting on the edge of her bed. His mouth moved, but no words emerged. Only mumbled sounds.

The door swung shut.

Bridget sat on the edge of the bed, arms crossed, grasping her shoulders, and rocking till the trembling began to lessen. Gradually, gradually, she began to inhale and exhale with regular breaths, and the room around her returned and light swam into focus. One breath, then another, assured Bridget that he'd not broken her. Body or spirit. She pulled the quilt around her shoulders and placed her hands on her arms and on her shoulders. She held one hand up to her cheek, to the burning spot where he'd struck her. Everything hurt, though she was sure her body was in one piece, unlike her soul. The trembling subsided. Shock numbed her senses. She felt nothing till she sensed, more than heard, a thud. It was the bumping of a body hitting stairs: a thump, a clump, and then, nothing. Bridget rose, listened, and waited. She heard no more sounds.

Clutching at her gown, the quilt across her shoulders, she walked to the top of the stairs where her body's dizzying tremor caught her off balance. Grasping at the railing, she looked below. Jack lay at the bottom. Bridget hesitated. What if? In this well of wondering, she began to move, to descend one step at a time, in a slow-motion rhythm. An overhead light in the hallway shone across his body. He lay, his head turned to the side, blood leaking from his nose. At the bottom step, Bridget stood over him. His eyes opened.

"Leave me here," he moaned.

It would be so easy, she thought, all she would have to do is press her foot against his throat. Instead, wrapping her quilt close to her body, she walked toward the kitchen. A glacial nothingness lay on her skin like ice. In a voice barren of emotion, she spoke.

"I'll call Dr. Winslow next door, ask him to come over. Don't move."

Time stood still for a moment.

Bridget walked back after calling the doctor and took a handkerchief from her dressing gown pocket. She bent over and wiped the blood from his nose. She stood, holding the bloody cloth, and, without wavering, she knew. She'd leave this house. She'd leave this man lying helpless on the floor. She'd leave him and never return.

Chapter Twelve

Dr. Winslow responded to her call right away and knew as soon as he saw Jack at the bottom of the stairs that he needed to call the local ambulance. Jack responded with a definite "No!" After the doctor determined nothing was broken, he asked what had happened. Bridget offered no answer, and Jack responded with a terse, "I tripped." There'd be no more explanation.

"Bridget, will you help me move him?" Dr. Winslow asked as he decided neither Jack nor Bridget had anything else to offer. She began to shake her head no and quickly realized if she wanted this nightmare to be over, he had to be moved. Jack leaned on both Bridget and Dr. Winslow to limp to the chesterfield, an act that meant he was physically touching Bridget. As they moved, she stared at the couch and used all her concentration to cut off the feel of his body and to keep herself from grabbing him by the throat. Getting him onto that chesterfield, was an act of will. She'd avoided that couch since her mother had died on it.

When it was done, Bridget walked to the archway between the hall and the living room. She turned and looked back at Jack lying there, hair bedraggled, his jacket rumpled behind his back. It occurred to her as she forced herself to stare over at him, that he was just a bad dream—an unkempt, contaminated wreckage. He lay back, groaned, and put his arm over his eyes, blocking out her scorn and the doctor's perplexity. "Is the light bothering your eyes, Jack?" Dr. Winslow asked. "Do you need a damp cloth for your forehead? Could you get one, Bridget?"

When there was no response from either of them, he looked to Bridget. "Is there something more I need to know?" Dr. Winslow had felt uneasy about the Blackwell family since Clara's death and George's departure. Something was wrong in this household. He looked over at the man lying on the chesterfield, his arm still shutting out the room and the people around him. Dr. Winslow asked again: "Jack, would you like Bridget to get a cloth for your forehead and your nose? And again, I ask, is there something I need to know?" His tone was edged in frustration.

Grunting, Jack tried to push himself up but slid back onto the cushions and growled: "I just fell down the goddamned stairs. That's all you need to know. And…could somebody do something useful and help me up so I can get the hell to bed?"

Dr. Winslow looked over to Bridget and shook his head. He silently asked, "*Do you want to help him?*" Still impassive, still standing in the doorway, she said nothing, nor made any move toward her stepfather.

When he saw that Bridget had no intention to help, he sighed and turned back to Jack. *Definitely something going on in this house,* he thought. Dr. Winslow felt a sick dismay collecting in the back of his throat as he looked over at Bridget and the angry red blotch on her cheek. He said nothing.

Jack pushed down against the cushion to raise himself, a grimace of impatience and pain contorting his face. His antagonism filled the room like toxic air.

Dr. Winslow was close to shouting at him. "Lie back and be still Jack. I think you need to stay there for the night.

You've probably bruised yourself badly and moving around after that fall is foolish, if not harmful." His tone not at all sympathetic, he called over to Bridget, "Might you talk some sense into him?" Not hearing a response, he turned toward her, but she'd gone, starting down the hall toward the kitchen, tossing her answer over her shoulder.

"Probably not. Anyone want tea?"

Jack, who realized she'd left, mumbled, "Girl doesn't give a care what happens to me. She'd as soon I died." The doctor wondered if he might be right.

Jack lay back on the couch. "Toss me that wool blanket on the chair there. Think I'll stay here." He reached over his head and clicked off the table lamp. A sense of dead air settled in the room. Without saying anything more to the patient, Dr. Winslow walked to the doorway into the kitchen, and seeing Bridget holding the phone receiver, waved and let himself out the back door.

Bridget was calling Mrs. Lowell, the neighbor across the street, who answered on the second ring. "Bridget, everything all right over there? It's late and your lights are all on." For a moment Bridget was glad Mrs. Lowell kept track of everybody's comings and goings in the neighborhood because she was going to need her. Neither Mrs. Lowell nor Dr. Winslow knew just yet that they were going to be caretakers for the man lying on the couch in the dark.

"Mrs. Lowell, I know it's late, but I need your help. Could you come over now?"

BRIDGET SLEPT DOWNSTAIRS IN THE BACK BEDROOM which had been her brother George's. The thought of going back into her room nauseated her. She'd taken her nightdress and her kimono, rolled them into a ball, and stuffed them into a trash can on the back porch. Her bath would have to wait. She stood at the kitchen sink with a warm cloth, washed her shoulders and her arms, and lay a heated cloth against her cheek.

One leather case, a cloth bag, and her handbag sat by the front door.

All was ready. Determination fueled by a buried fearlessness allowed a few hours of sleep. She'd thanked Dr. Winslow and Mrs. Lowell for coming so quickly to her distress call. And Mrs. Lowell, who relished the responsibility Bridget had asked her to assume, said she'd be back in the morning with breakfast, and she'd bring her needlework so she could stay for a "few hours." The fiend within Bridget relished the thought of Mrs. Lowell taking over her father's care and the household "for as long as she felt she needed to." Bridget knew that Mrs. Lowell annoyed Jack, just by being in the room.

Before the light appeared, Bridget slid out of bed, smoothed her skirt, draped a shawl across her shoulders, and bent to tie her shoes. Each was a gesture of goodbye. The house was silent as it ushered her away.

Across the street was the taxi Mrs. Lowell had called as she'd promised. The lady herself stood by the open door of the car. There were few questions about why Bridget needed a taxi at five o'clock in the morning. Mrs. Lowell was a curious woman; however, she was also observant, and someone Bridget had learned to trust over the years. Mrs. Lowell had her suspicions of what might be happening in the Blackwell household.

"You look after yourself, dear girl, and don't worry about a thing. I'll be sure he's well looked after. Between Dr. Winslow and me, he'll be fine." And unexpectedly she drew Bridget into her arms. "You're doing the right thing. Not sure what's gone on, but you need to go."

Just before Bridget climbed into the back seat of the taxi, she looked up to the second floor of the house she was leaving. A dim light shone from Jack's room. A shadow lingered for a moment and was gone.

Chapter Thirteen

"ALL ABOARD, TRAIN EAST LEAVING FOR TORONTO."

The pink lights of dawn were just beginning to penetrate the morning sky as Bridget boarded the Grand Trunk Railway train for Toronto. Only Bridget and four soldiers in their wool khakis climbed from the station platform into the passenger car, each person lost in a world of their own quiet thoughts of what waited for them at the end of their journeys.

Not many were traveling on this train. Most passengers sat separately except for a couple near the front exit, she with her head on his khaki shoulder, he holding her hand. Other uniformed men sat here and there throughout the car, reminders that Canada was at war and Bridget was heading to her new job at a munitions factory. Seeing these men gave her renewed commitment to the decision she'd made.

Walking along the aisle, leather case in her hand, a cloth bag and her handbag slung over her shoulder, Bridget experienced release. A knowledge that she'd never have to see him again. A knowledge that he could do no harm to her ever again. When the train began to move, she reached to the overhead rack and lifted her case, both hands holding firm.

"Here, ma'am, let me help with that." A soldier who'd been sitting by the window stood and eased out to the aisle beside her. Rising to his full height, he offered his hand to take her bags. "May I put your luggage on the rack over your head, and would you like your handbag at your feet?"

Bridget was shaken for a moment. What does a woman do when a man offers goodwill? In her world, Jack had not ever represented kindness. As the soldier brushed against her, she felt the rough wool of his khaki jacket against her arm. Immediately she moved back, as though a shock had passed through her body.

"Oh, my apologies, ma'am, I didn't mean to startle you." He turned to her while he lifted the case. "May I give you my seat by the window?"

"Thank you, sir." Placing her hands on the back of the seat in front, she edged her way toward the window and sat down. Bridget let the moment pass, took a breath, and smiled up at the soldier who stood as though waiting for an invitation. "I took your seat, sir; please, do you care to sit here?" And she patted the empty place beside her.

Folding his tall body into the seat, he turned to Bridget and offered his hand, "I'm Peter Radcliffe from Westover." Reaching to shake his hand, Bridget regained her usual poise that Jack liked to describe as her "just-too-sure-of-yourself" posture.

"I'm pleased to meet you, Mr. Radcliffe. I'm Bridget Blackwell." Smiling, she continued, "Also from Westover, although not for long."

Peter Radcliffe settled back into his seat as the train began to move. He seemed to be preoccupied, which for Bridget was a relief, not wanting to get involved in idle conversation, only wanting to hold herself together, get to Toronto and move on from her old life to whatever might lie ahead. But as she took another breath, Peter faced her with an abrupt turn of his body.

"Bridget Blackwell?!" His eyes were alight. "*The* Bridget Blackwell?" His exclamation was so comical that Bridget couldn't help a small chuckle and decided to play along. "The very one," she said, with just a bit of an upper-class tone.

"No, seriously. Bridget Blackwell, writing student at Western University, Class of 1913? Bridget Blackwell, who wrote the short story 'Footsteps in Our Garden'? Who won the McClean's writing award for short stories? I was there when you read it for all of us in the English Lit Department."

"You were there?"

"Yes. I remember you now. I'm thrilled to be able to tell you what a beautiful story it was."

Bridget watched his face as he spoke, a man on his way to war, who for a time was given a reprieve from fear—a chance to shut out his future. And for Bridget, life presented a gift in the person of Peter Radcliffe.

"Oh, yes, I remember you well. I was a visiting writer-in-residence in poetry for a few months at Western before I decided to join the army. What a happy coincidence to meet you here, now. Must be fate." He smiled. His greeting was warm and welcoming, and Bridget felt able to rest easy in his company. An interlude in life gave this woman and this man something precious—it gave them time. And they began to talk as people often might when tomorrow seems precarious and life uncertain.

"You are *that* Peter Radcliffe. The poet Peter Radcliffe?" Bridget grinned.

He laughed. A deeply heartfelt sound. "Touché, Miss Blackwell, touché. Truly I am, or, should I say, I was Peter Radcliffe, poet and writer, and now I'm Private Peter Radcliffe."

"You joined the army. Like so many other young men. What's brought you into this war?"

"Duty, Miss Blackwell, a strong sense of duty." When he spoke of duty, Bridget caught an edge of regret. She let his words sit in the air for minutes, while she turned to watch the fields drift by, some dotted with cattle, some with the fresh green of new barley. She watched the scene pass from view, letting her shoulders relax into the cushioned seat, and for a while, her bruised soul felt some respite.

"Please, Peter, call me Bridget." She turned to him. "We are two university friends, authors meeting unexpectedly, each on our way, traveling to a place neither of us knows."

"Well. There she is, right beside me. Bridget Blackwell, the storyteller." Peter sat back, folded his arms across his chest, and lifted one booted foot onto the rail in front of him. "Do you remember your story, 'Footsteps in Our Garden'? Do you remember where it came from? What the seed was?"

It'd been a long time, or so it seemed to Bridget, since someone had taken a moment to see her—the writer, the storyteller, that part of herself she'd buried after leaving university, and after she'd begun to work in her stepfather's furniture business. Jack had only contempt for her storytelling; words and writing were only relevant in business. Any other use was a waste of time. And air.

Here on this train, traveling away from him—his factory, his brutality—some parts of Bridget began to feel a healing rhythm rather like the steady motion of the train.

"Bridget?" Peter spoke with concern. "Are you all right? Did I say something to upset you? Did my question upset you? I'm inclined to be intrusive, maybe a little forward."

"Oh. Oh, not at all, Peter. No. I was just thinking how nice it is to be thinking about that story again. It's been a few years since I wrote that tale. And I can surely tell you where it came from. Do you have a while?" Bridget grinned again. Twice in the space of an hour she'd felt like grinning. As they talked, the hours melted. Bridget told Peter about the stories her mother, Clara, spun of the garden folk who arrived dressed in glorious colors every spring, and who befriended the bees, the hummingbirds, and the butterflies. "She'd take me into the garden where she'd paint, and she'd tell me stories of the flowers as though they were living beings, and to me they were."

Peter watched her face come alive as Bridget told him how her short story of mysterious footsteps in the garden had unfolded from her mother's fantasies and her paintings. He in turn heard the poetry in her telling, and he heard the sadness. He knew about sadness.

"Bridget," he said, as she paused, hands in her lap.

"I'd like to tell you some of my story, if I might." Before she could say yes or no, he put his fingertips to his lips, looked away for an instant, then looked back and said: "I'm not going to war entirely out of duty. I'm going, if I may say, out of love; love for my young brother who was declared missing last April in a battle at Ypres. I'm not going because I think I might find him, even though I'm sure Mom thinks I will. I'm going because I can't think of him out there somewhere by himself. Guess it's the poet in me after all, and the older brother."

Both let a gentle silence touch them.

Neither noticed when the train began to slow, neither felt any sense that time had moved them from where they'd begun till now. They sat, side by side in the comfort of newfound friendship. As the conductor moved down the aisle announcing their destination, Bridget became aware of a feeling of normalcy, and anticipation.

"Thank you, Peter. You've made what could have been a troubled journey, a happy one. My hope is you will be safe and come home unharmed." As she spoke words that felt like a farewell, she was aware of regret that their brief encounter was over.

Sitting up, she placed her hand on the top of the seat in front of her, turning to ready herself to stand. Peter hadn't moved. He sat, staring past Bridget, seemingly watching as the train pulled into the covered iron and glass train shed. A moment passed as the train shuddered to a halt.

"Excuse me, Peter, I'll need to get past you." Bridget stood. Without moving or letting her by, Peter looked up at her. "Are you meeting someone?" he asked. Something in his tone, a measure of hope, gave her reason to pause before she answered.

"Not really. I'll get a taxi and make my way to the residence where I'm staying." Peter stood, moved out to the aisle, and turned back, "This is possibly very presumptuous of me, but…" He smiled. "I don't have to be anywhere, I mean the coast, I mean I don't have to report in for another couple of days. Bridget? Would you have dinner with me tonight?"

The moment hung there as he waited, and she felt the second of uncertainty become ease. She answered, "I'd be honored to have dinner with the noted poet Peter Radcliffe." The words were in the air before any reason to say no might stop her.

"Then this is just fine." Peter's smile became wider.

"I'll need to check in at my residence and take my bags to my room…" Before she could finish her sentence and tell him what she needed to do, he reached up, took her leather case from the overhead rack, and set it on the aisle floor.

"Let's find you a cab, Bridget Blackwell. I'm here at your service."

Chapter Fourteen

ALL AROUND WERE THE SHOUTS OF PORTERS PULLING LUG-
gage wagons, the huffing of trains eager to be on their way
like horses pawing at the ground, and calls from conductors
announcing arrivals, departures, and city names: "Montreal
leaving, track four. Kingston, Brockville, Montreal, board-
ing in fifteen minutes. Connections with Quebec City and
Halifax."

Soldiers with duffel bags over their shoulders strode
along the platform, intent on going to war. Bridget and Peter
stood watching, each wondering what war meant to their
lives—Peter setting off soon to sail from Halifax with others
like him, to become part of what was being called The Great
War, and Bridget who would soon be creating the shells that
one day would kill German soldiers, men like Peter.

How much time could they steal from the futures they'd
chosen? What possibilities were waiting to give them life
here in the present?

They walked toward the stairs that would take them out
to the street, where taxis waited in a line at the curb. Bridget
was conscious of Peter beside her, shoulder to shoulder,
his haversack high on his back, his wool khaki grazing the
sleeve of her long trench coat. He carried her leather case
and her cloth bag; her protests having fallen on his deaf ears.

"You may be a modern woman of your time, but I will still
offer to carry your bag," Peter had laughed as they set off along

Milree Latimer

the walkway. For the first time in recent memory, Bridget felt a lightness in her step. She wondered if those around making their way within their worlds saw the two of them—he in uniform, she taking his arm—as a couple. In her imagination, Bridget hoped those in the crowd milling around them were wishing them well. Whatever that might mean.

One woman in the crowd was watching them.

As Bridget and Peter made their way to the line of taxis outside the station, the woman wove in and out among other passengers and headed toward the couple. She called Bridget's name.

"Peter, I just heard someone call out my name." Bridget stopped. "Who knows I'm here?"

Turning to look into the crowd, she spotted a woman waving and walking swiftly toward them. For a moment Bridget thought she might be conjuring a vision. The woman making her way to them was dressed in a red coat, sporting a floppy black hat that covered a mass of red curls. As she approached, her luminescent green eyes smiled with an open greeting.

A feeling of lightheadedness swept over her, and she swayed, grabbing Peter's arm.

"Bridget, are you not well?" Peter put his hand over hers as she grasped his arm.

"No, I'm fine. I'm only a little startled because I think I know this woman coming toward us." Without hesitation, she walked away from Peter, put her hand out, and smiled. The woman was only a few feet from her when Bridget spoke. "Hello. I know you. How did you find me?" There was no doubt in Bridget's mind that the woman approaching was Sophie Watson, her mother's friend, and hero of the stories she was told throughout her childhood.

Everything about her—blazing red hair, green eyes, hands of an artist—told Bridget this was her mother's friend, Sophie.

"Bridget, I found you," Sophie said. "For a while I wasn't sure I could."

They stood, holding hands. It was Bridget who spoke, asking the question again: "How did you find me?"

"Mrs. Lowell. Dear Mrs. Lowell," Sophie said. She released her hands from Bridget's and reached into her large bag, pulling out a note and a train schedule. "She called me when you left this morning. Gave me your train times and where you're going to be staying." Sophie was keeping her promise to Clara. She would protect her girl and she had Mrs. Lowell's help.

Peter stood by as the two women greeted one another, wondering if it might be time for him to make an exit. But at that moment, Bridget turned and beckoned to him. "Peter. Come meet a special person, an artist who was a friend of my mother."

Just as Peter began making his way to introduce himself, Sophie lifted her arm, reached out her hand, and, when he was close enough, grasped his large, rough hand in hers. It was a surprisingly warm gesture toward this man who was to her a stranger.

"Your name is Peter? Peter Radcliffe, perchance? The poet and writer?"

People continued to bustle, running for taxis, greeting friends. Sounds of clanging street cars rang out across the street, but Bridget, Sophie, and Peter stood in a moment that seemed to enclose them in wonder. No one spoke until Bridget couldn't contain herself, "How could you two know one another?" And as though a lighted fragment of a memory shone, Peter clapped his hands together and laughed. "You're the painter, Sophie Watson! I wrote a poem inspired by one of your paintings—it was a sunset over a lake, might have been Lake Ontario..." Bridget saw a side of Peter Radcliffe she hadn't had a chance to notice: excited, jubilant. He was a man showing passion inspired by meeting the painter, Sophie Watson. All the pieces of three lives began to coalesce on this early afternoon in May, and each life gathered a connection to the future, one to the other.

"Now that we've discovered we're all friends, Sophie, why don't you come with Peter and me, we're going to have an early dinner, together." Peter nodded in agreement.

"Thank you both, but I need to get back to work. I'm painting some scenes at a munitions factory and they're waiting for me to return. But Bridget, I may see you again."

Sophie left her comment hanging, didn't say where, didn't say when. "And you, Peter, what a pleasure to finally meet you, I was given the poem you wrote about my painting, but never had a chance to meet you or tell you how beautiful it was." She paused and placed her hand on his shoulder. "Are you leaving soon for Europe?"

Peter nodded. "I am, Miss Watson, I'll be leaving for the coast very soon." He cast a glance in Bridget's direction, maybe wondering if she might, at this moment ask him to delay, but her gaze was trained on Sophie.

"Well, Peter," she said, her hand still resting on his shoulder. "I wish you safe travels and a safe return from this war." Her eyes clouded, knowing it was possible she'd not see him again. "And you, Bridget, are you staying at the Warren Hall? Most of the girls working at Ashbridge Bay Munitions live at Warren." Bridget again was left perplexed:

how would Sophie know where she was living, and, even more curiously, know the factory she had been assigned to? Bridget had only herself received her placement letter from Canada War Records.

"Yes, I'm staying in Warren Hall, and I'm to report to Ashbridge Bay no later than Friday. But then you…"

Sophie waved her hand before Bridget had any chance to question her and began walking away. "Lovely to meet the two of you here. I hope you'll have a chance to taste some of the finer food this city has to offer and try to get in a walk by the lake. Now, I must run." And as quickly as she'd appeared moments ago, she was gone.

Peter and Bridget watched her weave her way through the crowd emerging from the station—one hand holding her black floppy hat, the other arm still waving above the heads of those trying to stand out of her way.

"Well, that was strange," Peter said. "She appears, she disappears." He tossed his open hands to the air. "Mysterious lady." Bridget wondered at the happenstance of it all. Her mother's artistic friend, who somehow knew Mrs. Lowell. How did that happen?

Amid her quandary, Peter picked up her cloth bag and leather case and walked with intent to the taxi curb. Ten paces maximum he turned to her. "OK, Bridget. Let's get ourselves a taxi, and take you to your new home, then dinner?"

Another thought occurred to the young woman while she watched him move her life along. "You know, I'm thinking let's go get me checked in at Warren Hall and find a cozy place where we can sink into a deep chesterfield, be served a bottomless teapot, and continue where we left off on the train."

The response from Peter came with no hesitation. "Just the place comes to mind. If you agree, I have a room at a hostelry for soldiers, coming and going…and downstairs is a living room, where ladies and gentlemen can sit, have tea, or stronger. If you're comfortable with that, I can get us there."

"Let's go!" Bridget was already standing at the curb, hailing a taxi. Jumping into the back, Peter at her right hand, she called out. "Warren Hall."

Chapter Fifteen

SERENDIPITY PRESENTED BRIDGET WITH SEVERAL GIFTS that afternoon in May.

Peter Radcliffe—poet, storyteller, and friend—entered her life and began to soften the sharp images of Jack's brutality—replacing his cold-bloodedness with a generosity of nature that Bridget hadn't experienced for years, since George had left.

Jack Blackwell was someone from her past.

Bridget felt convinced that her mother's spirit was nearby, possibly in the person of the woman Sophie, who seemed to know much about Bridget, and whose warm spirit reminded Bridget of a mother she'd known such a short time. Thoughts and hope crowded her mind as she climbed the steps of Warren Hall and rang the doorbell. Peter sat waiting in the taxi.

Within a few minutes the door opened to a woman whose navy and white middy blouse hung to her hips over a long navy skirt. She was such a small woman that she seemed to be all blouse and skirt, with a head of silver-gray hair and a shining, open face peering from the top of her collar. "Ah, you must be Bridget," she said and offered her hand with the assurance of preknowledge.

"Yes, oh yes. I am." Bridget felt as though her path had been charted and dotted with landmarks.

"Well, my dear, come in. I'm Miss Bishop, the house mother here at Warren." As she welcomed Bridget, Miss

Bishop peered around her at the taxi and saw Peter sitting in the back seat. "Is that your taxi, dear, and is the young soldier with you?"

Bridget couldn't resist the smile that played at the corners of her lips. Miss Bishop was curious. Rather than explain the story of meeting Peter on the train, that he was a poet who'd heard her prize-winning story, and that she had every intention of having dinner with him tonight, she said, "Yes, he's a friend on his way to Halifax to ship out on Friday."

Miss Bishop, who loved romantic stories, beamed. "Oh Bridget, he mustn't sit out there, I'm sure he'd be so much more comfortable waiting in the gentlemen's parlor, while you get your things to your room. May I invite him in?" Bridget had little chance to say yes or no or thank you, because Miss Bishop was already making her way to the taxi, beckoning Peter to come in.

Warren Hall was a residence for young (and some older) women who needed room and board while living and working in the city. When Bridget had sent her letter to the Canadian War Records Office to ask for a job at a munitions factory, her acceptance letter suggested she might be comfortable, as a woman alone in the city, staying at Warren Hall, a place that would be her home, possibly throughout the war. Here her new life awaited.

Lost in her thoughts, Bridget realized Peter had come up beside her, followed by Miss Bishop. "Come ahead, both of you. I'll register you in at the desk, Bridget, and sir? Private?"

"Private Radcliffe, ma'am. Thank you."

"Yes. Private, you may make yourself comfortable in the waiting room. May I bring you tea?"

BRIDGET HAD BARELY TAKEN TIME TO PLACE HER leather case in the small wardrobe, fluff her hair, and wash her hands before she'd headed back down the stairs to join Peter.

Later, as Peter and Bridget were leaving Warren Hall, she felt she'd entered another world. Every person she'd met since leaving Westover, and Jack's overbearing presence, had given her a glimpse of kindness and graciousness. Peter, Sophie, and now Miss Bishop were opening her to a world she hadn't known for a long time, a world where people were considerate of one another.

"Thank you, Miss Bishop," Peter said. "Your hospitality is much appreciated. Your biscuits are delicious." Peter shook Miss Bishop's hand as he turned with Bridget to walk down the steps of the reception area and out to a taxi waiting at the door.

"Take care of the young lady," Miss Bishop said as she waved them off, thinking what a lovely couple they were, and *he, oh my, heading off to war.*

"Where to?" the driver asked from the front seat.

Bridget settled in beside Peter, who looked to her as he called, "Soldiers' Hostelry just across from Main Station."

When he said, "Across from Main Station," Bridget shook her head back and forth, surprised. "We're going back to the station?" Peter, looking abashed, nodded yes. And offered no explanation.

"I'm thinking there's a story." Bridget began to wonder if she'd misjudged this man, someone she'd met only hours ago. "Want to tell me what's going on?" A touch of her inner voice sparked a cautionary note. A note that Peter detected.

"Remember I said we could go to the hostelry where I'll be staying overnight?"

She nodded her head.

"Well…it's across the street from the station." The man Peter, the man in the khaki uniform, the man going to war, was staring at his hands like the boy found out. "I worried that if I suggested we go straight across the street to the hostelry from the station, you'd think I was being bold, maybe even presumptuous."

His sidelong glance at Bridget made her laugh. "You thought I'd think you were kidnapping me? Whisking me away?"

"I wouldn't go that far, but…"

"Oh, Peter." Bridget sat directly facing him as much as was possible in the back seat of the taxi, her long black skirt picking up dust from the floor. "That's possibly the nicest thing you could have done for me today. The nicest and kindest." And her laugh escaped in mini gasps.

A red flush was appearing over the top of Peter's collar, which gave Bridget warning that laughter was not the best response right now. "I'm so sorry. I didn't mean to embarrass you." Without considering or hesitating she placed her hand over his, there on his knee.

The moment warranted a pause—a poetic pause, one of them might have said.

When the taxi pulled up by the hostelry, Bridget felt anticipation. Of what, she wasn't sure.

Peter regained his composure and offered his hand to Bridget as he stepped from the taxi. While he paid the driver, Bridget stared up at tall, arched wooden doors giving a churchlike feel to an otherwise plain, red, brick building with the Salvation Army shield over the doors. Pressing the buzzer, Peter readjusted the haversack on his back and reached down to pick up Bridget's large purse. "It's all right

Peter, I can handle it." Her voice softened as she looked up into his face. Seeing him there, stiff crowned hat, the peak hiding his forehead, his eyes bluer than the sky hanging over the May afternoon, she couldn't decide whether to turn and run or circle him in a "don't go" embrace. Choosing neither, she linked her arm in his and waited for the door to open.

High-backed chairs and cushioned chesterfields filled a spacious room, grouped to create small, intimate places for soldiers to sit, read, or doze, while others, like Bridget and Peter, were talking, holding each last moment up to the light. A Salvation Army Sally Ann, volunteering here at the hostelry, brought them a late afternoon supper of biscuits, tea and honey. After she set the chinaware cups and plates on the mahogany side table, Bridget sat back into the soft velour of her chair, smiled over at Peter, and said, "Thank you, and again thank you."

Peter turned to her, a curious light in his eye. "Thank you? Maybe it's me who should be saying thank you, for your company, for making this journey more gracious than I could have imagined."

Perhaps that was the moment when Bridget felt her soul begin to mend, if only for now, if only for this time together.

Taking a sip of tea and honey, she gathered herself and crossed her ankles, letting her black leather-booted legs rest together. She, facing full-bodied toward him, felt the warmth of his smile; he, in turn, thought she was an apparition who'd appeared from some magical place. How quickly life offers hope and how cruel to offer it now, he thought.

She placed her cup back onto the saucer and considered reaching for his hand. Possibly their thoughts were colliding, because precisely when Bridget speculated what it might be like to have her hand in his, he stretched his arm across the space between them. "Would you mind if I took your hand? I want to ask something of you."

His expression assumed such seriousness—she wondered if he might be proposing marriage.

"Of course, what do you need?" The Sally Ann who stood by the door watching them thought how poignant they were; she believed they might be another couple saying goodbye, neither knowing for how long. She might eventually be right about Bridget and Peter, but at this moment he had no thoughts of goodbye. His hopes were for an extended hello—now and when he'd return—whenever the war that called him away ended.

"You may think all poets are romantics, like Lord Byron, or Shelley." He took his hand from hers and reached into his jacket pocket. "I've never thought of myself as a romantic. I guess I'm more the 'well-what-now' kind of realist. If you've read my poems...and I've never..."

Bridget watched his face, his eyes looking down at a paper he'd taken from his pocket, his fingers worrying the paper, folding, unfolding. "Peter, whatever you are wanting to say, say it."

Unfolding the now wrinkled paper, he smoothed it across his knee, and began to read:

> *"Remember me,*
> *think of me,*
> *imagine me*
> *as I will you.*

There was a second of time that Bridget believed she'd stopped breathing. Nothing up to now had prepared her for the feelings that rushed to the surface of her skin: no fear, no dismay, only an awareness of something new, something possible.

"Peter?"

Without looking up, he shook his head, "Let me finish. Or I'll never...I'm afraid, I'll regret it forever if I don't."

She took a breath and sat back. He read on.

And when I go—as I will
let mornings dawn
let evening stars fade
let the earth
continue to revolve.
And know
I will return.
Till then,
Remember me.

When Peter turned to her, he smiled a peculiar smile, a mischievous smile. "Possibly the worst poem I've written in a long time but sitting sipping tea in the men's parlor while Miss Bishop greets you and takes you to your room at Warren Hall doesn't lend time for perfection."

Bridget chose to be silent, to let his words fall into the air. When she spoke, her thoughts rose from a place she'd not known for many years, if ever.

"Here I sit, the writer, and I have no words. For me, whether you believe or not," and she took the paper into her hands, "it's perfect."

A bell rang somewhere outside the sitting room. It was the supper hour at the hostelry. In an instant, without words, they agreed. There'd be no meat loaf in the cafeteria tonight.

Looking at one another, they stood, walked out through the reception area and down the front steps. Peter lifted his hand and hailed a taxi. As they settled their backs against the seat, the driver turned. "Where to, folks?" He was greeted with laughter. Neither Peter nor Bridget knew where they might land next.

"Sir," said Peter, "take us to the swankiest hotel in town, with the finest dining." Bridget laughed, grabbed Peter's hand, and raised both their arms in the air. Two people winning the golden chalice.

"Well, folks, one of the best hotels with the best food is right there." He pointed to a tall stone building down the street there on the corner, a place that Bridget and Peter could walk to within five minutes. They exited the taxi as they'd entered, laughing. Peter paused to pay the driver a handsome tip, then took Bridget's hand and stepped over the curb. Still smiling, they walked the one block into their future.

THE MAÎTRE D' AT THE HOTEL YORK STOOD BY THE entrance of the breakfast café and greeted the young couple once again, as he had at dinner the previous night.

"Good morning, and welcome. May I show you to a table by a window?" He tried to keep that special table for couples he sensed were either newly married, about to be married, or in his romantic view of life had promised themselves to one another. As he seated them, he glanced for the wedding rings but saw none.

He noted that the gentleman wore the new wool khaki of the soldier soon to leave, and the chestnut brown of the young lady's eyes rendered a gaze on the soldier that the maître d' wished for every man. As he turned to walk away, having taken their order of coffee, eggs Benedict, and fruit, he heard the gentleman speak, his tone soft, almost a whisper. "Bridget, I'll not forget. And I will return to find you." The old maître d' felt a wrench in his chest. How many times had he witnessed these farewells in the last year and a half? How many times, he wondered, did the gentleman return?

FOR BRIDGET, THE NEXT THREE DAYS WERE A DOORWAY into her new life. Peter's words echoed in her head long after she'd watched him climb the steps onto his train. He'd stood where she was standing now, looking down at her. She wanted to memorize him. His dark, brooding eyes (Peter's words); the bump in the middle of his nose, from an altercation with a tree when he fell off a speeding sled (Peter's words); his ears that were too large for his long face, like open doors on a taxi (Peter's words). How could she forget him!

He'd started to speak, "Bridget...," and when his voice gave out, she waited. Everyone on the platform had faded into a mist. A train whistle blew. His train. A conductor called out, "All aboard."

As he turned to go, she said, just above a whisper, "I know."

After Peter's train was far out of sight, Bridget stood on the platform, hat in hand, wondering where to go. The platform was empty, but still she stood watching where his train had been.

As she lingered, she let the days, the nights, the moments, float within her memory. Laughter, stories told, poetry quoted, every word clear, every sigh a place in her chest, every touch still on her skin. In that moment, Bridget felt the tug of desire to be back there in that room.

"Ma'am, you'll need to go, we're shutting this platform down for the night." A gentleman—overalls, cap, gloves up to his elbows—was standing, leaning on a push broom. "Oh, oh yes, my apologies." Bridget turned to go by him and down the stairs to the street.

"No need to apologize, ma'am. Goodbyes are hard." As she hastened down the stairs and out to the street, she felt the silent tears on her cheek.

Back at Warren Hall, Bridget sat at a table by the window, the small lamp casting a glow across the blank sheet of paper. She wrapped herself in a gray wool blanket, feeling the roughness of the bristly threads. Rather like army issue, she thought.

And in that instant her skin remembered the feel of soft sheets and Peter's gentle hands. She picked up her fountain pen and began her first letter to that soldier.

Dear Peter,

How long has it been since first you beckoned me to sit beside you on the train? You are like one of the characters from one of my stories, ephemeral and a bit magical.

What a joy it is to know someone like you who I know will appreciate words like ephemeral and magical. Being a poet, you'll know that people like us who love words are hard to find sometimes in the worlds we live in.

Bridget took her pen from the page; she knew that the words she'd written were not what she needed or wanted to say. Putting the page aside, she took another paper from her folder.

Dear Peter,

What do I say? Am I what is called a fallen woman? Would my mother disown me? Something says no. My stepfather, yes, and that would please me.

I want you to know that when you asked me to consider waiting for you to return from France, I was stunned, but somehow, I was convinced I wanted to. Totally without reason.

I'm known for figuring out conundrums, but never one so complicated or unexpected.

You are going off to war, I'm going to make weapons, and yet we stopped time for a while, together.

What we experienced throughout the three days and those two nights has shifted something in me like a rock splintering and finding gems inside. (Forgive that simile—it wasn't one of my better ones.) Whatever happens, nothing can erase those moments. I will write to you wherever you are.

I'm glad you gave me your sister's address, because it helps me know I have a connection, at least till I hear from you. But if you can, please write, and let me know how you are.

I'll need to rise early to catch the streetcar out to the munitions factory, so I'll sign off for now.

She paused and picked up the letter, then put it back on the table and added one more thought.

Yes, Peter, I will be here when you return.

Bridget

Folding the page, placing the letter in an envelope, she turned it over to write his address. All she knew was his battalion and his number, Canadian Expeditionary Force. Halifax.

Lessons in not knowing and wondering were about to begin.

Maybe someone in Munitions will know.

Next morning, Bridget awoke feeling as though she might have dreamt the past three days, until she saw Peter's poem lying on the table beside her letter.

An hour later she was on the streetcar.

Chapter Sixteen

IT WAS THE NOISE.

Workers shouting. Drills drilling. Hammers hammering. Small open trucks trundling.

Bridget stood beside a tall, formidable woman whose gray overalls covered her from shoulder to shoes. Miss Morrison had greeted her at the doorway of Ashbridge Bay Munitions Factory and with little ceremony had ushered her into the noise and cacophony.

There appeared to be an endless row of women seated at high-back chairs working in rhythm, one that Bridget couldn't fathom but soon would come to understand. She'd been assigned to the shell fuses section, which to her untrained eye was a mass of lines, of strange machine-drills; hanging wires and pullies; women sitting at machines that bore the appearance of sewing machines, but machines that created war matériel, not fancy dresses. Bridget watched while the working women sat, their feet on a press, driving a needle into a plug that would ultimately become part of a shell one day fired by artillery into wire fences, deep trenches, and the bodies of young German soldiers.

"We'll go no farther now until we find you a uniform, so come with me." Miss Morrison, businesslike and straight-backed, beckoned her to move along. Bridget followed, attentive to the concentration of the women at their stations; she'd learn later that concentration on your work in a munitions factory was necessary, possibly life-preserving. In less than an hour, Bridget was back out on the floor wearing a long, dark, heavy cotton coat and a white cap that covered every tendril of hair. Nothing about her outfit spoke of beauty, only a high need for protection. The woman who directed her to the change rooms and brought her to the floor had left her standing at a station where she'd be creating fuse needle plugs. Bridget had an impression of déjà vu. As a young girl she'd come to know the machinery that created fasteners and screws, an experience she wanted soon to push out of her memory. That memory was part of her old life, now gone.

She stood by the machine wondering if she was expected to figure this out for herself.

Within moments a cheery young woman bustled up to her and introduced herself, breaking into Bridget's thoughts. "Hello." She reached to shake Bridget's hand, her grasp firm and confident. "I'm Elva, Elva McKenzie, and you must be our new girl, Bridget, is it?"

Bridget had a sensation of being welcomed for tea, not a person trained for building bombs and ammunition.

"I believe you've been assigned to this station. You'll sit here." Elva pointed to the chair that accompanied the machine. "Come sit." Elva stood at her shoulder, and in clear, uncluttered language began the training that soon took Bridget into the real, dangerous, sometimes exciting, sometimes repetitive world of creating bombs that somewhere, someday would be on a trajectory to kill. She learned in a short while to insert a security pin into a shell fuse. That accomplishment alone cast away any doubts about her decision to join this war effort. "I can do this," she said aloud as she left the women's washroom during her break.

On the day she began to make bombs, she met two extraordinary women.

One of these women was Elva, daughter of a doctor who was in France treating wounded men of the 1st Canadian Division at a battle that would be known as The Battle of Kitchener's Wood—the Second Battle of Ypres. Elva, Bridget soon learned, was passionate about doing everything she could "for all those boys over there, and for my dad."

And there was Irene.

For the rest of her life, she would remember Irene, who walked into the canteen at lunch with Elva and dropped onto a chair beside Bridget.

"Elva tells me you're a pretty fast learner, took to that machine like a duck to water." Her tone was colored with an edge of doubt and a bit of an Irish brogue.

Eating her ham sandwich, Bridget took a couple of seconds to take in Irene Flynn and her comment. Very black curls escaped from under her white cap, and she wore trousers and a blousy overtop, not the long dress coat that had been issued to Bridget. A red, raised scar ran down one cheek from the corner of her eye, result of a near-fatal accident, which Irene described as a moment when she looked away when she should have looked down. She told this with some degree of bravado. Or so Bridget decided.

"So, are you smart?" Irene's gaze penetrated as though she were trying to decipher who Bridget was.

Elva interjected, watching what she thought to be Bridget's hesitation. "Hey, Irene. Give the girl a chance to finish her lunch before you start on her."

"No, no, I'm fine. Just startled, I guess. No one's ever asked me whether I'm smart. Particularly someone I hardly know." Bridget's words were on the point of sharpness.

"Oh ho. Now we're talkin'. She's smart, and spirited, too."
Irene's face lit with the joy of sparring.

"All right, I need to say something here." Elva once again.
"Bridget, this lady is Irene Flynn, and yes, she has the Irish
in her…"

"Sorry if I startled ya, but I'm a woman who likes to get
to the point."

"And what might that be?"

"Elva and I are always on the lookout for…"

Bridget had an uncomfortable feeling that she'd been
noted or pinned or identified. These days with a war raging,
suspicion reigned. "You think I'm a spy?" She spat out the
words, wondering how fast she could leave this place.

"Hey, slow down there. Not one bit, but Elva and I are
part of a small group who'll be what you might call working
and observing. We're thinking you could join us."

Bridget shook her head no and started to rise from the
chair. "I know what's happening here, I'm not a fool. You're
spies! What I need to know is for which side?"

"If you'd sit back down. And slow up, we'll talk. We're
here…" and her voice lowered. "At the wish of…" and her
voice lowered again. "The imperial munition's board and
Sophie Watson who runs this floor. We're making bombs,
you know, and we need to be very sure no one here or out
there is messing with what we do. Now, will you sit down?
We need to talk."

"Who are you?! And why are you talking to me?"

Irene looked over at Elva. "Go ahead and tell her," Elva
said. Irene nodded.

Irene shifted closer to Bridget and spoke in an even
softer voice, "The woman who heads up security for this
factory, and a few others, mentioned to me and to Elva that

she knows you, and that you might be a natural to work with us. Apparently, according to Sophie..."

Bridget swung in her chair, her hand up to stop the flow of words. "Who?"

"Sophie Watson. She's an artist but she supervises our section. An artist. Can you imagine?" Irene grinned and Elva's eyebrows connected, making her look quite fierce. "Ah, Elva take it easy, I'm only havin' a bit o' fun."

"I know her. I've met her," Bridget said. The conversation, all that was happening and all that had happened in the last few days, was making her stomach feel queasy and her head a little light. "You're looking a little pale, dear," Elva broke in. "Maybe we're being a bit hasty, Irene."

"No, no." Bridget leaned back into the chair, shaking her head. "No, I'm fine, it's just that everything seems to be happening so fast."

"Ah, girl, we did land on you, didn't we." Irene looked over at Elva again. "Maybe we need to give her some time." As she spoke, Irene put her hand on Bridget's shoulder. "We'll be around if you need any help at all. For now, we'll leave you in peace."

It was at this point that Bridget grinned. "Peace might not be a word I'd use around here." She pointed to the machines clanking, the people shouting over the din, the rolling open cars carrying shells, and over by the window a line of women were singing. Singing!

Elva, whose face had begun to crack into a smile, and Irene, whose grin had broadened, gathered themselves to walk back down the aisle toward the supervisor's office. Bridget realized they'd dispensed their duty for now, and she was left to get back to making bombs.

THREE WEEKS LATER AND SEVERAL SESSIONS OF TRAIN-
ing in covert surveillance of the factory floor, Bridget was
assigned to another section where she continued building
shell fuses.

This time with an added responsibility, to listen, to
watch, to see. Word had it that sabotage was ever a threat.
Mysterious fires were breaking out in certain factories
south of the Canadian border, and everyone was on the
alert. Being the observer she'd learned to become, the
added duty overrode the repetitiveness of her work, which
in some ways took her mind off the queasiness that hadn't
lessened. Some days her stomach rolled and heaved, to the
point she had to request more than one or two bathroom
breaks in a morning. It was during one of those breaks she
caught a woman at a sink, penciling a note. One of the rules
of work was that nothing written could go outside the factory. It turned out when Bridget mentioned it to Elva and
Irene that when questioned the woman had been working
on a grocery list. Feeling chagrined, Bridget had started to
apologize for wasting their time.

"Hey, Bridget those notes could've been code going out
to some agent," Irene had retorted. "Anyhow, the supervisor's firing her and wants to see you."

After work that day, Bridget walked across the factory
floor to the super's office, opened the door, and found
Sophie sitting behind the desk. "Come in, Bridget, you and
I need to talk. We've needed to have this conversation for
a long time."

Chapter Seventeen

BRIDGET MUNCHED ON THE CHEESE SANDWICH THE WOMAN from the canteen had brought in. Sophie sipped on a cup of tea that was no longer warm. Bridget waited. Night created shadows across the room. Women on the night shift had begun to arrive, bringing the burble and buzz of voices across the floor of the factory. An hour had passed since she'd walked into the office, where she'd been beckoned by Sophie. An hour that had taken on the mantle of another life change for Bridget. Sophie, the same Sophie who'd discovered her at the train station. The Sophie from her mother Clara's stories. The Sophie who'd warned Clara about Jack was cautioning Bridget and upending her life. A warning that stunned her, a lightning bolt because she believed without doubt she'd left Jack behind to gather dust in her past. But according to Sophie, this was not the case. She spoke of him in cold, biting language.

"Your stepfather is a dangerous man; he is a menace. He will try to find you, Bridget, and you must. Not. Let. Him. I failed your mother. I will not fail you." Time felt measured while Bridget composed herself, trying to take in what Sophie was saying, trying to understand why Sophie was telling her this. Placing the sandwich plate on the table by her chair, she spoke. "Why are you doing this? What are you telling me? More importantly, how can you know any of this?"

Sophie began to tell Bridget a story of regret. A regret at not being able to save Clara from Jack. How she believed he'd poisoned Clara's mind, criticizing her artistry, telling her she was a hack.

"Bridget, I'm not convinced about how your mother died—what actually took her—but I do believe a broken heart was part of her demise, her belief in herself gone, her life's passion shattered. He did that. I'll not allow him to destroy who you are. Which is one of the reasons I want to send you away from here. As far as we can to get you away from his bitterness and his ruthlessness."

Without acknowledging the words, Bridget knew the man Sophie described.

A hushed moment punctuated Sophie's words while she stood and walked to her desk, opened a drawer, and pulled out two letters.

One appeared to be formal, typewritten on cream government issue; the other handwritten with a distinctive flourish, one that Bridget recognized immediately to be her mother's script. She felt the world tilting on its axis, and she was slowly sliding off.

Lifting her hand to her forehead, leaning her elbow on the arm of the wooden chair, she shook her head from side to side. "You're right, Jack is a hideous, loathsome man who destroyed my mother." It was the first time Bridget broke her own silence about her hatred for her stepfather. Speaking the words caused her to gasp for breath. For the first time since leaving him, she wept.

"Oh, my dear girl, whatever it is, please, please tell me." Sophie placed her hand on Bridget's, whose fingers were cold to the touch.

"I can't. I can't." Bridget's body shook. All the pain of

the last months, the horror of her stepfather's attack, the intensity of all that life had dropped into her lap, meeting Peter, wondering what she'd done giving herself so willingly to a man she hardly knew. In that moment she wanted him there telling her everything would be all right, they'd figure it out, just the way he'd said on that night. In that moment, Bridget couldn't depend on anything being all right. Jack would pursue her, she knew, to kill her spirit as he'd done her mother's. And Peter, a man who'd walked in and out of her life, might never return as he'd promised.

Sophie sat, one hand on Bridget's shoulder, just as she'd done many times with other young women like Bridget, women confused and lost in a world that had changed their lives overnight. Yet Bridget was not like other young women—she was Clara's daughter, and Sophie had promised.

Sophie stood and walked over to her office window overlooking the factory floor. Pulling down the shade, she turned toward Bridget, who sat hunched over, her arms crossed, holding her shoulders.

"Bridget," Sophie spoke in a whisper, "you don't have to be here alone. I'm here and I will help in any way I can. You need to tell me what happened." She paused. "Did something happen with Jack?" She drew in a breath, letting her next question flow on the air. "And Peter?"

The sounds out on the factory floor were strikingly muted behind the walls and closed door of the office; only a rumbling and vibration of trucks moving shells, the unintelligible shouts of the women and the lower basses of the foremen leaked through the walls and the heavy curtains that Sophie pulled over the blinds. The banging and clanking seemed far away.

Sophie pulled a chair from behind the desk. A carved lattice back and cushioned seat set it apart from the solid austerity of the chair where Bridget sat, straight-backed, wrapped in the long cotton coat, her boots barely showing below the hem.

As Bridget turned to look at this woman, Sophie, she felt the despair lifting. Jack was a person, only that, a person who no longer could damage her, no longer destroy her spirit. An unfamiliar confidence took seed. And Peter? Peter was hope.

Stirring herself, Bridget placed her hands on the arms of the chair and moved to stand.

"Will you talk to me?" Sophie asked. "Sometime, some-day? If for no other reason than that you know you're not out here in a desert, wandering. I'm here.

"There are women out there," she pointed to the factory floor, "who have stories, maybe not exactly like yours, but their stories. They'll be here with you. Women like Irene."

"Thank you, Sophie, I think I know that, and I'm grateful. For now, I need to figure out where my life is taking me. And for a while, I need to do that on my own." Standing away from the desk she reached her hand out to Sophie, who picked up one of the letters she'd mentioned earlier.

"I want you to stay a few more minutes. I think with everything we've said you need to read this letter. It's from your mother to me. She wrote it after she'd come to see me."

"I'd know that handwriting anywhere." Bridget smiled, letting her breath ease, her shoulders relax as Sophie handed her the letter. Images of Clara rushed into the room, her way of leaning over a desk, her hand curled under her chin as she wrote the letter, her hair falling around her face.

Bridget sat back to read the thoughts and the hope that Clara had left in Sophie's care.

Westover, Ont.

Late night,
June 1902

Dear Sophie,

I needed to say some of those things I might not have expressed very well when last I saw you. Bear with me, Sophie, I'm failing.

You know how unhappy I was after everything that happened at the gallery, a chance that you set up for me, an opportunity to follow my dream. I felt like I'd lost my spark—life's essence, you used to call it.

Possibly I was and am ashamed because I didn't stand up to Jack when he undid all you had arranged. I'm ashamed and embarrassed about how he went to the owner of the gallery and demanded she have nothing more to do with me as one of her artists.

He's no longer a man I recognize. He used to be someone who marveled at beauty, who told me how much he loved my paintings...and me. He said that my paintings enchanted him. That Jack has disappeared and someone dark and menacing has replaced him. I fear him, and I fear the dark places he enters. He's a man who's lost his soul.

You are the only person in my life now who knows about the inheritance left to me by my mother and father when they succumbed to typhus. My will is with Aunt Vivian's solicitor who looks after her affairs. She gave me sound advice, not to tell Jack about any bequest, particularly the size of it. He believed my resources were my teacher's salary. When something happens to me, George and Bridget will each claim their portion. It's important that Jack not find out about the money. They must have a way to be free of him.

You, my friend, know that my constant worry is Bridget. I fear what her life might become left in Jack's care. She is a strong girl, but I know he will try to break her.

George has already confessed to me, even at fifteen, that he can't stay in this house much longer. I worry about what life will be like for Bridget left on her own with Jack. She's only a child yet keenly intelligent and a beautiful writer, even at her age. She has my creative spirit, but I worry he will somehow shatter that part of her as he has mine.

Rest might come more easily to me if I knew you could find some way to be there for Bridget. Without me or George, Jack will transfer his bitterness to her, in some way. I fear he's going to try to suppress her vital spark. I pray she will find it within herself to withstand his heartlessness, because yes, he is without heart.

You may not be able to see Bridget or contact her, but I ask you to somehow in some way, know how she is, over the years. I'm going to ask Mrs. Lowell, our neighbor across the street, to mail this letter to you. I hope you receive it at the address I still have.

This may be my last letter to you, Sophie. My life's energy is gone.

Thank you for remaining a spirit and a light in my life. You are and have been a magical friend.

Affectionately,
Clara

The wheels of a trolley carrying shell fuses trundled under the window of Sophie's office. In Bridget's head, it was a sound—only that, a sound. Nothing registered or placed her in this room. Bridget's mind had shut out everything except her mother's words on the page.

She spoke, barely a whisper. "Have you been looking for me, all these years, since you got this letter?" It seemed an impossible thought, yet, what if?

"I can only answer that question by telling you that your stepfather kept me away from you, in every way he could. I tried to contact you at your school but was told I couldn't see you without his permission. I've never stopped wondering how you are, where you are. I've carried my promise to your mother. When Mrs. Lowell wrote to me that you were coming to the city, and bless her, knew what train you'd be on, I went to find you. Finding you outside the train station that day was your mother's spirit reaching down and placing me there."

"I've never believed in spirits, until lately." Bridget sat back against the laddered wood of the chair and smiled. "Now, I do."

A whistle blew in what seemed to be another world. First break for the night shift. Sophie rose from her chair, went to her desk, and from a drawer pulled a photograph. "Clara sent me this with her letter."

As she reached across to hand it to Bridget, the two women held the photograph. Possibly in the magical world Sophie spoke of and believed in, Clara had entered the room and left, knowing that now her girl had a warrior on her side. Moments passed before Bridget was able to lift her head and speak.

The picture lay in her hands, like a memento of a time sewn into the memory of her childhood. They were all there. Clara sat on a curved settee, with Bridget beside her, a hand resting on her mother's knee. George, who would have been fifteen years old, five years older than his sister, stood next to them, a young man in his first tie and stand-up collar, a gray suit jacket giving him the look of prestige his stepfather required.

Jack stood just off to the side; his hand placed lightly upon Clara's shoulder—more a possessive gesture than love. Each stared into the camera, faces immobile, eyes steady. No one smiled.

"This is the last photograph we had taken. Mama didn't want any more because she thought she looked too old and sick." Bridget smoothed her fingers across the photo, possibly wanting to re-create the touch of her mother's hand. The tall clock by the desk punctuated the moments holding Sophie and Bridget in balance. They were like two women wanting to step into the flow of the river together, one step at a time, one wanting to trust, the other wanting to be trusted.

"Sophie...?" Still, no one moved.

"I'm here. I'm listening."

"I want to take this letter and the photograph, go back to my room at Warren Hall, and consider all you've said today. And tomorrow, when I come into work, I'll be ready."

"Ready for...?" Sophie sat, still at her place, daring not to move.

"Ready to tell you what's happened to me, and ready to decide what I must do."

"Will you be all right tonight?" Her concern revealed, Sophie stumbled for the first time. "I mean...do you need me to go with you?"

"You needn't worry, Sophie. I have much to carry me through till tomorrow. I have hope and my mother's friend."

As Bridget stood up from the chair, she took her mother's letter and the photograph in her hands and held them to her chest, like a prayer.

"Thank you, Sophie."

Without a glance back, Bridget walked to the office door, pressed the latch on the handle, and slipped out into the noise and cacophony of the factory, the letter and photo still at her chest.

Chapter Eighteen

THE NIGHT AIR GREETED BRIDGET WITH A SOFT SPRING breeze. A place in her chest, where her heart had been locked in for many nights and days, felt softened. Everything that had happened over the past hours flowed within Bridget as she made her way out through the high iron gates of the factory. Hope, anticipation, sorrow, understanding, and beginnings.

The overhanging globe of a streetlight across the way cast a lackluster glow upon a group of women from the factory standing by the corner. Bridget turned to walk away in another direction. The last thing she wanted right now was the buzz of gossip and chatter and questions about why she'd been called into the supervisor's office.

But her attempt to slink into the shadows was too late.

"Bridget. Bridget. Over here, my girl," a distinct Irish voice called out. Irene waved her arm, beckoning. "We're here waiting for the tram. Elva's here, too."

Seeing no escape, Bridget gave a casual wave and walked toward the corner.

"What's kept you so late?" Irene asked as she stepped from the curb into the shadows and waited. Before Bridget could think of a response, Irene reached for her hand. "Why don't you and I walk along to the next stop?" Her voice lowered. "You look kinda pale. Are ya all right?"

Maybe it was the kind gesture, maybe Irene's hand on

her arm, maybe it was the softness of her brogue—whatever the reason, Bridget knew she wanted to trust Irene. "I need to talk with you. Could we just keep walking?"

The rain started about the time Irene and Bridget realized they were walking farther than anticipated. Deep in conversation about their jobs and the new surveillance role Bridget had been asked to play, they'd soaked themselves in the prospect of growing friendship, but now they were feeling the effects of a true rainstorm.

Laughing and running, they dodged into a streetcar shelter.

"Where are you going?" Irene asked. Neither had talked about where they lived in the city. The topic of where home might rest did not often arise in the conversations among the munitionettes. Home was not here in this city for most of the women. Home was somewhere each had left, some painfully like Bridget, some with adventure in mind, some who felt this place, this city, this job, were only temporary pauses till the war ended and they'd go home.

The pelting October rain had given in to a soft autumn dampness. Bridget put her hand out beyond the shelter and peered into the darkness.

"Let's wait a couple more minutes to see if the rain is going to stop," Bridget suggested. They were dressed back in their civvies, both wearing the new ankle-length skirts and three-quarter jackets now coming into fashion. Neither was eager to let the falling rain, or the dampness, spoil outfits upon which they'd spent their newly earned government money.

They waited there in the shelter, only the dim glow of the streetlamp bulbs lighting their faces. An expectancy hung between them, one wanting to say more, the other waiting to listen.

"Bridget?" Irene shoved her hands into the sleeves of her jacket and faced out into the street. "Are you freezing?"

"Mm, mm. Not freezing, just coldly damp."

Irene pointed through the gloom. "Look, on the corner across the street. Isn't that a deli just by the streetlamp? I bet we could get a cup of coffee, maybe a sandwich. It's just the supper hour and the dining room at Warren will be closed soon."

"Irene! Are you living at Warren Hall?"

"Yeah, I am. Don't tell me...?

"Me, too. Well, we're practically family. Let's go eat." Once again, laughing like young women will when friendship blossoms, they strode from the shelter arm in arm.

"And...they're open. What luck." Irene dropped Bridget's arm and with an exaggerated flourish opened the door, ushering her into the warmth and smells of freshly baked bread, which spoke of home in Ireland and back kitchens where loaves lay cooling. A table by the window and a potbellied stove beckoned them like a friend who'd been waiting, anticipating Bridget and Irene might come by eventually. Bridget pulled a chair and placed her bag at her feet—she needed to know where the letter was. She needed to feel it near her.

"Why don't I get us a bit of their warm stew and a coffee, while you sit there." Irene was eyeing her friend with an attentive gaze that spoke concern.

"Here, I have change." Bridget reached down to pull out her small coin purse, one that had been Clara's, flowered with her distinctive needlepoint designs. As she retrieved the purse, she caught the edge of the scripted paper and Clara's letter fell onto the floor.

Irene chose that moment, wise woman that she was, to pull her chair closer to Bridget. She reached down, picked up Clara's letter, and placed it in Bridget's hand, each motion careful and gentle. Unspoken words floated between the two women, neither of them feeling an urgency to explain or mend. Bridget sat now in the comfort of Irene's sustenance. It might be that for the first time since her life had been swallowed up, she imagined a world where Sophie's words "I'm here" could be true, and Irene's gentle silence offered a door.

Silence became the marrow between them.

But then…three women from the factory blustered through the door, bringing the sounds of the night rain falling on the road, the rattle of the street rail car moving to the next corner. Without looking to the door, Irene sensed the three women walking to their table, ready to pull up chairs and chat away the tensions of the day.

Looking to them, she shook her head back and forth, with the gentlest of motion. Elva in the lead motioned the others to turn back, move away. Irene smiled gratitude over to Elva.

"Let's you and I find a cab and go back to Warren. I can get us some stew to take with us. There'll be coffee in the dining room still." Like the protective friend, Irene, arm on Bridget's shoulder, waved to the others and walked the two of them out into the rain.

BRIDGET AND IRENE SAT, LETTING THE DARKNESS OF night overtake the room. Only the faint sound of horses' hooves and rattling Model Ts rose up from the street below. Irene sat at the small desk, letting her feet rest on the footstool. Bridget, wrapped in a wool blanket that Irene assured her was straight from her hometown Kinsale in Ireland, sat across the bed, leaning against the wall. For the first half hour, she'd eaten her stew, drunk her coffee, and said nothing.

Irene let the silence be. Until Bridget whispered. "I think I may have done something, something wrong, yet it doesn't feel that way. Things have happened in the past weeks that've been awful and wonderful. I may pay the price for both." Irene strained to hear but said nothing. Bridget's words floated on the air like a whisper. "There's been someone. Someone I met, he's gone, he's a soldier—he's a poet—"

Irene took her feet from the stool and leaned into the darkness, leaned toward Bridget. She knew this story. "You're not alone in this. Other young women have been tricked and persuaded, it's nothing to be ashamed..."

"No, no, Irene, that's the point, I wasn't tricked or persuaded or whatever you're thinking. And this isn't about shame. I keep waiting to feel some kind of remorse, but truthfully, what I'm feeling is, don't laugh, a kind of grace. And I think I'm going to vomit. I gulped down that stew too fast."

Bridget placed her hand over her mouth and leaned forward. Irene stood to switch on the hanging lamp over their heads. She grabbed a bowl from the side table and held it for Bridget. A dry retch escaped, shook her body, and without hesitation brought back the stew she'd just eaten.

"Jesus, Mary, Joseph...Are you sayin'?" Irene reached for the lamp.

Bridget moved across the bed, set the bowl at her feet, and set her feet firmly on the floor like a woman looking for solid ground, a place.

Irene could see the shadow of Bridget folding herself into herself, like an animal balloon slowly losing air.

"Come, let me sit there with you." Irene moved her chair closer to the bed and placed her hand on Bridget's shoulder. "We'll figure this out."

There it was again, *we'll figure this out*, and with her head over the bowl again, Bridget knew Peter, Irene, all those who had entered her life…and now this sense of grace… were here to help her figure it out. While she continued to lose her supper.

AN EARLY MORNING LIGHT CAST A DIM BEAM UNDER THE window blind. Irene sat up in her bed, trying to stay still. Bridget lay beside her, face turned to the wall, her hands folded and tucked under her cheek, as though in prayerful supplication. Her breathing was even and sure, as one in sound sleep. The clock across the room measured the moments with a quiet ticking.

Bridget had given into exhaustion, no longer insisting she'd get up, go to her own room on the second floor. She'd accepted Irene's suggestion that they stay in her room. "Come stay with me tonight" had held a welcoming sound, a feeling of being attended to, and a memory of who last said those words—Peter, in the hotel dining room, reaching for her hand.

That night Bridget set sail on rough seas but knew she'd weather them. This was Bridget who'd lost a mother she'd loved; Bridget who'd been the force helping her stepfather become rich; and Bridget who'd left after he'd tried to devour her soul. Bridget who'd found a miracle on a train.

Bridget was the woman who said, "I feel grace."

AT PRECISELY EIGHT O'CLOCK THAT MORNING, IRENE knocked on Sophie's office door. Bridget had insisted on going to her station. "I have work to do here. Whatever happens, I still have work to do." She'd left Irene's room at six o'clock, gone to her own place to change into a fresh uniform, and, without waiting, had made her way back to the factory. Not knowing what the fallout might be now that her story had been told, she made up her mind to work as long and as hard as they'd let her. Bridget was sure today would be her last at the factory. She'd have to find another escape route. In her world, in any world, she was damaged goods.

Nine o'clock. A whistle sounded for morning break. A line of machines for drilling needle holes into detonators ground to a synchronized halt. Irene emerged and walked down the aisles toward Bridget's station, a determination in her stride. Bridget believed the moment she dreaded had arrived. She'd be asked to gather her things, report to Sophie in her office, and receive her exit pay. Stepping away from her station, she began to collect her bag that held a lunch sandwich, and her wallet. Bridget straightened her back, picked up her belongings, switched off her machine, and turned to be ready for the news.

"Bridget," Irene beckoned as she approached. "Will you come with me? Sophie and I need to talk with you. Oh, you can leave your things on your chair." Confusion rattled Bridget's reckoning of why she was being summoned. Why leave her things if she would be making her exit from the factory very shortly? "I'll need to take my bag with me when I go. I'll take it with me now."

Irene's brow crinkled into a puzzled furrow. "What are you saying, 'when I go'? Your shift won't end till later this afternoon." A flash of realization crossed her face. "Oh no, you're thinking...because you're...or believe you're..." her voice lowered, "...expecting his child?"

Bridget's shoulders lowered half an inch. "I'm not being sent away?" Other workers were making their way around the two women standing in the middle of the machinery aisle. Aware that workers were curious and liked to gossip about one another, Irene motioned toward Sophie's office and strolled away. Bridget followed, her bag back under the seat of her station. When she arrived at the door, she looked through a small window to see Irene already seated at Sophie's desk, and Sophie herself in her usual place.

An inhale and a long exhale ushered her into the room. "I understand you need to talk with me." She spoke as if she might be one of the suspicious women she'd been asked to observe, only a month ago when Elva and Irene had secured her to be a "watcher and listener."

Sophie waved her in, pointing to a chair opposite her desk and a teapot that sat on a hot plate. "Tea, Bridget?"

That feeling of being readied for something prompted Bridget to sit tentatively on the chair. She shook her head no to the tea and uttered a quiet "thank you."

Sophie's easel sat off to the side by a window looking out onto the factory floor—her painting of women creating munitions had been commissioned by the Canadian War Records to document the war effort in Canada. It was another recognition of Sophie's talents. Jack had disliked her influence over his wife, a resentment that Sophie knew had mutated over time into bitterness and rancor. Her fear for Bridget arose from firsthand dealings with his vindictiveness. She'd seen how he'd fractured Clara's spirit, and now she knew all about the horror he'd brought into his stepdaughter's life. Bridget had described the brutality of his attack.

And Sophie feared for Bridget.

"I'll not linger on any more discussion. I think you've told us how excruciating your life has become. With your stepfather. You are my friend Clara's daughter; you hold her gifts and spirit, so I'll be as plain spoken as I can. I believe, and now so does Irene, that he will try to find you, and because of what he has done, he will do even more harm than he already has, although it's hard to imagine how much more damage he might do." She leaned across her desk; hands folded.

"I've already suggested what you need to do. Irene, too, has an idea. Both of us…"

Bridget put her hand up to stop the words. "I'm not leaving. I'm staying here, I've made my bed…and if either of you is thinking…well, that's not an option."

"That's just shite. Forgive me, Bridge." Irene, who was sitting off to the side, threw her arms into the air, hands coming down and landing on the top of her head. "None of what has happened to you is yours. He is the devil!"

Sophie unfolded her hands and brought them sharply flattened onto the wood of her desk. A sound like a gunshot. Both women jumped.

"First," Sophie spoke with the compelling tone of a woman who had made her way through an unfriendly world.

"I know what it means to have to create a new life and so does Irene. But. Nothing will occur if you, Bridget, waste time torturing yourself. You carry no blame, none, for what's happened. As a matter of fact, you've rescued yourself."

Another whistle blew out on the floor, and the unhurried swish of leather-soled footsteps joined the sounds

THE SHELTER OF EACH OTHER   125

of machines. Bridget moved to the edge of her chair and started to rise. "I need to get back to my station, I have work before me."

"Elva is replacing you till lunchtime. Please sit down and hear us out." Sophie spoke in a tone ringing with white clarity. Doing as Sophie said, Bridget sat back, yet without real compliance; instead, she took Sophie's stance. She leaned across the desk and folded her hands.

"I've told you both my story because I decided to trust you. Now, there's nothing left to say. If you are asking me to continue working here, I will. But if you are telling me I need to leave, which you seem to be saying, I won't and can't do that." The room became quiet, with only the accompanying sounds of drills and the thuds of machines breaking into their silence. Sophie stared straight into Bridget's eyes, willing her to listen.

"He will find you. I tried to convince your mother to stay away from him, but he was like a charlatan, a sorcerer. He charmed her, at first thinking her talent could bring him the wealth and fame that he desired—but he couldn't accept she was so much more talented than him. He's a sick man, Bridget. You cannot do battle with his vindictiveness by yourself. We can't do battle with his brutality…he is a man who has power. We don't. What we will do is outmaneuver him."

Bridget dropped her hands into her lap and leaned against the back of the chair. A sense of disbelief turned an inhale into a gasp.

"How do you know this?"

"There's more. Remember that your mother had an inheritance from her family which was given to her in trust after her parents died, to be collected at her twenty-first birthday. However, she never did. She kept it in a special account, without Jack's knowledge…" Sophie began.

Bridget interrupted. "Mama told me the same things when I was a girl. What happened to the inheritance? Why didn't Mama use it and go to Paris? That's what she wanted. I know it was. Does George know all about this, too?" She paused. Her face showing a glimmer of realization. "How much does Jack…know?"

Sophie shook her head back and forth. "You need to know. After Clara died, he discovered from your mother's solicitor how she'd kept all this from him, and that the inheritance was to go to George and you. Your mother was wily and smart. She came to know what a dark man he really was. She made very sure, as much as she could within a less-than-helpful system because she was a woman, that he would never benefit. I'm sure he wants you, Bridget, and… he wants that inheritance."

Sophie spat out the words and curled her lip in disgust. "Knowing how loathsome he was, my deep regret was, and still is, that Clara wouldn't leave him.

"She could have, you know, with the resources she had, but she knew Jack would wrangle to keep you and George away from her if she dared leave. In many ways she was a woman ahead of her time—she was braver than most, yet she was dealing with the devil himself."

Bridget sat frozen, nauseated, and horror-stricken.

Irene sat forward in her chair. "I need to say something, Bridget. I know what Sophie is saying, and she knows a whole lot more than I about this man, but I know something about leaving to find safety. I come from a family of brothers, five to be sure, who all belong to something called Irish Volunteers—which scares me because I know they're the old revolutionary brotherhood wanting to fight the British. And…will not ever fight for the British in this war we're in now."

Bridget cocked her head to the side and looked over to Irene, "So, what are you saying? I don't see the connection."

"What I'm saying is…I disagreed fiercely with my family's politics and that made me a traitor to them. I couldn't hang around with what was about to happen. To watch the violence I knew they were planning…That's when I decided to emigrate to Canada. A short while ago. All I'm saying is we women need to make up our minds to be brave. Take care of ourselves. You're on that road, Bridget. But you're not walking it alone."

A quiet whisper slipped from Bridget. "Thanks, Irene."

"With that said." Sophie stood from her chair, walked around, and leaned against her desk; ankles crossed. "I have something you need to look at. I'd decided to keep this locked away. But it's time." She reached into the side pocket of the long cotton coat she wore and pulled out a ring of four keys. She took a brass one from the circle and handed it to Irene.

"Could you go into the closet, please? On a shelf just behind my street clothes is a small wooden box—would you bring it to me?" Irene, who looked as puzzled as Bridget, took the key, unlocked the closet, and for a moment disappeared inside. When she emerged, she held a carved box.

Bridget gasped with surprise. "That's my mother's jewelry box, why do you have it?"

As she started to rise from her chair, Sophie motioned her to stay seated. "I'm going to come sit there beside you. Irene, why don't you go sit behind my desk." Sophie sat, moving her chair to face Bridget. "Your mother gave this box to me two weeks before she died. It was when she came to the city to meet the curator of the gallery where we were going to show her paintings, until your stepfather barged his way in."

Sophie took another key from the ring and handed it to Bridget.

Chapter Nineteen

INSIDE THE BOX WAS A SMALL COTTON BAG TIED WITH A red ribbon. As Bridget reached in for the bag, Sophie delayed her hand. "Before you open that bag, I need to show you a letter I've been keeping, one you need to see." Bridget placed the bag back into the box and reached for the envelope. Addressed to Sophie at the munitions factory, the heavy black scrawl was Jack Blackwell's.

Bridget took the envelope and placed it on Sophie's desk. No one spoke. No one moved. An air of horrified expectancy floated in and around them, but Bridget sat, staring at the letter. Sophie and Irene waited. "Would you like us to leave you while you read?" Sophie asked. "Or do you need us to be here?"

"I'd really like you to stay. Just seeing his handwriting makes me sick to my stomach." Sophie was alarmed by how pale Bridget had become, like a person seeing the ghostly figure of someone at her heels, someone who meant harm.

"Irene, would you go to the canteen and get us some more hot tea and biscuits?" Without a word, Irene walked to the door, opened it, and sprinted down the aisles of machinery to the canteen.

When tea arrived, Bridget had moved to sit on a large chesterfield by the office window, her ankles crossed, her long cotton coat wrapped around her body like the protective covering it was meant to be. The letter lay on her lap, and she was in midsentence. "…he was threatening you, my mother's friend. Damn his soul if it isn't damned already." Turning to Irene, she held the letter up. "Have you seen this?"

"No, this is the first I've heard about it."

"Listen to this." Bridget's words spit into the air like crackling fire. She leaned forward, feet flat on the floor and elbows on her knees, and read, her voice tight with anger.

To: Miss Sophia Watson
May 1915

From: Jack Blackwell
President of Blackwell Fine Furniture

It took some doing on my part to find you; however, I am not a man who is easily daunted. As difficult as it was, all it took was a little detective work with the help of some business friends who are manufacturing munitions for this war and connections I still have with the Society of Artists. It seems you've made a name for yourself, Sophie Watson. If that is your name now. Supposed art critic, painter of some talent, now munitions worker. It's been difficult tracking you down, but I've done my homework.

I understand you've been commissioned to create a record of women in the war effort as a painter. And that you in fact may be working in one such factory. You've always been an opportunist. I do remember.

You led my wife, Clara, to believe she was a gifted artist. You made a very difficult situation for me and my family, causing me to have to intervene.

I said it then, and I'll repeat, how dare you let her believe she was talented and persuade her to have a showing at a gallery?

Clara passed on years ago, but I still resent the claim you placed on her life. She was meant to be my wife and my children's mother—not some short-lived painter looking for fame. You went beyond the boundaries of propriety—interfering in the life of my family. Now it appears you are still meddling with my life.

My daughter, Bridget, has left her home and left me. With much shrewdness on my part and my connections, I've discovered she's taken on a job at a munitions factory. It would not surprise me if you've had something to do with her leaving and with her gaining employment as a machine operator.

I intend to find her and, as I had to do with her mother, bring her home where she rightfully belongs.

I feel it my duty to demand that if you know of her whereabouts, you contact me immediately.

Jack Blackwell

Bridget threw the letter to the floor and stood up, fiery determination flashing in her eyes. "I'll leave. I'll leave tonight."

"My God, are you going back there!" Irene said.

Sophie, who'd been watching Bridget's every move, listening to the rancor in her words, walked to the chesterfield and sat beside her. "Realize what you are saying. You mustn't, you can't."

To their amazement, Bridget laughed, picked up the paper, crumpled it, and tossed it across the room. "Do you honestly think that's what I meant, to go back there, to him?"

"But you just said…" Irene lifted her shoulders, looking baffled.

"Irene, give me some credit. I meant, I need to leave here, go somewhere where he can't find me."

"How about Ireland?" Irene piped up.

Sophie reacted first. "In the midst of the trouble that might be bubbling there. Probably not."

"Well, he'd never think of looking for me there, would he?" Bridget grinned and then some dark specter dimmed her eyes. "Seriously, where can I go? He's relentless. Sophie, you know what he did to my mother."

A look crossed Sophie's face, a flash of knowing. "Have either of you ever heard of…hiding in plain sight?" Sophie asked, a slight smile coloring her words.

"What does that mean?" Bridget asked. Irene's brow furrowed. Puzzled.

"It means exactly what it says. Hiding right under someone's nose. Or where he thinks is under his nose."

Silence greeted Sophie's notion.

"I have no idea what that might look like." Bridget sighed. "And, you don't know how mulish this man can be. I expect he'll overturn every rock to find me." She sank against the leather back of the sofa and folded her arms across her chest. "Maybe I should just go back and confront him."

"That's not an option, Bridget," Sophie said, shaking her head. "Don't ever think for a moment he's not planning his revenge for leaving him. He is deluded. If you go back he'll believe he's won and from that point on, he or his hired cronies will find a way to punish you." She paused. "I won't see you go back there, ever." Her eyes darkened.

"Where do you suggest I go? And am I not being a coward by not facing up to him?"

"This is not about being cowardly. Understand Bridget, I know what I'm talking about. He's gained power in dark places, and those who have, in his eyes, betrayed him have paid the price. And regrettably, being a woman is fodder for his vengeance. In his eyes and in his world…we're…nothing." Sophie spit the word "nothing" into the air.

Irene, who'd decided it was time to move the conversation into action, broke in.

"It's clear to me, to Sophie, and should be to you, Bridget, it's time to move beyond this man's grip." She looked out the window at the lines of wires, the machines clanking, the women in their white caps and long coats. "When you told him you were going to work in a munitions factory, did you give any indication of where?" Bridget shook her head, "No. But…"

"Hear me out."

Sophie opened her arms, palms up. "Of course. There are factories in all kinds of places: Ontario, Quebec, England, and Scotland! There are thousands of women working…"

Bridget slapped her hands on her lap. "No, wait. Why didn't I think of this sooner? My brother, George. He'll help. He hates Jack enough to delight in the thought of outsmarting him." For the first time since the conversation began, Bridget's energy entered the room.

"Look. I'm an unmarried woman, expecting a child. What factory will want to hire me? But…what I…what if, I have my baby and then…then go to Quebec or England or Scotland…wherever there are munition factories?"

"What on earth are you saying?" Sophie's voice rose in disbelief.

"Here, Bridget, I think you need a sip of tea and a bite of sweet bun." Believing that her friend wasn't thinking with a clear mind, Irene handed her a cup of tea with sweet bun on the saucer.

"I don't need tea right now. I need you to listen." The vehemence in Bridget's voice gave both women the shock needed.

"All right, we're here. We'll listen." Sophie beckoned Irene to put the tea aside.

THAT NIGHT, BACK IN WARREN HALL, BRIDGET SAT AT the small desk near the end of her bed, took paper and pen to begin a letter to her brother. By the side of the paper lay her mother's turquoise butterfly brooch.

Warren Hall, Gerald St.
City of Toronto.

Dear George,

Now it seems sitting down to write to you is the wisest and the clearest way to explain what's happened. Jack had a serious fall down the stairs—he tripped and fell headlong. Why he didn't break his neck I'll never know.

Bridget paused and read back through the words—why she wondered, did she begin this way, a fall down the stairs, and questioning why he didn't break his neck. Now, all these weeks later, was that where she wanted to start her story? She felt as though she were dissembling, clouding what she really needed to tell him. Was this wise? A letter, words on a page, no chance to watch his face or hear his reaction.

With a small sigh, she put the pen to paper and continued.

I was packed and ready to leave, for good, before he had his fall. He couldn't be left on his own because the fall injured him. Dr. Winslow came over when I called him, and he suggested I take Jack into the local hospital just to check him over. Nothing was broken, he's a tough old bird, but he was bruised. His body and his ego. For which now, I care little.

A voice within was struggling for airtime; she could both feel it and hear it. *"This is not about the bastard; nothing any longer can be about him. Get to what you need to say."* She let her shoulders drop, realizing that the act of writing about this man was drawing her into the darkness of that night in her bedroom. Blocking her from opening herself as she'd done with Sophie and Irene. Bridget knew if she were ever to dislodge herself from the quagmire her life could become, she needed to stay the course and tell her truth. George must know what happened. Each line fell from the pen as a recognition of what she must do.

I'm in a predicament, well actually it's more than a predicament. There's more to this story to explain but I'd rather do that face-to-face with you.

I've left home. Some of my reasons I believe you'll already know, but the final straw, the shattering moments, I'll save to tell another time.

Jack and I reached the end of our relationship the night he had the fall. I want nothing more to do with him.

I've a job at a munitions factory outside the city on the east side—that's why I was packed and ready to go that night. Something's happened that's pushed me and yes, Jack, into the abyss.

Mrs. Lowell, remember the neighbor across the street, the widow who knows everything about everyone? She's going to watch out for Jack for a while, take him meals, and the doctor will check in on him. That's all I can or am willing to do.

If my words somehow don't make sense, forgive me. Luckily, I've discovered friends here who are willing to help me as I work through what I need to do next.

I tried several times to convince him I needed to be out and away and on my own, but he'd have none of it. He convinced himself I'd never survive. I believe for his own warped purposes. Over the past year he's become more possessive and possessed about knowing my whereabouts, who I'm seeing, even questioning why I need to leave the house. My decision to leave has been coming for a while, maybe even years. He's even locked me in my room once, can you believe!

He's never said aloud that I'm the one who's helped increase his business, never said thank you for the furniture designs I created or acknowledged me at all. I've written all the copy for the descriptions in the catalog—and him—he takes the credit and the money. He's caught up in becoming wealthy and only sees me through his accumulation of money. This is a man whose view of the world is about how large his bank account is and who helps him do that, without being beholden to anyone, particularly me. I'm some-

one he must control in any way he can. There's more to that story which you probably know better than I because you were there all those years watching how he broke Mom's spirit.

My resentment is hatred of who he is: an angry, dangerous man.

Our mother gave up a promising career as an artist. I don't know the whole story, but I do know he crushed her spirit.

I wish I'd had a chance to talk with her about why she let him do that, but I was too young to understand. I will always blame him for her death.

I ask nothing from him. Nor do I want anything. With my planning, putting away the pittance he paid me over the years, I have a bank account.

When you receive this letter, I'm hoping you'll write back to me. I'm going to need your help.

Bridget took a deep inhale and wrote *I may be asking you to take me in for a while.*

"There. It's said." She spoke aloud as though to assure herself.

With my fondest regards,
Bridget

There, in the solitude of her room, she sat looking down at what she'd written. There was nothing about Peter, nothing about what was happening in her body. Why? The ends of her fingers itched with apprehension. Picking up her pen she wrote:

P.S. Remember, shortly after Mom died, we sat out on the porch one night and we told each other that if one of us needed the other, no matter the reason, we'd be there. This is one of those times, George.

Without rereading any further, she took the envelope, wrote George's name and the address of the farm he'd given her across the front, and licked the seal before she could change her mind.

Early the next morning, she dropped it into a mailbox by the steps of Warren Hall. Then she walked to the streetcar stop and stood watching the city come alive with people heading into their lives.

Clarity and possibility rose in her body, straightening her back, softening her furrowed brow.

She knew a path forward.

Chapter Twenty

Broadview Farm
June 1915

Dear Bridget,

*I wish there'd been some way to get my letter back to
you faster. The only thing that kept me from rush-
ing to Westover and bursting into the house was the
knowledge that you are no longer there. I hope that
is still true.*

*Six, almost seven years and I haven't laid eyes
on you. I feel I've let you down. Selfish in my need
to get away from him, not thinking about you being
left there.*

*When I didn't hear from you for days after that
last letter I wrote to you, I admit I was afraid he might
have done something, maybe even something awful.
Or you were done with me. I'm glad to know you are
somewhere safe, or are you?*

*Something is wrong. I haven't known you to ask
me for anything, except when you asked me to teach
you to ride my bike. And we both know how that
turned out. You ended up with a brand-new bike and
I kept my old rattly one.*

*Gladly for both of us, money is not a problem, but
if for some reason it becomes an issue, let me know.*

I have invested some of my part with, may I say, the wise advice of Edna my now wife. I can help.

Toronto where you are isn't far from the town of Milboro, which is close to our farm. If I'd only known or tried to contact you, I realize you and I have not been far from one another all this time! If you need a place to stay, if that's part of your worry, you can certainly come here. Picking you up at the train station is easy.

One thing you need to know. Remember the family I told you about, the widow and her two sons, I haven't told you the whole story. You and I have some catching up to do.

Edna Murphy and I were married. She is a good woman and I've grown very fond of her. It matters not that she's older than I am. In fact, I receive the benefit of her life experiences, especially her know-how as a farmer and as a financier...She carried on after Mr. Murphy passed and in fact has prospered. No grass grows under her feet, not a bit! And I've gained two young sons. Harry is ten and Edward is seventeen. You'll like them both, I hope, and Edna, too. Harry is rambunctious and needs a firm hand, while Edward is a quiet boy—the kind you'll find in the barn up in the haymow with a book. They have taught me a lot about what it means to be a good father.

The farm is called Broadview for a good reason: I can go for a walk from the back door past the barn and see for miles. Acres of grain, cows grazing, and the horses that still pull the ploughs. If I'd ever wanted something approaching peace in my life, this is it.

Are you smiling, imagining your brother, a farmer? Bridget, I've discovered my place. I've found a good family and I'm hoping you'll consider coming to stay at least for a while.

About this trouble you mention. Have you done something to anger him? You haven't done anything that's against the law, I hope. Whatever it is, I'm glad you wrote to me. Please let me know the soonest you can get a train. Bring whatever you have, and I will meet you.

Fondly,
George

P.S. Edna is eager to meet you. I've told her about my sister who is so much smarter than I am.

P.P.S. I do remember that promise we made, and I'm here.

"ALL THOSE LEAVING THE TRAIN AT MILBORO, WE'LL BE arriving in eight minutes. Please descend from the train at door B." The conductor walked through the car. "Milboro, next stop. Milboro."

Bridget gathered her skirt and lifted her cloth bag from the seat beside her. She stood to move down the aisle but first leaned to look out the window as the train slowly rolled into the station. A few people stood waiting on the other platform, passengers ready to board a train on the opposite track headed for the west of Ontario, back in the direction she'd left almost two months ago, determined not to return.

As she scanned the station platform, she grinned at

the sight of her brother, George; he was leaning against a black car that to her appeared to be a large and intimidating vehicle. Seems George is doing okay, she thought, as she clambered down the aisle with her cloth bag in tow.

A woman dressed in a long cotton coat and a wide-brimmed straw hat boasting yellow flowers stood on the platform just in front of the car. She was smiling.

The air was light with a scent of summer as Bridget stepped down from the train. She strolled toward them at first but then picked up speed as she walked along the platform toward the car. Her bag swung at her side. Holding her hand up, she waved like a girl returning from a long journey. By the time she arrived to greet them, she was trotting like an excited colt, her skirt flapping at her ankles.

Edna moved toward her; arm extended. Her face shone with open acknowledgment that spoke welcome. George started toward Bridget, tentative at first. It had been almost seven years since brother and sister said their goodbyes, George leaving in anger, Bridget inconsolable to see him go. But the sorrow melted into the air as they moved toward one another. George, first to reach out, lifted his arm to take her bag, but Bridget dropped her cloth luggage onto the station platform, grasped his hand, and stood looking into his face, which appeared to her more weathered, more seasoned.

"George." She spoke in a whisper that rode on a sigh. A promise made to herself was soon broken when tears found their way to the corners of her eyes.

"Bridget, I've missed you." George's voice cracked and he closed his eyes for a moment, composing himself. At that moment, the sadness they'd felt during their separation began to heal. Bridget knew her decision to come to George and seek his help was the right one.

George placed his hand on her shoulder and drew her into his arms. Bridget's breath filled her chest like a lament, one she'd held since he'd left that night long ago. She felt safe here. When they drew apart, the world resumed. George turned away and beckoned to Edna. "Bridget." He reached toward his wife as she walked to them. "Meet my wife, Edna." He stood like a gate swinging open between the two women.

"Edna, meet my sister, Bridget."

BRIDGET MADE HER WAY DOWN THE BACK STAIRS TO THE kitchen later that evening. The scent of cinnamon, cloves, and baked pies wafted up toward her as she stepped down to join the family waiting to greet her. The ceiling above the stairwell felt low and confining, and being as tall as she was, she ducked when she arrived at the doorway into the kitchen. Edna, George, and Harry greeted her with smiles and grins. Edward looked up for an instant and went back to his books and writing.

"Everyone does that. Has to duck," said Harry, a ten-year-old self-assured boy with fierce brown eyes and a smile that strode straight to Bridget's heart. "Those stairs are this house's booby trap. You thought you were about to crash into the ceiling, didn't you." He grinned.

"Harry. You haven't been introduced yet, manners please." Edna, over by the stove, waved a large spoon in Harry's direction. He stood by the stove, where he'd been piling cut firewood into a steel bin. Dressed in blue overalls and a red plaid shirt, he appeared to be the center of everyone's attention in the room. George sat in an old rocker by the stove, his eyes fixed on Harry.

"Careful there, boy, you'll be sending chips all over the floor." But Bridget noted a slight play around the edges of George's mouth—Harry had won his stepdad's heart.

And Edward, older brother. He sat at a table, books lying in an arc around him. Pen in hand, he wrote with an intensive focus.

"Edward. Edward? Our guest is here. Manners," Edna said, with a soft edge.

He looked up at Bridget who stood in the doorway, hesitant to break into the fold of this family. When he stood up, there behind the table—more a desk than a table—he seemed to unfold till he stood full height, all six-feet one-inch of him.

"Welcome," he said with a soft resonance.

"Meet our family scribe," George offered from his place by the stove. "You'll need to show your Aunt Bridget your stories. He's had some published, Bridget, in our local library's magazine."

Bridget walked to the table, shook Edward's hand, and said quietly: "I hope you'll let me read one. I like to write myself. And so did your dad's mother. I won't interrupt you now. Why don't you go back to your writing? We authors need our moments when they happen."

Edward smiled for the first time.

"Come on over here, Bridge. Sit by me. We're about to have evening supper," George beckoned. His face clouded at Bridget's mention of Clara. His eyes searched her face, looking for that sister he'd known all those years ago. He saw a woman, no longer a girl, with sadness in what used to be bright, alive eyes, yet her lips parted in the beginning of a smile.

It'd been seven years since last he'd seen her, then a young girl. The woman who stood in the doorway at the bottom of the stairs was someone George didn't recognize. She was Bridget, yes. She was his younger sister, although a taller version. Yet she seemed to hold an expression and a stance he couldn't reconcile—the woman before him was the same self-possessed Bridget, yet tentative. Her eyes, whose luster he remembered, seem to have dimmed. Edna was first to go to her. With a hand outstretched, she moved from where she'd been cooking supper, a woman used to taking charge, a woman who'd known difficult times, and recognized hesitancy in Bridget.

"Come sit here beside your brother. Let me bring you tea before we sit down to eat."

Before Bridget could say yes or no, Edna spoke to Edward who was again immersed in his writing. "Edward, the teapot is steeping, would you be a good man and pour a cup for Aunt Bridget." It was a strange moment. Lives in freeze frame, awaiting what might happen next.

Bridget was first to move. "Edward, you stay with your writing, I don't want to disturb you. I know exactly what it's like when thoughts are interrupted. I'm happy to get my tea, if that's all right with you, Edna." Edward looked up. Smiled. His aunt whom he'd just met had given him a gift—she'd recognized that what he was doing was important to him. He mouthed, "Thank you."

George saw the girl he remembered. That girl who had an uncanny instinct for others.

"Bridge, can I help you?" He began to get up from his chair. With George's invitation, Bridget moved into the kitchen and gave him a gentle shove, which landed him back in his rocker. "I'm not going to be a guest in my brother's home," she laughed. "I'm willing and able to do my part. My thanks to you, Edna, for teaching George some manners."

"Well, some things haven't changed." George grinned. "My sister is still as sassy as ever." Color rose in Bridget's cheeks for the first time since arriving, and her eyes brightened. She laughed and waved a hand over to her brother just as a sister might have done those years ago.

Her news could wait.

THAT NIGHT A FULL MOON GAVE BRIDGET LIGHT ACROSS her bed, and the quilt—flowers and trees stitched carefully by Edna and her neighbors—gave her comfort. She lay watching a cloud drift across the moon's face, the window framing the sky beyond. Murmurs of conversation in the kitchen below drifted up the stairs and into her bedroom. George's deep, gravelly voice, like a low rumble, spoke to her of safety and refuge. Edna's, husky with fatigue, responded occasionally.

They'd given Bridget peace and contentment, if only for this night. She knew tomorrow would jar her tranquility when she announced her news, but for now, tonight, stomach satisfied with beef stew, roasted vegetables, pumpkin pie, and cider, she felt the momentary ease of sanctuary.

Her dream broke into the night, like a thief grasping at the covers. She woke, grabbing onto the quilt, gasping, and gulping for breath. The room that had been bright with moonlight now was dark and threatening. A branch cracked against the window.

"Who are you?" Bridget whispered. "Why are you here?" Only silence responded, a menacing silence. A shadow like a paper doll crawled from the floor across the ceiling and made its way down the wall beside her bed.

"Bridget…Bridget! Wake up. Wake up. You're having a nightmare."

She flailed at the hand wanting to smother her. Thrashed at the dark presence that threatened to overwhelm her.

"My baby. My baby," Bridget screamed into the dark.

"Shhh…shush…shh, you're all right Bridget, you're safe. There's no baby." This time the voice was softer, gentler. Someone familiar with comforting frightened children. "George, go make some tea. I'll stay with Bridget." The voice sounded like someone she knew.

"Edna?" Bridget crawled from under the flannel covers but held the quilt close to her chin. Finally able to open her eyes, she saw the shadow of Edna sitting by her.

"Yes, dear. It's me, Edna. You've had a terrible dream."

"Where am I?"

"Oh my. Let me light the lamp by your bed, you need to get your bearings."

With the gentle strokes of a mother's hand, Edna brushed the strands of hair back from Bridget's face and wiped at the tears that dampened her cheeks. "You poor dear…" she murmured almost to herself.

Bridget sat up, now fully awake, while Edna lifted the chimney of the kerosene lamp, took a match from the top of the small table, and lit the wick. As she turned the knob on the side of the lamp, a luminous glow from the flame warmed the dark and revealed Edna, hair in rag curlers, a patterned knitted shawl across her nightdress. Her eyes affirmed her words. Bridget was safe.

"Can I come in?" George stood at the doorway. He held a tray with a cup and saucer, steaming hot tea to comfort his sister. "Here, Bridge. I brought this for you." His manner was attentive, wary.

"You're all being so kind and I'm such a nuisance." Bridget tried to sit up but fell back against the pillows, her hands cupping her face, like a child afraid to reveal herself. "Here, George, pull that small table over to the bed. Bridget, let me prop those pillows for you, so you can sit up and have your tea." Edna spoke gently but firmly to both George and Bridget.

But before Edna could reach for the pillows, Bridget pushed back the covers and swung her legs over the side of the bed. She sat, her hands bracing her on the bed's edge, bare feet on the wooden floor. "I have something to tell, and I don't know what you are going to think of me."

George set the tray on the table by the bed and walked around Edna who was sitting, her arm across Bridget's shoulder. He sat on the bed by his sister. The moment was quiet; only Bridget's breath broke the silence. Leaning down, he placed his head against her shoulder, the way he'd done when as a small girl her fear overtook her at night. He'd been the comforter even then. He whispered, "Do you remember what I'd say when you thought the monsters were there in the closet?" Bridget, without looking at him murmured, "If you open the door and look them straight in the eye, they'll say 'Close the door please, I'm sleeping. We'll talk in the morning.'"

Edna looked over at George, smiled, and remembered why she loved him.

Bridget took her hands from her head, put one on George's knee and one on Edna's. "That monster has decided to leave, and I've decided what to do."

"Will you tell us?"

Sitting straight up, Bridget swallowed once, closed her eyes for a second, and spoke with a soft but clear resonance. "The night I left Jack, I was packed and ready to go the next morning." She paused, one breath in, one breath out. "When he realized I was leaving, he was like a madman. George, remember how he was? How he'd say cruel things? He got so much worse over those years."

George took Bridget's hand, grasped it, and intertwined his fingers with hers. "Oh Bridge, I'm so sorry I left you there."

"No, no. Please don't take it as your fault—he is an evil man—you could never have changed that. And look how life has opened for you." With a smile, she squeezed Edna's hand. "George, you needed to save yourself, as I have done. You've created a place for me to run to. You and Edna. And now, I need to tell you what I've decided to do."

The moments carved themselves into silence. Each one—Bridget, George, and Edna—waited. None seemed to want to break into the moment. It was Edna who stirred, grasped Bridget's hand, and held it with a fierce clasp. George sat silent, then took his hand from Bridget's.

"You don't have to tell us now, maybe in the morning," Edna sighed.

"No, no, it's important, I need you both to know what's happened."

"Bridget, what did he do?" George looked at the floor.

"I'll tell you." Bridget lifted her hands from Edna's grasp and folded them on her lap. "Please know, I'll understand if you ask me to leave, because there is more to this story, much more, and I want to tell it all."

They sat, brother and sister-in-law on either side of Bridget, shoulder to shoulder with her, as though to let her know they'd be there, and they'd listen. And she told them.

She described how Jack threw her to the floor, slapped her, tried to strangle her, and now she said aloud, for the first time, "I thought he wanted to kill me, or worse." Her voice dropped; the words became raspy with disgust.

"What do you mean, worse?" George whispered. Edna sat, eyes closed.

"At that moment I screamed at him 'Jack, it's Bridget,' and it was like he woke from a trance. Walked out of the room and fell down the stairs."

Edna, who'd been sitting motionless, said aloud what Bridget had been wondering since then. "Did he throw himself down those stairs?"

George thrust himself from the bed and turned. "No god-damned way he threw himself—he's too much of a coward!"

"George. Language," Edna said in her best firm tone, and the tension floating everywhere snapped. The three of them grinned.

"Sorry, Eddie," George said. The moment gave Bridget a chance to collect herself, to take a long breath and tell them why she'd come to them. She began the story of Peter Radcliffe, poet and soldier.

WHEN SHE FINISHED TELLING THEM ABOUT PETER, George and Edna were still there beside her, still shoulder to shoulder. Bridget's voice was softer, the tightness gone, as the memory of those days and nights with Peter flowed into the room.

No one left. No one sighed. No one shook a head with disapproval.

Bridget watched for the signs from them that she'd be asked to leave. None arose.

"And I'm pretty sure—no, very sure—that I'm expecting his child."

Edna whispered, "Oh, Bridget," her voice quavering. She looked away as though she were searching for the right words, then returned her gaze to Bridget and grasped her hand.

"What can we do? How can we help? George? How can you help?"

In that moment, Bridget knew she'd found a home, not for her, but for her child.

"George?" Edna said again. George stood from the bed and walked to the window, where he stood with his hands behind his back. When he turned, Bridget thought she might cry. His face crumpled and his eyes were bleak.

"Oh George, I'm ashamed, and I know I've disappointed you and probably Edna." The lady, though, was shaking her head back and forth, with some fierceness.

"And I'm so sorry."

"No, Bridget," George answered. "No, you haven't disappointed me. I'm only grateful you had us to come to. I'm sad because you'll be raising your child by yourself. And what if he—Peter—doesn't return?"

Bridget stood and walked to her brother at the window. Turning to face him, she straightened her shoulders, held her arms across her body, and with a clear voice told him why she'd come to them.

"I want you and Edna to adopt my baby. Because then… I'll know she has a home where she'll be loved and safe."

Edna stood from the bed, and in her take-charge manner joined the two of them at the window. As they stood, Edna reached around Bridget's back and grasped George's hand. In that moment Bridget felt the energy of their care.

"This is that time we promised one another," George said. "Isn't it, Bridge? Remember when I gave you my promise, that wherever, whenever, you need me, I'll be there?" He looked over at Edna.

Edna spoke, not taking her eyes from George. "You took Edward, Harry, and me into *your* life…and now Bridget offers us a new life?" She dropped George's hand with one small squeeze and turned to Bridget. She fastened her eyes on Bridget's face. "Whoever the little one might be, this will be her home."

Gratitude, sadness, and hope flowed through Bridget's body.

"Thank you," she whispered.

ON A SNOWY DAY IN FEBRUARY 1916, WITH DRIFTS PILED across the fields and over the fences at Broadview Farm, George hooked up the horses to his sleigh and drove to his neighbor's farm down the road. There he bundled Mrs. McNally, the best midwife within fifty miles, into blankets, with hot stones at her feet.

Dr. King had called to say he was on his way. But when Mrs. McNally arrived, she took one look at Bridget, and said in her matter-of-fact way, "Looks like we're doing this together, Bridget, you and I."

Edna, having experienced Mrs. McNally's gifts, said, "I'm here too, Bridget."

George, still in his boots and winter wool jacket, scarf wound around his neck, left the house and walked to the barn. It wasn't till Edna and Harry burst in yelling, "It's a girl!" that he left his perch on the hay bale and walked back through the snow.

FIVE DAYS LATER, GEORGE AND BRIDGET DROVE THE snow-covered roads in silence. If there were any words that needed speaking, they would have to wait, or never be said. The sun glinted off snowdrifts along the road. The oak trees stood like sentinels appearing to bow their empty branches to the brother and sister making their way to the train station.

"Bridge, if you…" George started to say, wanting to reach over to her hands sitting gloved in her lap, fingers intertwined. Her back was straight against the leather seat, her shoulders square. He tried one more time. "Edna and I talked, and we both would like you to change your mind…"

Before he could finish his thought, Bridget shook her head, and for a moment said nothing.

When she spoke, her voice was steady, her gaze straight ahead. "You know, don't you, that in a while he'll search me out here. Staying puts you, Edna, the boys, and now especially Meg in danger. I can't allow that. Let's get me to the train and I'll be gone."

Only on her last word did her voice break.

Part Three

I tell you this to break your heart,
by which I mean only
that it break open
and never close again…"

—MARY OLIVER

Chapter Twenty-One

June 6, 1944

MEG HAD ALWAYS FOUND PEACE WANDERING THROUGH the woods that lay beyond the barn. George and Edna had sold off the workings of the farm and left the house to her when they moved into town. She had missed the lowing of cows, the bleating of sheep, and the whinnying of Russell, her brother Harry's horse. Yet after finishing the renovation of the old farmhouse, she had found living the solitary life restoring. Now, everything, every memory, felt like a story someone else had lived. A story that no longer belonged to her.

It has been almost three days and she'd heard nothing from Bill about the letters he'd taken with him. Detectives have other business and other people's lives to attend to, she told herself. *Just because my life has blown up in my face doesn't mean he must drop everything for me.*

Still, I wish he'd call.

The rays of an early morning sun wove their way through the branches of the red maples and touched the leaves like a gentle wand.

The feel of this fresh June morning on her face summoned memories of walks through the woods with her brother Harry who, though ten years older, had chosen to spend time with his little sister, looking for mosses and fungi, flowers and ferns, shrubs, and tree seedlings, all the array that forms a carpet of life on the forest floor. Remembering those mornings aroused memories of other hours when she'd felt the familiar intimacy of family. With those memories, a wave of sadness washed over her, a felt loss for her big brother who'd some days gallop across the fields, Meg sitting in the curve of his body, grasping the horn of the saddle.

This morning as she walked among the maples, her mind was on Harry, with the Third Canadian Infantry army, landing on some beach, far off in France. She'd not had a chance to come to know Edward her brother, who'd gone to France in 1917 when she was barely a year old, but somewhere in her skin was the memory of Edna's grief when she received the letter that confirmed he'd been killed at the Battle of Hill 70. Edward gone. Harry taking his place back at another frontline twenty-seven years later.

Her images, her recollections, brought her to the bench in among the woods, one she and Harry had fashioned from old pieces of lumber—the poignancy of something lost invited her to sit and remember. What did those memories mean to her now? Now that they were no longer real or belonged to her.

Chapter Twenty-Two

September 1916

WHEN BRIDGET HAD PICKED UP THE TRAIN TICKETS TO Montreal at the station seven months ago, she'd sent George on his way, asking him to please just drop her off, afraid if he stayed with her too long, she'd climb back into his Ford coupe and go back to the farm, back to her girl.

Once on the train, she'd taken a seat by a window, bringing memories of sitting with Peter that time so many months ago. She remembered the feel of his shoulder brushing against her blouse and how his smile had eased her fears.

Now it had been months since she'd climbed aboard the train to Montreal, heading for Verdun and La Poudriére Munitions in Quebec. Throughout the months in Verdun, an outrage spread throughout her body, birthed in her anger, one that fed her determination.

All the threads of her life intertwined and created a steadfast intent in her soul: war and its horror; Jack's brutality; his relentless pursuit of her; a baby daughter she'd left behind and might never see grow into a woman; a man she loved gone into battles. Each thread fed a fearless determination that one day she'd set her life on course. One over which she might have a measure of control. Bridget would not let her mother's story become hers.

Her days at Le Poudriére were again about the business of war. A business she knew well. Bridget kept to herself most times when she was away from the factory.

Her heart yearned for the letters that arrived sporadically from Peter. She wrote every week, telling him that she'd joined a company of women who too waited to hear. He'd given her his sister's address, which was the only way she could discover if something were to happen to him. He gave no indication where he was in his letters from France. Bridget knew there was reason—soldiers were not to give details about battles or places. But, oh, how she longed to be able to place him somewhere safe.

Some days were worse than others, when the wondering if he was alive or dead consumed her. On those days there seemed no respite, nowhere to go and hide from the fear.

One morning the supervisor on duty came to ask Eloise Nadeau to follow him to the office. Eloise's station was beside Bridget's. Genevieve, head girl on the shell fuses line, told everyone around Eloise's station to be ready.

Bridget knew the practice well, for she'd witnessed it time and time again over the months she'd worked in munitions. The difference was, now she felt a chill whenever the supervisor walked out of the office, his face tight with grim news.

But then, one morning as Bridget stood at her station, her eyes locked on the machinery, she heard a familiar voice. She shut her machine down and watched Irene moving among the women, her face smiling, her eyes steady with intent. Bridget knew she was on the move once again. Before Bridget could ask what on earth Irene was doing here at Le Poudriére, her words were in the air seconds before she arrived at Bridget's side.

"You need to get your things and come with me, Bridget. Jack is on his way to Montreal as we speak. Sophie's keeping track of him, in her own way. She and Mrs. Lowell. And I'm here to make sure you're safe." For a moment the old grin broke through. "He doesn't stand a chance."

As Bridget turned back to her machine to be sure it was shut down, Irene took her hand. "Sorry to do this friend, I've spoken to the supervisor, who tells me he's had a call from a Mr. Jack Blackwell, wanting to know if his daughter, Bridget, worked there. Luckily, Sophie has a network and the supervisor called her."

"Do you mean we have to go, now?"

"Yes, now. Please trust me, we need to leave." Irene handed a short letter that Sophie had written hurriedly.

Bridget, it's time for you to leave Canada. The last communication I had from Jack was a letter threatening to hire a private detective to find you and force me to reveal what I know about you. I'm worried, very worried. He's in a world filled with his own demons. He's obsessed with finding you. Knowing what I know about him, I fear for your safety.

Bridget read the letter, looked at Irene, and asked with a tone of resignation, "Where am I going?"

"A village in Scotland," Irene replied. She was already walking away to a waiting taxi. Bridget followed with the suitcase she carried to the factory every day, ready for this moment when she'd need to flee.

She thought, *across the ocean?* Wasn't everyone being a bit alarmist? But then the death of her mother flashed through her mind—the bizarre circumstances, the mystery surrounding it. And the harsh reckoning that maybe…he'd had something to do with how she died. Something more than breaking her heart.

Bridget realized now that in his demented way he would be relentless and keep tracking her down—even, as Sophie had emphasized, wanting her dead.

Settling herself into the taxi, she looked over at Irene. "He's a madman, isn't he."

For a moment Irene stared out the window, then turned to Bridget: "Yes, he is. I've known men like him in my lifetime, here and in my country. They hate. There's no sane reason, only their own unglued loathing that, for him, seems directed at women." Irene's lips pressed into a red slash, and she threw up her hands. "God only knows why...but let's not try to figure that out here. Let's just get you to the ship."

The ship... Bridget felt like Alice going down the rabbit hole.

When they arrived at the docks, Irene handed Bridget a ticket for passage to Liverpool. And folded inside the envelope was a train ticket from Liverpool to Glasgow.

"I'll leave you here, take your passage, my friend. Safe travels. And safe arrival."

Bridget stood at the open door of the taxi, took the envelope that Irene handed out to her, and in the same motion reached to Irene. The two women clasped hands for only a moment before letting go. "Go on there now, *a chara*...o friend, you need to get on with your adventure." Irene's eyes clouded. "And I need to get on back to the factory. Go on then. The supervisor of the munitions factory in Kirkcudbright will look after you."

Bridget shut the taxi door, gave a gentle wave, and turned toward the passenger terminal, leather case in her hand, cloth bag and handbag over her shoulder. Bridget on the move once again, and Sophie, Irene, and Mrs. Lowell clearing her path forward.

Bridget was headed to a small village in southern Scotland, a remote place with the invisibility she needed. It was tucked at the confluence of two rivers, a place at one time only known to the few who chose to live there, but now, in the third year of this war to end all wars, the site of a munitions factory. Sophie knew about the place, and she knew, too, that the factory administrators wanted to attract women to make shell fuses, women who might continue after the war and become engineers. It was a perfect place for Bridget's disappearance.

NOTHING COULD HAVE PREPARED HER FOR THIS Scottish factory, built and designed to train women engineers and, in this wartime period, a munitions factory.

Bridget was convinced that Sophie with her mysterious connections had found a place where her talents and skill could be recognized—a place where her experience in other factories would all come to bear. But Bridget couldn't fathom where working and living in a Scottish village might eventually lead.

What happens, she wondered, when the war ends? Will I stay here when I'm no longer useful, making shells? Do I want to become part of an experiment, training women engineers? Is it my fate from now on, to do what's only necessary to stay out of harm's way, avoiding my stepfather's unbalanced mind? And how can I continue working in places that are only about creating death? Is there a chance, when this is over, that Peter and I might find one another?

Is he even alive?

Questions moved through her body as she made her way into the vastness of the passenger terminal, soon mingling with uniformed men, women in nursing capes, and a few other civilian passengers. She put questions aside and, moving in among the crowds, took up her journey away from country, friends, and family.

Possibly closer to Peter?

Chapter Twenty-Three

BRIDGET SAT ON THE EDGE OF HER NEWLY ACQUIRED BED in the Kirkcudbright village hotel, a quilt wrapped around her shoulders, her feet propped on her unopened suitcase. She'd arrived at the hotel two miles from Tongland where the munitions factory had been built. The letter she'd received told her she'd be picked up in the morning.

Now she'd found her way to her room on the second floor. All was quiet, yet her brain was chaotic, trying to take in all she'd experienced in the last ten days—sailing from Montreal to Liverpool, spending most of the time in her cabin, not wanting to venture out except to the dining room or the ship's library. Her body was asking for sleep, but her experiences summoned her to pen and paper. Clarity appeared at the end of a pen for Bridget. Her questions flowed onto the page.

I've been living like a runaway, possibly that's exactly what I am—I've run from a dangerously demented man who would harm me once again if he could. I wonder if it's true that he wants to see me dead?

Could he be that twisted? Sophie thinks so, and for some reason that she's not told me, he wanted my mother dead.

Am I being a coward, running as I am, or am I saving my own life the way George possibly saved his, by leaving? What would that little girl I left there on the farm think of me? Will my life ever matter to her? Somewhere, sometime, I hope I'll be able to explain to her. Will she listen?

I'm here in a strange country preparing again to go about the business of making weapons that kill. If I'm honest with myself, I'm hating that I do this and get rewarded for it. There's a part of me who wonders how I'm able to do this, how I can feel such sadness and rage, yet have this odd sense of adventure. What is that all about?

Where are you now, Peter? I'm fearing that you're becoming more like a dream. But you were real, as real as our girl is, back there, at Broadview Farm.

Bridget left that question on the page, closed her notebook, and sat drifting into a place of detachment. It felt safer there.

She leaned against the pillows at the head of the bed, looking for a dwelling in her mind, in her soul, and in her body that felt like clarity. As always, it was the pen and the paper that brought her to the clear place. Rising from the bed, she walked across to a small table by the window that looked out on the village street below. Her pen and paper rested on the shining mahogany of the table. She pulled the chain to turn on the lamp, then sat down and started to write.

The words came—words that felt like truth.

I am exactly where I'm supposed to be in this life. My feet rest on the carpet, I hear the sounds of a village outside my window—an unfamiliar land, yet I feel as though I belong here. There is no rationality in feeling such (what's that word Edna used?) stillness, yes, stillness it is. I remember her saying one time, "Just wait, Bridget, the stillness will come." I'm discovering she might be right.

All those threads, those pieces that seem out of sync, will make sense, somehow. I'll keep a distance from Jack's irrational obsession; this war that goes on and on will end someday soon. I'll stop making shell fuses that kill.

Most importantly, I must trust my body's conviction that I will see my girl again.

I remember Mama taking my face into her hands and telling me with an urgency that I didn't understand at the time, telling me to listen to the wise person who lives inside of me. My regret is she couldn't do that for herself.

Bridget realized her odyssey was not over, yet she wanted to settle in and work here in Scotland for a time. The possibility she'd have to move again was real and thinking about it was practical. This was not the life she had imagined for herself. Picking up her pen she added a thought, one that just now occurred to her:

Were it not for Jack and his unfathomable hatred for me, were it not for Mama's far-sightedness leaving a bequest, and were it not for Sophie's rather unusual need to be vigilant on my behalf, I believe I'd still be writing copy for furniture designs back in Westover. And fearing the next time he'd come to find me.

A knock at her door brought her back into the moment, here in her room.

She opened the door. A young woman stood in the hallway. Her gloved hand reached to Bridget and a smile lit her greeting.

"Bonsoir, Mademoiselle Blackwell. Je suis ton novelle ami."

Without hesitation, Bridget returned smile for smile. "I'm sorry. Je parle un peu français. And please, my name is Bridget."

"Ah, Brigitte," she replied. "We will be fine. I speak English. I was saying, I am your new friend, Suzanne."

Both women laughed for reasons unknown to either of them, except the unexpected pleasure in greeting one another. Instant friendship blossomed there at the Hotel Kirkcudbright on that September evening in Scotland.

"I've been expecting you," Bridget said, reaching for the leather case that Suzanne was holding. "You're the roommate mentioned in my letter of acceptance to work here. I'm very glad to meet you." Bridget turned and placed the case on the second bed, the one near the window over the small table where Bridget had been writing.

"I wasn't sure what to expect. What a pleasure to be here and meet you," Suzanne said. "How long have you been here, in Scotland? I understand from my letter that you are Canadienne. What a long way you have come. Pourquoi? Ah, pardonnez. Why all this way? From Canada."

"We each, I'm sure, have a story to tell. Me from Canada. You from France. But for now, why don't you settle yourself and I'll go find us some tea."

"I can settle anytime, for now I'd like to have a tea or possibly some vin?" A soft grin lit Suzanne's face. "You agree. No?"

Bridget felt a moment of pleasure. She was drawn to Suzanne's gentle way, a kind of graciousness, one that seemed incongruous for a woman about to make shells to kill young men. They stood in that early moment of kinship, feeling a friendship awaken.

"I agree. Yes. The concierge at the desk mentioned a typical Scottish pub I might like to visit for supper. Why not go there? I think it was called something like the 'Wheat and the Chaff' or the 'Wheat and the Barley.' Regardless of name, apparently it has good beer and food. And I'm sure they'll have wine…vin."

"We must go then." Suzanne took her purse from the bed where she'd dropped it and threw it carelessly across her shoulder.

"Oh, my," Bridget declared. "That is a beautiful handbag. The embroidery so delicate." Red flowers seemed to move among leaves and yellow buds across the blackness of the material. For a moment Bridget sensed her mother's spirit in the room. Clara, who loved beautiful things, would have carried such a purse.

"Brigitte, you appear sad, are you all right?"

"Your purse reminded me of my mother who died many years ago. I was just a child. She loved beauty, and I guess I've inherited that." Bridget wondered at the instant connection with this unknown French woman, in this remote Scottish village, a village where Sophie had sent her.

"He'll never find you there. Never," Sophie had said. "And it's a beautiful place. You need beauty, Bridget."

"I'm so sorry you have lost your maman. I too have lost mine, in this terrible war. We will talk. We have much to tell one another. I think maybe you and I are just where we need to be, in these sad times."

Two women walked from a hotel room down a hallway out into an approaching evening, each a story unto herself, each finding comfort in the other.

"Your English is lovely, Suzanne," Bridget remarked, as they made their way down the village street to the Wheat and the Chaff, or the Wheat and the Barley, whichever it might be.

Bridget and Suzanne realized that the evening was presenting possibilities in what might have been a gray time in their lives and a juncture of events neither had anticipated. The realization began with the mention of a mutual fervor for telling their stories—Bridget yearning to write novels and Suzanne, poems.

In the pub, called The Granary, Bridget raised her pint aloft. "To peacetime, to France, to Canada, to story, and to poetry."

"Oui. To France and to Canada." Placing her glass on the table, Suzanne sat back, folded her arms across her chest, and gazed over at Bridget. "Brigitte? Whatever brought you to this place?"

"I could ask you the same." Bridget smiled, enjoying the restful feeling in this unlikely connection. Life had propelled her for the past two years, with no respite, no sitting back to feel stillness move through her body. Her breath now spread from a quiet place she'd discovered while she wrote, back in her room.

"You are silent, Brigitte."

"I like the sound of my name when you say it—it's so much gentler than 'Bridget.'"

"Merci. There is so little that is tendre or gentil in our world, so I am glad that saying your name as I do is a pleasure."

"Suzanne." Bridget took a long swallow from her glass and set it firmly on the table. Her eyes darkened. "There's nothing tender or gentle about where we are, and what we're doing, which is why I want to find a way, sooner than later, to leave." She sat forward, elbow on the table, finger waving. "This war is a horror." Her voice penetrated the smoky huddles around tables. Two men at the bar turned toward them.

"Brigitte," Suzanne whispered. "You need to be careful."

The restful stillness Bridget had felt for a few minutes faded. "Let's go." She stood up and turned toward the doorway.

A man limped out of the shadows from the corner of the bar. "Miss," he called out as he came toward them. Suzanne straightened her back, frightening Bridget with the defiance she showed, her eyes darkening. Bridget witnessed her new friend's fierceness, as did the man strolling toward them.

"Whoa, there." He stopped. "Ma'am." Bridget noted she'd been called "Miss," but Suzanne was "Ma'am." Fierce Suzanne daunted him.

"Ma'am, I mean no harm. I wasn't eavesdropping, but I couldn't help hearing the young lady's pronouncement of this hellish war."

There it was again: "young lady." Bridget began to feel like the innocent in the room. *If they only knew.*

The man continued. "I just wanted to come say I'm with you. I've been there. I know." It was then that Bridget and Suzanne, who'd begun to soften her shoulders, saw his wooden leg.

"Let me buy you both a drink." When he discovered they were munitionettes, he bought them another. And told them his story.

He was proud. He was dauntless. His body broken. His spirit unblemished.

Back in their hotel room, Bridget rested against the tall back of the cushioned chair and considered the words she'd written across the page of her notebook. She wrote by the glow of the lamp that shed a low light across their room. Suzanne snored gently in her bed by the window.

Of course, she'd have a gentle snore, thought Bridget. *She's elegant and fierce.*

The glow from the lamp reflected the concentration on Bridget's face as she remembered the man who'd come to their table in the pub. She thought about his story, and how the short time spent in his presence started to shift her view of what she wanted to say and write about this war.

Geordie McKinney, a wounded soldier, had touched her in unexpected ways. For his words and his stories had brought her to this table to write about the women in the factories and the men on battlefields in France. What if, she wondered, her stories might be life-giving, countering the killing intent of shell fuses she handled every day?

Bridget had felt irritation prickling the back of her neck when he'd first begun talking there at the table. Suzanne had sat very still, her hand wrapped around her glass, and listened with a quiet intent, seeming to urge him on. Soon Bridget, too, realized how engrossed she'd become in this story of a battle in a place called Loos in France, near the Belgian border. "I know where that is," Suzanne had said, her eyes brimming with sadness.

Geordie McKinney had been seriously injured in that battle in 1915. Weeks of armies launching bullets, bombs, and shells at each other. Landscapes of shattered trees and broken men.

The two women had listened as he told of being sent to a Casualty Clearing Centre and from there shipped back to Scotland. Bridget was stunned by the way he talked openly of his agonizing pain, of being afraid "almost all the time." The artillery explosions, the unending shellfire, the lack of sleep, the knowing that any moment he could die.

"You speak to Suzanne and me, total strangers to you, about such horror. How is it you can do that?" Bridget asked this question from her own damaged place, a place searching for answers. In that moment, Suzanne saw something in Bridget, possibly a horror of her own, and broke into the conversation.

"Geordie, how have you made your way back from all that, to this place, here, having a beer, being in this ordinary time? This untouched place?"

Bridget turned to her friend. "It's not untouched, Suzanne—walk up the road two miles where we're creating the kind of shells that might have penetrated his leg." Her words pierced the air. Suzanne reached for Bridget's hand. Geordie placed his glass on the bar and turned away for a moment. When he returned his gaze, he pointed across the room.

"There's a young woman sitting at a table by the fireplace. Her name is Emily, and she comes in every night and sits at that table. Her fiancé is missing in action, and she sits each evening and writes to him."

"Why here?" Bridget asked.

"Because this is where he sat each night when he'd finish his work at the farm. And she believes somehow that she can bring him home if she just keeps writing and believing he'll walk through that door." He looked over at the woman, her head bent, her pen to the page.

"Who's to say?" he murmured.

"And you? How have you found your way? What has Emily to do with your story?" Bridget asked, her words a bit softer now.

Geordie moved his head and looked down at his peg leg.

Without looking up, he said: "Each day, she goes to an auxiliary hospital nearby and cooks, reads to wounded soldiers, writes letters for them home to families. Emily's the reason I'm here today talking with you instead of putting a gun to my head."

Sounds of glasses clinking, voices beginning a song, rose into their silence.

No one spoke. Bridget wondered at this moment. Maybe there was redemption somewhere, maybe a way to ease the scarred and scared places in her soul. Maybe. Maybe she could do what Emily has done and become inspired in other ways. A thought occurred.

"Are there hospitals in France?" Bridget asked. She wondered if a nurse might be there for Peter if he fell to the artillery fire like Geordie.

Geordie looked over at her. "You have someone there?"

For a moment, Bridget felt almost fraudulent. *I hardly knew him. Yet...*

"Yes, a young man from my hometown." She said no more.

"Do you know where he is?" Geordie asked.

Bridget realized she was among friends, as brief as the time they'd known one another. She knew they'd understand. "I hadn't known him very long before he left, but..."

"You need say no more," Geordie interjected. "Going to war doesn't give the luxury of time—sometimes we have to make life happen quickly."

Bridget wanted to take his hand and that's what she did. "Thank you, Geordie. I know that when he comes back, we'll be married, we'll have family, and one day we'll tell our children how it was...." There seemed nothing more to say after that.

Geordie remembered all those men lying in the muddy trenches. He wondered if her young man might have been among them. Suzanne, remembering the bodies of her mother and father, swallowed the sadness collecting in her throat.

The threads of an unforgiving war stitched together three people who'd not known one another only twenty-four hours ago.

Chapter Twenty-Four

November 1919

"IMAGINE," BRIDGET SMILED TO HERSELF. "SUZANNE AND Bridget traveling first class."

She'd neglected to tell Suzanne, who believed their tickets had been funded by their munition factory salaries, that Clara's care and generosity had given Bridget the freedom to follow where life might take her—and to travel first class! Today, they were on their way to France.

God bless you, Sophie, and Western Union money wires.
And Mama, wherever you may be.
Thank you.

Bridget and Suzanne sat in a finely appointed first-class compartment of the train from Glasgow to London, where they would change trains to Dover and there take the Empress ferry across the channel to Calais.

Bridget pressed her nose against the window as they began to move away from the station platform. Silent words like a blessing filled her soul. "Goodbye again, my sweet girl, may all the colors of the rainbow paint your days." Meg would be three years old now. Knowing the possibility she'd never lay eyes on her, she tried to picture how she might look. George had written to describe how she was growing, already asking continual questions, needing her favorite books that both Edna and George would read to her. Bridget had smiled when she read that Harry liked to take her out riding double on his horse. George's stories gave Bridget comfort, feeling that her decision to give her up had yielded a good life for Meg.

Looking at Suzanne there beside her, Bridget felt a kinship toward her friend—another woman in her life opening a new path. Like Sophie, Irene, and now Suzanne, these women believed in their own life-giving strength, and Bridget's.

For Suzanne, head back against the soft cushion, the excitement of going home to Paris flowed through her body like the French champagne she soon would be tasting.

Three people stood on the platform: Geordie McKinney, Emily from the pub, and her fiancé, the very fiancé who'd been missing in action.

All three lifted their arms in a salute as the train gathered speed and left them behind. Bridget regretted the goodbyes yet knew that this village and these friends would always be a safe haven if ever she needed them.

Her good friend Geordie McKinney, Emily, and her fiancé Arin Baird had each of them offered Bridget a place. "If ever you need a haven, it's here. Always will be," Geordie had whispered into her ear as he placed his hands on her shoulders to wish her farewell and without hesitation pulled her close into his broad chest.

Bridget with an exhale relaxed into the feel of him.

"Thank you, Geordie," she'd whispered before the demons could undo the feeling. For a year now, Bridget had gradually stopped talking about all the reasons she'd not heard from Peter. The war had ended November 11, 1918, but Bridget had heard nothing from him. She stopped talking about why, and she stopped talking about Peter. Suzanne waited. Geordie wondered.

As he gathered her into his arms on the platform, Bridget's conscience screamed "No!" But something in the way he held her—his gentle, sheltering manner—stirred a mixture of uncertainty and yearning. In that dreamlike moment, she felt a glimmer of hope, not for Geordie, but for the dream in her body, in her soul—Peter, who rested there still.

Untangling herself from Geordie's hugeness, Bridget looked into his face.

"You've been my brother, my listener, my keeper of the faith. You've never interfered with my hope…if we ever meet again my dear friend…" She stopped her words.

"I know, Bridget. I know." Geordie paused. Taking her hand and placing it between his two palms, he said: "Bridget, I've asked Suzanne to talk to you when you arrive in France. To talk to you about writing to Peter's sister."

His words were soft and gentle, yet Bridget blocked them, ignored them. Drawing her hand away, she bent down, picked up her cloth case, and turned to Suzanne.

"It's time." And putting her hand on his cheek, "Goodbye, Geordie. Thank you for everything."

She walked away.

BOTH WOMEN WERE FROZEN IN TIME ON THEIR WAY TO France. Suzanne, eyes closed, rested her newly bobbed hair against the head cushion. Her smile reflected images of returning to France, and once again being with her sisters she knew would be waiting at Gare de Lyon in Paris.

Bridget, hands tucked into the folds of her wool shawl, let her mind wander back over the goodbyes. Back to Geordie's words about writing to Peter's sister. Her thoughts crashed against one another. His suggestion was like an eclipse that blocked the sun. *What if...*

A short blast from the train whistle. "France, here we come," Bridget said, blotting out the farewells. "And to my amie française," she turned to Suzanne. "When we step onto French soil, I shall buy you a rose from those flower sellers you've described to me."

"Non. We shall buy each other one rose." With those words Suzanne settled herself into the soft plush of the seat. Bridget leaned her head against the window and watched Scotland disappear.

Suzanne's invitation to come back with her to Paris had given Bridget a way forward, to begin to let go of what she once thought her life might become. Lifting her head, she turned to Suzanne who'd been sitting quietly, conscious of Bridget's pensiveness.

"Suzanne?" The moment arrived.

"Yes, Brigitte." Suzanne turned full body to face her. "What do you need?"

"Geordie said he'd spoken to you about Peter's sister. What did he say? Is there something I should know?"

It was a few moments before Suzanne found her voice and the words she wanted to say. "Brigitte, cheri, I want to ask you to do something that could be difficult." She paused and watched her friend's eyes cloud over, her shoulders stiffen. "Would you consider writing to Peter's sister?" She offered nothing more, knowing she'd said enough.

EVENTUALLY, BRIDGET BROKE THROUGH HER RELUCtance to confirm what her heart knew could be true. She wrote the letter she'd been avoiding. Soon after, a reply arrived from Peter's sister, Sally. Bridget, sitting in her new apartment on Boulevard Saint-Germain, read the letter aloud, engraving each word on her soul. Suzanne, by her side, listened to every nuance and waited.

Dear Bridget,

When I received your kind letter, I needed to gather myself to write back to you. It's been a terrible year. Yes, the war is over, but the aftermath is devastating for our town, for my family, and for me. So many of our young men have been cut down, and Peter. Oh, Bridget, Peter was one of them.

I'm so sorry to write back to you with the news that Peter was killed during one of the last battles in northern France. How unfair that he made it to the final hour and was shot by a sniper. He was going out on a last watch on November tenth, taking it for one of his buddies—when he stepped out of the house where they were hunkered down, he was fatally shot by a German sniper. Eleven o'clock the next morning hostilities halted.

Bridget dropped her head, covered her eyes with her hand; Suzanne thought she'd stopped breathing till she heard a ragged sigh escape from her friend's lips. She placed her hand on Bridget's back and listened as Bridget read on.

I believe he's been buried in a Canadian military cemetery in northern France. Neuville St. Vaast is the village nearby.
All of us, our family, our friends, the professors

he worked with at the university, were and still are broken-hearted. A son, my brother, a friend, a teacher, a poet, was killed that day…and for what? Please forgive my bitterness. Peter brought beauty into our worlds, and there was so much more he was ready to give.

I have a sense you knew about and will remember the beauty of him.

Bridget looked over to Suzanne. Her eyes like dimmed candles spoke of the anguish of not knowing and now knowing.

"He's gone.…"

"Oh, Brigitte."

Bridget held the letter between her fingertips and read the last lines.

May you remember him always with love.
With regards,
Sally Radcliffe

P.S. Don't hesitate to contact me again.

Laying the letter aside, she sat motionless, her eyes staring into some distant place where memory lay. The words "Peter brought beauty into the world" sat on her breath, and the thought arrived fully formed and unfaltering.

"Suzanne, I've decided something." She paused. "Sometime in the next few years, I'm not sure when, I'll go back to Canada, for a brief time. I'll go back and see my girl, Peter's girl. The beauty he brought into this world. I'll go back and see Margaret Grace."

Chapter Twenty-Five

May 1923

"Come on Harry, make him gallop faster," Meg called to Harry, already digging his knees into Russell's flanks to urge him on.

"We don't want to tire him too much today, Meg. Soon we'll need to turn back. I'll give him his head while we cross the fallow field near the house."

But just as he turned Russell's head to make their way back to the house, he spotted his father out on the road in his new Ford coupe, driving faster than he should on the gravel, sending dust clouds reeling behind him. The distance between Meg, Harry, and their dad narrowed, and Harry could see him waving at them, his arm out the car window.

Harry slowed Russell to a trot, while Meg waved back from her stance up front on the saddle. Harry heard their dad calling out to them as they drew closer to the fence.

"Meg. You need to come back with me to the house."

Harry pulled the reins just as they reached the fence. Meg lifted one leg over the saddle horn and, with the ease of someone without fear, slid to the ground, climbed the wire fence, and ran to the car.

"Papa. What's happening? Why'd you need to come get me? Is Mama all right?"

"Mama's fine, just get around to the car door and climb in. Remember this morning I said we'd be going to the train station today for a surprise? I just found out the train's early. We need to go into town now."

MEG BELIEVED THE WOMAN WHO DESCENDED THE STEPS of the passenger train may have been the most beautiful lady she'd seen in her short lifetime. Nor had she ever seen her papa so close to tears as she watched him open the car door. Only once had she seen him cry—it was when the news that her brother Edward, missing in action during the Great War, had been declared dead. This time, unlike then, his tears puzzled her.

For a few seconds she wondered if he'd forgotten she was there; he stood by the car, motionless, his hands on his hips.

"Papa?" Meg grasped the car door handle, hesitant to move, not knowing what she needed to do. George moved away from his car and stepped onto the station platform— the woman was walking with measured steps toward him, dressed in a long-waisted navy suit, her dark hair bobbing around her chin. She emerged from the crowd like a wildflower, stopped, put her leather case on the wooden platform, and waved at George. Meg felt like she was standing outside a glass wall watching something mysterious unfold.

Next moment, George turned to Meg and waved to her to come by his side. Placing his hand on her shoulder, he leaned down to her and whispered, "Come, meet your Aunt Bridget."

A sense of a far-off story, a dreamlike image, floated just beneath Meg's gaze. And vanished. No one in the family has ever mentioned an Aunt Bridget, she thought, as she walked beside her father. His hand still rested on her shoulder. She wondered, did he expect she might bolt, like Russell was known to do when something felt strange?

A scent wafted through the air as they drew near to the woman, one that reminded her of the lavender garden she and her mother grew by the back porch, near the steps. Last summer Meg had asked her mom if she could tend it herself. Everyone in the family called it Edward's Garden, planted to honor her brother's forever grave in France. She wondered now, as she approached this beautiful woman, how someone could transmit the scent of a garden. What magical person holds the fragrance of lavender?

Her imagination circled in and around her. A story began to tell itself about this mysterious woman who smelled like lavender. Meg realized her father was standing, waiting.

The train pulled away from the station, wheels grinding on the rails. A whistle blew, people moved away, and the platform emptied. Meg stood back and watched, curious and cautious as the woman walked along the boards, her eyes never leaving George's face. She dropped her case a few feet from him and reached out her arms. "George." Her voice a whisper.

He moved toward her and gathered her into his arms. Meg heard him saying, "Bridget, Bridget, Bridget."

"Thank you for this," she said, her voice still barely a sigh. As she dropped her arms, she looked over at Meg who stood apart from the two of them, her hands shoved into the pockets of her riding jodhpurs. The shirt she'd tucked into the waist of the pants this morning was hanging loose. Her hair was tousled and fly-away, dark curls bouncing across her forehead.

The woman turned, smiled, and reached her hand toward her. Meg, not known to be shy, was tentative but unfolded her fingers in her pocket and with a small movement began to offer her hand.

"Meg, meet your Aunt Bridget who's come all the way from Paris to see us." George reached for Meg's shoulder, wanting to draw her into the moment. Wanting her to know what he was not able to tell her: this lady is your mom.

"I have an aunt?" Meg moved, and with an assurance beyond her seven years, grasped the hand of the woman whose name was Aunt Bridget.

"I'm very pleased to meet you." They stood hands clasped for a time. What reason could there be, Meg wondered, for feeling this strange warmth radiating from her aunt's hand? "I'm pleased to meet you too, Aunt…Aunt…" She paused.

"Bridget," her father interjected, his hand pressing a bit on Meg's shoulder, a slight smile flickering in his eyes, moving down to his mouth.

"Da-a-ad." Meg cocked her head and looked up at her father, one eyebrow raised. "You told me her name already," she said, a skittish edge to her tone. "I'm just trying out the word *aunt*. I like the way it feels on my tongue." The silent tension dissolved like the steam from the engine fading into the countryside.

Bridget grinned. "Are you perchance a writer, Meg? I think that's something a writer might say. And I'll tell you why I know that. I'm a writer too."

Her aunt's confession surprised and delighted Meg, her grin matching Bridget's. A school scribbler lay in a box in Meg's clothes cupboard, a notebook that held words, sentences, and stories that Meg had been printing since the day she began to form letters. Which for her began shortly after her fourth birthday. She'd proudly printed her full name, "Margaret Grace," when she was three years old.

But Meg wondered how this lady who had just appeared in her life could know she wanted to write stories, almost as much as she wanted to sing songs. Harry knew about her stories, and sometimes she'd share one with her mom, and maybe with her dad.

"She's an imaginative one, this girl, she surely is." George, hand back on Meg's shoulder, nodded his head. "She's our writer, that's for sure, Bridge." His eyes misted as this brotherly name for his sister slipped out.

Bridget put her hand on his arm, a silent gesture saying *"It's all right."*

Meg looked one to the other, sensing that something important had passed between them. She watched them straighten their shoulders, saw her dad's face redden.

Aunt Bridget smiled.

"You and I will talk. We could be writers together, how's that?" She bent to pick up her suitcase.

"Oh yes, yes! Are you really a writer, Aunt Bridge? Oh, sorry. Can I call you Aunt Bridge? You can call me Meg if that's all right." She glanced over to her dad.

George saddened as he listened and watched mother and daughter discover that mysterious connection that neither one knew existed, for he knew the mother of Margaret Grace would leave once again, all too soon.

THE BLACKWELL FAMILY CARRIED FRACTURES.

An embittered separation between a stepfather and a stepson; a stepdaughter's flight, wanting and needing to disappear; a brother's promise to keep the secret of who Meg's mother was; and a seven-year-old girl, who, for reasons unknown, wondered where she belonged in this world.

The feelings sometimes edged her thoughts after her mom and dad tucked her in and wished her a peaceful sleep. After they left her alone in the dark.

Some nights, she'd lie in bed listening to the murmur of Edna and George's voices while they sat by the fire, down below in the kitchen. Most nights there was comfort in their familiar sound, yet there were nights when she felt a knot in her belly.

One night she'd left her bed and crept into her parent's room where family pictures were on the desk by the window. Mama, Dad, and Harry were all there, and Edward whom she'd never known.

Meg, a small girl, sitting on her father's knee, her head on his chest. Meg laughing while she rode Harry's shoulders. She'd sat on the edge of their bed gazing at the pictures, lit by a full moon that gave them a ghostly sense.

Mama, Harry, and Edward all looked so much alike... her dad looked like himself. But try as she could, she could not see herself in their faces.

That night, when Edna and George came up to bed, they found Meg curled on the rug asleep, the picture of herself on George's knee tight in her hand. But on this night, with the arrival of an aunt she didn't know she had, and her family gathered around the supper table, Meg sensed herself part of something that undid the knot for a while.

Plates, empty of Edna's roast chicken, sweet yams, and green beans, sat waiting to be taken to the kitchen for washing up. No one was ready yet to break from the familial feel that surrounded the table and the allure of Aunt Bridget as she described a life that Meg thought enchanted. She knew interrupting was bad manners, but the words burst forth: "Criminy! You've lived in Paris! You wrote stories! You're like those storybook people I read about!" For a moment, George and Edna's inhales and Harry's snort-like snicker were the only sounds.

"Oh, Meg, manners," Edna said, her cheeks coloring.

"No, no." Bridget smiled. "Being thought of as one of Meg's storybook people is high praise." George saw that his sister's eyes glistened, but, before he could interject, Bridget carried on.

"I remember our mother talking about a magical woman. Do you remember those tales, George?" Bridget sat, elbows braced on the table, her hands around one of Edna's fine china teacups, her smile broadening. Each around the table looked to George, Edna with a quizzical look because she knew nothing of a magical woman and thought George to be much too commonsensical for gossamer ideas.

He was smiling as he turned to his sister, because the story between them brought warm memories. "I do remember, but she wasn't magical. That woman in Mother's stories. She was real. Wasn't her name Sophie? Wasn't she Mother's friend?"

Hearing her dad speak of Gran Clara, Meg sat up and looked down the table at George.

"Dad, maybe Aunt Bridget can tell us some of her stories about Gran Clara." At that moment, something happened and Meg noticed it, a glance between brother and sister and a shadow dimming Bridget's eye. The story of the magical woman faded. Neither George nor Bridget seemed to want to finish it. The familial threads that had previously wrapped in and around George, Edna, Bridget, Meg, and Harry seemed to dissolve. No longer were they a family telling old remembered stories. The coolness of separation was in the air. Painful memories entered the room—of a mother's death…a ruptured home…an angry stepfather.

George pushed back from the table, his fingers tight against the edge, looked over at his daughter, and with a weak grin spoke as a father might: "I think I know one young lady who needs to climb the wooden hill. It's a school night and that seven o'clock chime rings early in the morning. Time, Meg." George paused. "Time for good nights all around." He rose, unfolding his lanky frame from the armchair. The evening, as far as Meg could gather, was over.

"Papa, it's not even eight...." Her protest was met with a stern glance, one that she had seen only a few times in her almost seven years. She moved to push in her chair, feeling dismissed for no good reason. Her eyes smarted with confused tears, and a voice, Aunt Bridget's voice, interposed like a storyteller might when the tale needs a new ending.

"Why don't I come along and say goodnight as well, and Meg...you can tell me one of your stories?" Her glance over to George as she spoke was pleading. Amid a tense silence, Edna cleared a plate from the table, stood up and, in her inimitably conclusive manner, said: "George, why don't you go along with Bridget and Meg? Both of you can listen to her story—I think that's perfect." She glanced over at her daughter, who nodded, grinning.

GEORGE RESTED IN THE WHITE WOODEN ROCKER THAT sat at the end of Meg's bed, a familiar place that spoke of nights he'd rocked his girl to sleep, she a wee babe, curled into the curve of his arm, her breathing soft, her tiny fingers looped around his calloused ring finger. A tightness seized the back of his throat as his sister stretched out on the bed beside his girl. He caught the thought in midair: no, not *his* girl. A muddle of feelings crisscrossed in his chest.

He wanted to reach over, take his daughter's hand, and say, "You'll always be my girl." Instead, he folded his arms across his stomach and put his head back on the quilted cushion Edna had fashioned for this rocker when Meg was a baby. And he listened.

A girl, a daughter, pillows scrunched at her back, flowered pajamas wrapping her in the warmth of soft flannelette, sat inches away from Bridget's shoulder, no closer, not touching, as if something sat between, holding them apart.

"Let's hear your story, my girl." Bridget swallowed the sound of the words "my girl," crossed her arms, holding her hands against her elbows, seemingly becoming comfortable. The truth? She wanted more than anything to take Meg into her arms, hold her, and tell her how sorry she was. Instead: "Your papa and I are listening."

Sitting up straighter against the pillows, Meg placed her scribbler across the blanket that covered her knees, smoothed her hand across the pages, and began to read. Words fashioned in her way, pictures drawn amid sentences, a blossoming writer, a budding artist.

"My story is called 'The Lost Kitten,' by Margaret Grace Blackwell." Bridget glanced over at George who'd closed his eyes to listen, a habit she remembered from her girlhood when she'd ask him to "pay attention to what I'm about to read to you."

"Papa, are you listening? You haven't heard this one." Meg narrowed her eyes and tried to look fierce. George's eyes flew open. "Right here, Duffer, right here." Bridget bent her head and hid a smile behind her hand.

"I'm listening with all ears, my girl. Let's hear this story by Margaret Grace Blackwell."

LATER THAT NIGHT, QUIET MOVED THROUGHOUT THE FARM-house. The animals out in the fields moved among one another, cows watching for their calves, colts finding the warmth of their mother's broad bodies. Promises of summer rustled in the warmth of a breeze, and scents floated across the air—peonies, lilacs, lily of the valley. "Edna's garden," George said when Bridget lifted her head to sniff the essence of spring.

Bridget and George sat in the wicker chairs that rested on the back porch overlooking the fields and the vegetable garden tended by Meg and Edna. Green promise of tomatoes and lettuce colored the soil, tall poles along the side of the garden encouraged tendrils of green beans.

The whiff of flowers floated from window boxes and lilac bushes full of branches and blossoms that trailed across the porch railing, seeming to beckon Bridget to stay. Brother and sister rested in the quiet, knowing that soon enough, farewells and leave-taking could unravel any contentment. A full moon shone just over the peak of the new barn that George and neighbors up and down the road had built. Silence floated between them. Until.

"Where will you go tomorrow?" George asked, not daring to look to his sister. Not waiting for her reply, he asked, "Why do you need to leave right away?"

Bridget's sigh emerged from a soul place in her body. "I can't stay here, George. I've taken a huge chance coming as I have. He's still tracking me. I know."

George's jaw tensed at his memory of Jack's brutality. His mouth tightened into a thin line; his eyes darkened. Hatred. His hands curled into knuckled fists. "If he dares, dares to try to find you. If he dares to come here. I. Will. Kill. Him."

Bridget broke into the heavy silence that George's fierceness created. She reached for his hand. "Thank you for letting me come here. I know how difficult it must have been to say yes." George said nothing.

Bridget felt her breath tight in her chest, her next words almost a whisper. "You need to understand, I may never be back. Sophie is anxious that I go back to France as soon as possible." Her words gathered momentum as she spoke.

"She was beside herself when I said I was leaving Paris to come back, and she was only somewhat calmer when I said I wouldn't be staying here for long. I think she's more afraid of him than I am. I'm not sure what that's about."

George said nothing. And then: "Sophie is your friend and your protector. I know you do but keep listening to her. You are fiercer yourself and braver than I ever knew. Meg has you in her body, in her blood." He paused, leaning forward, head down, hands folded between his knees, a man considering what to say next.

When he lifted his head, he placed his hands against his lips, fingertips together like someone about to pray. "Bridget, I need to know something, but I've been afraid to ask." His voice was barely a whisper. "Have you come to take her back with you?" And as though he might not bear the answer, he covered his face with his hand. Thus, he missed her bewildered expression. When he dropped his hands, he saw her face had turned ashen.

"Oh, George, George," she whispered. "No, no, no." Grabbing his hand, she held it, wanting to set his mind at rest, forever. "Never. She's your daughter, she's Edna's daughter."

"I'm sorry, Bridge. Everything feels so unsettled. I'm not even sure why you've come. Or why you need to go back there. To France." For a moment, his voice caught an edge.

"What keeps you there, of all places you could be? It was a war zone, for God's sake. If you were even considering taking her..." He paused when Bridget dropped her hand onto his knee with more than a little force.

"I said, never. I meant it. You did something for me all those years ago that was miraculous, and who she has become in your care is equally miraculous." Bridget had to admit to herself that being here, experiencing this family, feeling the connections all around, was unnerving her. And now, too, she did wonder if seeing this young girl, recognizing the spirited being within her, and discovering her innocent childlike way, was unsettling her more than she'd anticipated.

Bridget wondered somewhere deep within, if she herself had ever felt such a quality of simplicity, of childlike wonder. No. She would never take Meg away from this place—away from her home. It was time. Time to unravel the story of why she'd needed to come.

"George." She spoke with a soft assurance that she'd closed one door and opened another. "I'm here because I needed to put a dream to rest."

Chapter Twenty-Six

BROTHER AND SISTER SAT ON THE FRONT PORCH SWING, watching the moon cast a glow over the fields beyond. Theirs was an ancient journey, finding the paths that reconnect two people who, for a while, had lost each other. They discovered that story was the way back, and that story could distance them from old pain. After Bridget quashed George's fear that she was there to take Meg away, he sat back. He relaxed into her presence.

Bridget closed her eyes as she talked, wanting him to hear her words. "George, just for a while, forget I'm your sister and try to put away all I've told you about what happened with Jack. Just for a while. Let me tell my story the way it is now. How I am. How I'm discovering what's possible."

"All right, Bridge. But before you begin, please promise you're not going to disappear again. I need to know you're all right. She…" he said, pointing back into the house, "… needs to know you'll be all right."

Bridget looked away for an instant. When she turned back to him, her eyes shone with old, unshed tears. "I promise. I'll be more faithful and write more often because I have more reason than ever now."

George leaned down from the swing and picked up a wooden box that he'd brought from the house.

When he opened it, Bridget laughed, "You kept my letters! My brother kept my letters."

His face flushed a bit. With that, he pulled a letter from the box. "Here, have a read. It's one of the first you sent to me after you left us."

"George. I know what I said in those letters. About Jack. About his brutal nature."

The years dropped away for a moment, and they were brother and sister living in the crackling tension of a home coming apart, a mother dying, a man capable of barbarism and cold separation.

Bridget continued. "I need you to listen. Let's not talk about him. Let's live in a world where he no longer exists. I know I can, because I've done that for the last eight years."

"Where who no longer exists?" Edna spoke from behind the screen door.

George shifted in his chair and turned around. "Did we wake you?"

"Not at all, I've been reading, but the two of you seemed so deep in conversation I didn't want to interrupt. Do you know what time it is? Bridget, if you are leaving at the time you mentioned to catch the early train...."

Bridget waved her hand to beckon Edna out onto the porch. "No, don't worry. I can leave later in the morning. You need to hear what I'm about to say. Will you come sit here?" She pointed to a rocker that sat by the railing.

Bridget took the letter from George, held it gently within her fingers, and put her slippered feet onto a stool by the swing. Leaning back, she read her words aloud. George closed his eyes and listened. Edna folded her arms about herself and sat watch over the two of them, brother and sister, as Bridget's words lifted into the air.

When I left here all those years ago, I left my child, I left you, and I left all that was familiar. I felt like something good in me had died. And what I felt was—guilt for leaving Meg. Yet I left.

We have that in us, George, you and I, grit that wouldn't and won't let us give in. Look at you now, a successful farmer, a good woman by your side. If you hadn't left as you did, Jack would have taken the heart from you, too. He took Mama's and he almost took mine. Because that's all he knows how to do. You saved your own life by leaving, and I'm still saving mine with the help of two remarkable women who came into my life exactly when I needed them. Call it magic, call it fate, whatever it might be, here's what happened. It's a story of one extraordinary man, whom I think I might love forever.

I haven't told you the whole story yet of Peter. He's the reason I needed to come back, to lay eyes on Meg.

When I stopped hearing from him, I thought of every reason why, but I pushed away the one reason I couldn't accept. I decided he might have fallen for one of the French beauties in one of those villages he'd described to me, or, on the dark nights, I thought I was just another port in the storm for him…but my brain, my mind, and yes, my heart, would not let me go to that one place. That he'd been captured…or was dead.

Not until my friend Suzanne in Paris, not until…

Bridget's chin dropped to her chest. When her voice quavered, Edna reached for her hand but sat back when Bridget shook her head no.

"I need to do this," she whispered. And began to read again.

…until Suzanne suggested I write to Peter's sister.
I still have the letter she sent to me…to tell me he'd
been killed.

"How was he killed?" Edna asked, gentleness softening the words. The moment hung in the air.

Bridget inhaled a breath and exhaled a sigh. "He was at the last battle of Ypres, 1918. He'd made it that far. The war was almost over, and a sniper shot him." Another breath. "He was doing double duty because he was standing another man's watch, someone who was sick."

No one spoke. George opened his eyes, now wet with sadness, and Edna bowed her head. Bridget picked up the letter again, folded it, and looked over to George and to Edna. "There isn't much more to say about what I wrote in the letter; except I knew I'd always feel unfinished if I didn't come back."

"And that's when I needed to see Meg. I wanted to see our daughter one more time. Peter's gone from our lives, but in those three days and nights together we created something beautiful, a daughter."

George, not known for revealing emotions, stood from his chair, walked to his sister, reached for her hand, and, as she stood, enfolded her in his arms, where they stayed in the silence of grief.

Chapter Twenty-Seven

GEORGE, BLEARY-EYED, STUMBLED TO THE PHONE IN THE front hall. It rang with an insistence that said, "Answer me, now."

"Hullo." Eyes closed, he leaned his forehead against the speaker and held the receiver close to his ear. The clock on the parlor mantel chimed four thirty.

"George? George? It's Sophie. Can you hear me?"

"Yep, I hear you." George could feel his chest tightening.

"George, Bridget needs to leave. She needs to go as soon as possible. Jack knows she's there. At the farm."

The peace of early morning dissolved into the darkness surrounding him.

"How? How?" George's drowsiness transformed into high alert. "How did he find out?"

"That's not the point right now, just let it be said he's hired a private detective. Jack's a deranged man, obsessed with his hatred. When's she catching the train to Toronto?" Sophie spoke with an urgent crispness.

"Not till this afternoon, but," he paused for a moment, "I'll get her up now and drive her to Toronto and get her on the next train to Montreal."

"That's good. I looked up the schedule. If you hurry, you could make the morning train."

"I'm on my way to get dressed and wake her up." George reached to place the receiver on its hook but took it back to his ear. "Did you say something more, Sophie?"

"Just, thank you, George. You're a good man."

Hanging up the receiver, George turned to move toward the stairs, unbuttoning his pajama shirt.

"Papa?" Meg stood at the top of the stairs. "Why are you talking on the phone in the middle of the night?"

"Meg, go back to bed. Aunt Bridget just needs to go—she needs to catch a train."

"Why does she have to leave so early? I want to say goodbye." Meg put one foot on the top step and began to descend toward her papa, who in turn raised his arm to beckon her back.

"You go back into your bed. She'll come in and say goodbye."

Another voice echoed down the hall. It was Bridget, fully dressed, leather case in her hand. "Do what Papa asks, Meg. I'll come say goodbye in…just a moment." Her voice spoke of sadness as she walked toward them. "It seems my train is a bit earlier." She lifted her eyes and caught the bleak expression on George's face.

"Yeah, you're right, Bridget. Your train is earlier. I was just coming to wake you."

They made a strange portrait, the three of them standing there: George climbing the stairs, half out of his pajama top; Meg sitting on the top step, her nightie wound around her ankles, her mass of shiny curls cascading down her back; and Bridget, straight-backed, holding her case, looking as though she'd been ready for this moment all night.

Continuing up the stairs, George reached down to Meg and lifted her into his arms. "Papa," she giggled. "What are you doing?"

"I'm taking you back to your bed, my girl, so Auntie Bridget can come give you a hug goodbye." Meg lay her head against her papa's shoulder. "You promise?" she whispered.

"I promise," he breathed into her ear.

THE SKY OFFERED NEW AND CERTAIN COLORS, REDS, oranges, and pinks—a morning to remember, Bridget thought as her train gathered speed, moving away from Toronto toward Montreal. Beside her sat Sophie, who, when she met George and Bridget at Main Station, declared she intended to stay with her friend until she saw her onto the ship sailing to Liverpool.

"And, if I'm so inclined, I will see you right to Paris." Bridget knew that look; the one Sophie could assume when she'd spoken the last word on a subject. There would be no fuss. George had handed Bridget her leather case when he'd helped her from the car.

Little had been said as they'd driven into the city, following the growing sunrise. Both wondered if this might be the last time together; neither spoke about the possibility. As he'd turned away from her, he held her hand for an instant, "I will take care of Meg as though she were mine."

With no pause or hesitation, Bridget had smiled. "Dear George, Meg is your daughter. I see that. I know she's safe. I know she's loved."

THE TRAIN SWAYED, ROUNDING THE CURVES THAT TOOK them away from the city toward Quebec. Sophie placed her hand on Bridget's arm and let it sit there, a gentle gesture that said, "I'm here." Placing her hand over Sophie's, Bridget turned to her. "Maybe I shouldn't have come." Her face gave way to anguish, her eyes shadowed with doubt.

"This was a journey you needed to make, I know surely, and more than that...Meg will remember someday that you were here."

Bridget took her hand from Sophie and leaned down to the case at her feet. She reached into it and grasped a notebook. Meg's notebook.

As she smoothed the cover bright with painted sunflowers, designs that Meg had created, she felt an overwhelming love for the girl she'd birthed. Bridget believed Clara's creative spirit lived in Meg, the same energy that flowed through herself. Three generations connected by their artfulness and their passion for beauty. Jack had not destroyed Clara's gift—her daughter and her granddaughter were carrying it out into the world.

"Sophie, I want to read you a story that Meg told to her dad. She gave it to me when I went to say goodbye." Bridget sat back into the cushioned seat, opened the notebook, and began to read. Sophie held her arms crossed as she might hold a child. Head down, she closed her eyes and listened.

Aunt Bridget.

I fond out today that I have an aunt. Her name is Bridget. She looks a lot like Papa, not a surpriz, because he's her brother. I don't know why he never told me he had a sister, but I think it's ok. Maybe she wanted to be a mystry, like me when I go hide under the porch with my book and my flashlight, or when I climb up into the attic with my cat Ginger, and I tell her stories that I make up.

THE SHELTER OF EACH OTHER   199

Aunt Bridget, Aunt Bridget sounds nice when I say it.

Right now, I'm up in the attic and I'm writing this story to give to her when she leaves. She's not staying very long, I guess she's a good writer and needs to get back to fnishing her stories I told her I'd keep writing and if it's all right I'd ask Papa to mail some of my stories to her. Paris is very far away, across the ocean, but I'll find out where it is on Papa's map, that way I'll know for sure where my stories go when I send them. There are other stories in my book

Aunt Bridget told me she's a writer, and when I said I wanted to be a writer, she laufed

(laughed) and hugged me, I think that meant she was happy I want to be like her.

I thought one time I wanted to be L.M. Montgomery and write stories about orphan girls like Anne but now that I know Aunt Bridget is a writer, I'd like to be like her, go to magical places where I'll have adventures and write about them.

When I'm older, maybe when I'm sixteen, I'll ask Papa why he never told me he had a sister.

For now, I'm happy I met her.

Whoever she is.

Bridget stopped reading and closed the notebook. That last line, *whoever she is,* sat upon her inhale of breath, hung there for an instant, before she exhaled and lifted the book to her lips. The clean scent of Meg wafted between her fingers. *What have I done, coming here?*

"Sophie. I wonder if I've made a huge mistake." Bridget glanced out the window of the carriage where an image shimmered for seconds—Meg in her flannel nightie, her tousled curls shining chestnut brown in the glow of her bed lamp, eyes drowsy with sleep.

The image faded and Bridget gazed over at farmers' fields, where groves of trees caught the early morning sheen on leaves wet with last night's rain. Seeing the beauty of the morning, remembering Meg's innocent gaze, Bridget felt an emptiness, a space where she knew her heart should be.

"What if she finds out somehow what I've done? She'll hate me."

Beside her, Sophie sat silent until, without turning, she spoke. "Yes, Bridget, she may find the truth one day but maybe not all of it. You can decide that."

"What are you saying?" Bridget, still holding Meg's book, turned toward Sophie, as the train leaned into a curve, sending her and the notebook lurching into her friend's shoulder. Sophie lifted her arm and caught Bridget, holding her while the train righted and traveled on forward.

The well-dressed gentleman across the aisle chuckled, "A very good catch, ma'am."

For a moment, neither woman found words, wound into one another as they were. In the end, it was Bridget who lifted herself back into her seat and picked up Meg's notebook where it had landed on the floor. Lights from a passing rural station flashed by as the train sped straight away to Montreal. A lake appeared below the banks and trees. Something about the glittering waters stirred Bridget to seize upon what Sophie might mean by "but maybe not all of it."

"Sophie. I think I know. Maybe Meg will someday know who her father is. Maybe there's reason…" Bridget's voice broke. She grasped the notebook in both hands and placed it on her lap, her hand lying atop like a blessing, an affirmation. It was a gesture of hope, that if ever or when Meg discovered her parentage, it would be all right. For now, speeding toward Montreal and back to France, Bridget settled into that possibility.

Sophie nodded.

Part Four

One can only go for so long without asking
"who am I?," "where do I come from?," "what does
all this mean?," "what is being?," "what came
before me and what might come after?"
Without answers there is only a hole. A hole where
a history should be that takes the shape of an
endless longing. We are cavities.

—RIVERS SOLOMON, *The Deep*

Chapter Twenty-Eight

June 11, 1944

MEG THREW ANOTHER OAK LOG ONTO THE FIRE. SHE WEL-comed her new brick fireplace on this cool Saturday eve-ning. Even though summer was on its way, the air felt the crispness of a fall day. The storyteller in Meg found that crispness befitting for the deed she was about to undertake. Bill McBride had finally arrived that afternoon with the let-ters he'd spirited from her seven days ago. She hadn't asked why it had taken him so long to bring them back—that would wait for another time.

"I'd like you to put them all away. For now," Bill had said, as he placed the boxes on her kitchen table. "At least till I come back tomorrow, Sunday. I'm not work-ing…we could sit together and…" Meg waved him over to the door.

"Bill, you're being bossy. Come back tomorrow, yes, I'll make lunch. We'll talk, but I can't promise I'll not read at least one or two—my life is written into these letters. And there's a crack there that needs mending." Her words faded into a whisper. "Now you need to go."

Bill, hand on the door latch, had turned. "Before I go. Have you talked to your mom and dad about finding these letters? Maybe they need to be there as you go through all these. Do they need a chance to explain?" He'd hesitated as he opened the door.

Her breath had caught somewhere in her throat, her next words strangled. "I don't know what to say. I don't know how to understand what they did."

Perhaps, like most policemen, Bill had developed the ability to remain apart from human despair, although his natural inclination was shared sorrow. Bill had watched Meg try to grasp that she was not who she'd believed herself to be. She was not George and Edna Blackwell's daughter, nor was she Harry's sister. So, who was she?

"I need you to go for now, Bill," she'd said, seeing him begin to come back into the room. "I haven't talked to my parents...I mean, George and Edna, all week...." Her voice broke. "I need to unravel who Bridget is...."

Meg's hand slapped against her mouth. A flash of a memory penetrated. A woman. Bridget. "Bill, I've met her. I was a child."

"That's it." Bill shut the door and walked to a well-worn armchair by the fireplace. "Here, come over here." He pointed at the plush of the chair. "I want you to sit down. And I'm not leaving. Yet, anyway."

In that moment their roles changed. Bill, who'd been that boy arriving in Meg's classroom all those years ago, became the protector, the one who'd help her navigate these unfamiliar waters.

Meg walked to the chair without protest, lowered herself into its comfort, and smoothed her hands across the soft wool of the arms. "This is Dad's chair. He gave it to me when they moved into town, so I wouldn't miss him, he said." She spoke softly, as though to herself.

Bill pulled a wooden chair from the kitchen table and sat forward, elbows balanced on his knees, his gaze intent on Meg's face. Although she returned his gaze, she didn't see him. Instead, an image floated: Aunt Bridget leaning down to wish her a farewell, "We'll meet again, someday."

"Bill." She looked into his eyes, an unwavering gaze. "I know her. I want to find her. And I want you to help me find her." Putting her finger to her lips, she cautioned him to stay silent. "There's more. I want Dad…George, to help too. I'll call him, ask him to come over tomorrow. It's Sunday. He could spend the day."

Bill knew this side of Meg. There'd be no more discussion. It was time for him to leave.

LETTERS LAY SCATTERED ACROSS THE KITCHEN TABLE, some still folded, others open, waiting.

Over on a table by the fireplace lay a local newspaper opened to an article outlined in ink. Headlines amplified her concern right now for Harry:

CANADIAN NAVY PROMINENT AS INVASION ARMADA SAILED

Meg wondered, did this woman, her mother Bridget, ever know Harry? Had she known Edward? Had she grieved his death like George, like Edna? Was she loved by this family?

On the bookshelf a small radio played out across the room, bringing to Meg's mind an image of George and Edna jitterbugging across the living room to "Don't Sit Under the Apple Tree." Those years now seemed long ago, when she, Margaret Grace Blackwell, was their daughter.

The chair by the fire beckoned. "Come, sit, be still."

But instead, she sat at the table staring at the spread of letters. Her body felt like concrete. When she lifted her hand, it flopped back onto the surface. She wondered if she might be having an attack. But no, she told herself, more likely she was shedding something, like birds that molt when time comes to grow new feathers.

That's what I'm doing, I'm growing into a new story of me. Meg picked up one of the letters Bridget had written in 1916. Thirty-two years ago.

Her thoughts whirled. Thoughts blended into questions.

As she often did when the unexpected arose in her life and she couldn't do anything about it, Meg took shelter in her imagination. Placing the letter on her lap, she smoothed her hand across the paper and imagined the woman who sat somewhere, maybe by a lamp casting a glow across her words, a favorite fountain pen between her fingers. Was she right-handed? Did she lean over the letter, her hand cupping the edge of her chin, in the same way Meg did when she wrote? Was the story of why she left somewhere here in these letters, in her words? Did she wonder if someday her daughter might discover that story? Was she hoping she would?

The music from the radio changed, becoming softer, slower, and Meg became aware that a new feeling drew her to take up the letter from the table. Confused, yes, but something that felt like curiosity crept in around the edges of confusion. She wondered, who is Bridget? Why didn't I know about her? Why did no one ever say anything? In the midst of her questions, a favorite line from *Anne of Green Gables* popped into her head: "There's such a lot of different Annes in me."

"I suspect there are a lot of Megs in me," she said aloud, and, with that thought, began to read the letter she held in her hand and tried to imagine the woman who'd written it.

June 1916

Dear George, dear brother:

This may be the last letter I write to you for a long while. I only want you to know that I am safe and, yes, well. Even though I know once again what heartbreak feels like.

No one, not even you, George, need know where I am for a while. I've left the munitions factory where I was working when I came to you last September. I don't want to say where I'm going. For all the reasons and everything that's happened to me over the last many months, I want to disappear.

There's so much I want to say to you, about your tolerance, but more than that, your act of kindness—you, and Edna. My girl will be loved and cared for; I know that as surely as I put this pen to paper. I wish I'd known all those years ago what a remarkable man you are.

Don't worry, George, because I know you will, whether I have resources to see me through. I do. Salaries from the munitions factory are satisfactory, and with our mother's money from Aunt Vivian, left to us, I am fine. I want so much to ask you to send me word about Margaret Grace as she grows, but that's not fair to you, and in many ways, I need to let her become yours completely. What I'm saying is how I began this letter. I'll not be in touch for a while.

But if you need to contact me, write to Sophie Watson at Canadian Records in Ottawa. They'll know how to find her and her address.

I'm so sorry, George, that I'm choosing to disappear like this, but because of the circumstances and him, I need to start fresh.

By now, Meg's head was approaching a dull ache. She knew something must have happened; whatever it had been, she was part of it.

Tires on gravel told her that George was arriving. This was not how she wanted to be when she talked to him. Meg's own sense of her dad was of a man who listened whenever she'd been hurt or disappointed. She knew without hesitation how much he cared. Yet this felt different. This felt like betrayal.

Meg roused herself from the chair, went to the table, and began to collect the letters to put back into the boxes, but changed her mind. If she and George, her dad, were going to talk, maybe they needed to have Bridget and her letters in the room. Maybe the three of them needed to be together: Meg. George. And the spirit of Bridget.

A knock at the door. A rattle of the doorknob.

"Meg, the door's locked," George called from the porch. She ran across the room and into the front hall, and called out, "Coming." As she undid the latch, she realized not only had she locked the door, but she'd also slid the bolt from the inside. What must he be thinking before he even gets in? she thought to herself. Ambivalent thoughts fluctuated: not wanting him to be hurt because the door was locked and confusion about why he'd lied to her all these years. Meg flung the door open and words burst from her mouth...not how she wanted to start but here they were: "Why didn't you tell me?"

Meg stood facing her father, her eyes boring into his face, tears brimming, arms outstretched. This was not how she'd planned to be. Nor did George expect his intrepid daughter to fall into his arms.

"Meg. Ah, Meg. I'm so sorry. So very sorry."

George Blackwell—stepson of Jack Blackwell, a man he hated, a name he despised, and brother of Bridget, a sister he loved deeply—felt as though the family secrets were unshackling themselves piece by piece while he stood holding his daughter. He wanted no more of locked-away skeletons. He wanted, more than his own well-being, to help Meg find her mother.

"Do you have that bottle of whiskey we bought for Harry's homecoming?" he asked, as they walked shoulder to shoulder to the chairs by the fire. "I believe we may need some inner warmth as we talk, but first." He turned toward his daughter. "Please, know this, you are my girl, now and always."

"How did you know, Dad? How did you know why I wanted you to come tonight?"

"Your friend Bill McBride. Came by the house this afternoon. Don't be annoyed with him. You are his hero. He wants to help."

Meg looked over at the table piled with papers. She pointed.

"There. Now that you know, and I know, secrets are over. Right? Answers are buried in among those letters. I need those answers. Dad…we need to find them, and her."

Chapter Twenty-Nine

August 1923

NOTRE DAME CATHEDRAL ROSE TOWARD THE SKY ABOVE the trees and shrubbery where Bridget sat. Gargoyles and flying buttresses seemed to dance and sway in her imagination, stories of hundreds of years caught within the stone's curvature and thrusts. She came here with her writing and her letters each afternoon to sit within the unusual quiet of an August in Paris. Many Parisians left during the hot days of August and gave their empty streets to those new to their city. Most days, since arriving in 1921, Bridget immersed herself in Paris's sensuous delights, and numbed places within herself became awakened.

This place, this city, uncovered her passion for writing, and she began to unravel her own story, painful as the words and images might be some days.

Other days Bridget felt she'd been transported and bit by bit could see her way forward, just as her walks by the Seine along the Quai de la Tournelle cleared her mind.

Each morning Bridget set out from her fourth-floor studio apartment on Rue de l'Odeon and stopped at Shakespeare and Company bookstore to return library books and search out new ones. If she arrived early, before the busy time began, she might have a chance to talk with Sylvia Beach who owned the store and, Bridget discovered, invited authors in who'd found a home in Paris.

Today, Sylvia had asked if Bridget could help shelve new books.

"Thank you," Bridget replied. "I'd be happy to." With those words she relished a sense of belonging. She'd found the perfect place, which, in an ironic way, her stepfather had provided. Here in Paris, while staying out of harm's way, Bridget discovered a life force within herself she'd not known before. She felt like an explorer finding new horizons.

No one here knew her story, only as much as she chose to tell, no one except her friend Suzanne Garnier. Bridget was the mysterious Canadienne, a role she played well.

Bridget felt comfort today, sitting under the soaring stone arches and stained-glass windows of the cathedral. Suzanne and her sisters had left the city for the beach, like so many others, but, unlike her two past summers in Paris, Bridget had turned down their invitation to join them. This year, 1923, held an ache of loss, one of the tattered threads that hung on after seeing Meg three months ago. Now she wondered if she'd ever see her again. She missed her daughter, that young vibrant girl, as a mother naturally misses her child.

Bridget had hoped that going back to the farm, after being away, would be like a family visit, or she'd tried creating that story. She'd be Aunt Bridget, dropping by to see her brother's little girl, Meg.

But the bond of mother and child was stronger than Bridget's attempts to erase their attachment. On that day in May, the seven-year-old Meg had looked at her birth mother through eyes that matched Bridget's clear-eyed gaze; she had a quirky way of raising her one eyebrow, as did Bridget, when she was puzzled. No, Meg was not "a little girl she didn't know at all," she was her blood, her heart, her soul.

And since the day she'd left, making her way back to France, Bridget longed for Meg, and her fear grew that she'd never go back. She knew that life for her was forever changed. This knowledge took her breath away.

Grateful for the fifteen-minute walk back to the bookstore where she had new books to shelve and library books to reshelve, she stood up from the bench, brushed crumbs from her new checked cotton dress, tossed her lunch papers into the garbage by the bench, and began her stroll to Shakespeare and Company. Later, she thought, she might walk over to the Luxembourg Gardens, a place full of beauty and light. She needed beauty and light after the world had taken on the gray hues of the last few moments when she found herself missing her girl.

When she arrived at 12 Rue de l'Odeon, she walked past the rolling bookshelves by the door, stepping over stacks of books waiting for shelving and library books brought back by frequent patrons. Her work awaited: tasks in exchange for a small space where she might write her novel, in what she considered rarefied air.

Since leaving Scotland and traveling to Paris with Suzanne, Bridget felt life as never before. All that she'd experienced as a young girl in western Ontario seemed a tintype, a photo of someone she hardly knew. Here in Paris, living among writers, artists, and musicians, she discovered that creative inner threads were replacing old, frayed, and slanted perceptions she'd held of herself. Threads of feelings gave words to letters written to George, to Meg, all of which she folded away and placed in the pocket of her leather case.

Sylvia was finishing with a customer when Bridget walked into the store. Like someone who might have known Bridget's yearnings, and someone who recognized a wanderer like herself, Sylvia flashed a friendly smile and greeted Bridget.

"Good, you're back. A letter arrived here at the store for you today. It's on your desk in back." Bridget smiled at Sylvia's words "your desk"; that scratched, shabby piece of furniture was a resting place for those like Bridget who showed up at Shakespeare and Company and were given a place to weave their stories.

Bridget anticipated another letter from George, and maybe another brief note from Geordie McKinney in Scotland. She'd had an unexpected letter from him early in 1920, short and to the point. A letter she carried with her because she needed to hold the threads weaving her journey.

She took it from the side pocket of her cloth book bag and read it one more time.

Tonga Village
Scotland, UK
March, 1920

Dear Bridget...

I hope it'll be fine with you if I drop a line to you every so often.

I'd very much like to hear about your time there in Paris and how your writing is coming along. There was much we talked about, there in the pub, that gave me reason to consider. I thank you for those days, because as you know, my experiences during the war left me bitter, at least until Emily, the nurse you met in the pub, took time and care. We rather looked after one another, she and I, while she yearned for her fiancé. (Remember Emily the auxiliary nurse who sat writing letters there in the pub?) By the way, Emily and her fiancé split up! That's all I'll say about that…for now.

It seems to me that you might be troubled, being far from your home, and without friends or family, although, I believe Suzanne was and hopefully still is a good friend.

I feel I may be rambling, so I'll close off for now with the hope you'll see your way to sending me a note every so often, just to let me know how you are and how that novel you're writing is coming along. My friend Bridget, the writer!

She'd kept the letter. And the others, over the two years she'd been in France, always with news about the village, and, yes, about Emily. Bridget thought in the beginning, when Geordie's notes started arriving, that he might have notions of something more than friendship between them; however, that thought soon ended when she got the letter announcing Geordie and Emily's nuptials. The news spread warmth through her chest, and a seed for a new story, someday.

Making her way through the store, weaving her way around stacks of books, she walked into the back room and saw two letters propped against the wall behind her table. The manuscript of her novel lay by a shelf, where she'd left it earlier. As she picked up the letters, she recognized George's scrawl, the feel of the thin airmail paper gave breath to the moment. A welcome deep breath of the familiar.

The impressions she gathered into her body, here in this writers' community, sometimes gave Bridget the feeling that she'd climbed to a higher altitude where the air was thinner. Out-of-the-ordinary people moved in and out of this bookstore, one owned and run by an extraordinary woman. Yet Sylvia welcomed her in each day, giving her pieces of the familiar: the nutty smell of freshly brewed coffee; the scent of pages and books, hundreds on shelves, piles in hallways; and, during winter, the warmth of the coal stove. Something felt like home to Bridget, yet she couldn't quite fathom what that might be. Was it possible that Clara's spirit and her artist's heart had taken up residence here, while she waited for Bridget to arrive?

Shaking her head at how she'd become lost in surprising thoughts, Bridget set the mysterious letter aside, opened George's letter, dropped down into the wooden armchair cushioned with a red velvet pillow, and proceeded to read.

Broadview Farm,
Milboro, Ontario.
July, 1923

Dear Bridget,

There's some excitement here at the farm, for Edna, Harry, Meg, and me. Two of our mares have had colts almost at the same time. One of those mares is Harry's Gracie. (He renamed her after Meg was born—she was Goldie originally, but he decided after Meg came along that she needed a horse named after her. Well, that's Harry for you.) The other mare who dropped a foal is Luna. We've had her for eight years.

I could probably go on about farm news. The lambs born last February are already producing wool and Bill Anderson our neighbor came over to help me with shearing before the ewes gave birth. Can you believe that your brother has learned how to shear sheep?

When you were here that time seven years ago, when Meg was born, we were mostly a dairy farm with cows and a few horses, but now Edna and I are expanding our farm. She is one of the most enterprising women I know, and she puts a hand into the work, as does Harry. He's a good boy, well—young man now. He's already eighteen and going to high school in town. We're proud of him, and I think he could be whatever he chooses to be. Right now, we hope he thinks about staying on the farm for a while.

Meg thinks the world of him, and she, as far as he's concerned, is his little sister. He's never asked much about what happened and how he acquired a sister who arrived just when his aunt left. I know you wanted us to say as little as possible, and we've done that as he's grown up, but he's a young man now. So, Bridget, I have to tell you that Harry and I had a talk just a while ago, shortly after you were here and left, mysteriously as far as he was concerned. I told him part of the story, how you were in "trouble" as they like to say around here, and you didn't feel you could look after a child on your own. And do you know what he said? "Well, I'm sorry Aunt Bridget was in trouble, but we got a great girl in Meg, didn't we, Dad."

Almost brought me to tears. Edna was stunned when I told her. She said she always thought Edward was the sensitive one.

Harry will never ever say anything to Meg, you can be sure of that.

Bridget held the letter to her chest and folded her hands over the words, letting her chin drop. Another person held her secret, another person close to Meg. When she'd gone to the farm last May, Harry had been polite but seemed preoccupied, not the energetic, sometimes boisterous boy she'd known when first she'd gone to stay at the farm those years ago. Those years when she'd left her baby behind.

Maybe he's been judging me, maybe he thinks I abandoned her... The demons collected in Bridget's head until, sitting up, she smoothed the letter onto the desk and, with a determined sigh, began reading and hoping that the next sentences might quell her uncertainties.

But what George continued to write did nothing to bring any composure—instead, his words set her heart pounding. Her mouth dry.

> *To be plain-spoken, Bridget, I'm not so worried about Harry at all, what concerns me is what seems to be going on with our stepfather, and my reactions. With all the time that's gone on since you arrived here and left, I assumed he'd given up. Maybe even done what he did with me, blocked you out of his life. I was wrong. He is a man obsessed. I don't want to alarm you; however, Sophie has been in touch with me. She's working as an art critic writing under a pseudonym for the Toronto Telegram. She may have news about him. All she said was she had disturbing news. Have you heard anything at all from Sophie?*

By now, all the calm she'd experienced sitting by Notre Dame had vanished. In its place was a sick sensation, and anger. *How long will this man's evil haunt me?*

Bridget stood from her chair, placed George's letter in the side pocket of her leather case, and threw the other letter into the deep drawer of the old desk where she placed crossed-out pages of her manuscript. Not knowing the address in the corner of the envelope, not recognizing the neat script on the front, she decided to put it away, for now. When the nauseous feeling let go, she'd come back and see about this unknown mail.

Taking the leather case, she threw the strap across her shoulder, opened the flap, and stuffed her rough draft deep inside. On her way out and through the store, Bridget called over to Sylvia, who was leaning against the counter in what seemed deep conversation with one of her well-known authors.

"Bridget. Come over and meet another one of our authors," Sylvia called to her. Bridget felt a moment of pleasure to hear the owner refer to "our authors," as though she had a place within Shakespeare and Company. This moment reminded her that she had a life far away and apart from Westover. A place she'd escaped from, a man she'd run from.

Bridget walked to the counter where Sylvia and her author leaned, each with ankles crossed, arms folded, comfortable in one another's presence.

"James Joyce," he said and extended his hand. A rather languishing handshake. What Bridget remembered later, when she wrote to Sophie, was how thin he was, a bit stooped, yet there was a grace about him. And his pleasurable Irish lilt.

This moment, this meeting, highlighted the acceptance she felt here in Paris at Shakespeare and Company. Bridget Blackwell, author, meeting James Joyce, author.

Bitterness and fear dimmed. For a time.

Chapter Thirty

September 1923

PARIS STREETS WERE COMING ALIVE.

The summer hiatus was winding down.

Suzanne and her sisters were back from the beach and in their apartment on Rue des Écoles. Suzanne and Bridget had resumed their afternoon coffee ritual where it had left off in early August. A wedding was in the offing in Suzanne's family, and Bridget had been invited. Life in her adopted country was becoming comfortable and familiar. If Suzanne would only stop asking questions.

"When are you going to open that last letter?" Suzanne looked over at Bridget who was sipping on her coffee and biting into a warm croissant slathered with butter.

Bridget regretted that she'd said anything to Suzanne about the letter she'd decided not to open. And she was feeling childish, as though something dangerous lay in that letter she'd thrown into the drawer. Like the monster in the closet.

How could anyone hurt her now? How could anyone except George and Sophie even know she was living across the ocean in France? And, if her stepfather found her, what harm could he do? Soon he'd be just another old man. A man who had hurt his stepdaughter deeply, a moment in time that happened years ago. A moment locked away in the darkness.

"Bridget…Bridget? Where did you go?" Suzanne waved her hand across the table. "I've been talking to you for five minutes and you disappeared. What are you thinking?"

"Mm…what? Oh, oh, Suzanne. I'm sorry. My thoughts took me away. What were you saying?"

"Will mademoiselle have more café?" A young waiter stood by them, French coffee press in hand. He smiled and greeted the two women, his favorite customers, both open and gracious, especially the Canadian, the one who had a lightness in her spirited manner. But this afternoon her smile was dimmed, her eyes darkened. He leaned in with his coffee pot.

Bridget held her oversized cup up to him and he broadened his smile as he poured. "That's fine, thank you, monsieur." Her tone, edged with a curt dismissal, caused him to back away. Suzanne looked over, her head tilted to one side, eyebrows raised.

"Tu es énervé?"

"No, Suzanne, I'm not upset," Bridget said, a tone of finality coloring her words.

"If I may be bold, and you know I can be, I think it's time to read the letter. You're like a frightened child not wanting to look in the closet. How long…?"

"Stop right there, Suzanne. I've told you, my story. I don't need any advice. You live amid family and can't know how it is…." Suzanne's smile slipped, her eyes welled.

"Oh God, Suzanne. I'm so sorry." Bridget, in her own fit of pique, had ridden like a tank over the fact that Suzanne's family had been torn apart during the Great War, with the death of her mother and father. "You're only trying to help, to get me unstuck. I so didn't mean to open a wound."

Suzanne, who'd gathered herself together, took a ser-
viette from the saucer of her café and wiped the corners
of her eyes. "Brigitte, I did know about family, once
upon a time. And I have my sisters. I feel you may not
know family in the same way. Although…" She paused,
looked away for a second, and when she looked back,
smiled. "You have George, your brother. I don't know
many women whose brothers remain as faithful. And
Sophie, isn't she family?"

Bridget dropped her cup onto its saucer, a cracking
sound that brought the waiter running. "Mademoiselle,
est-ce que tu vas bien? Are you all right?" She raised her
hand and shook her head.

"No, pardonnez moi. I'm fine." Both women grinned,
each convinced that the waiter was taking extra good care
of the Canadian lady. He dusted crumbs from the table-
cloth and walked away, occasionally glancing back over
his shoulder.

"I think you've made a conquest," Suzanne quipped.

"No, I think he's worried I might break something or that
I'm a bit unstable. He could be right." Their shared laughter
eased the taut place between Bridget's shoulders.

"All right, I'll open the letter. I want to go back to the
bookstore. I told Sylvia I'd reshelve library books later this
afternoon, and I want to finish the last part of a chapter I've
been working on. This novel is becoming a kind of fantasy
rather like the stories my mother told me."

"There, see? You have family. You have your mother's
stories." Suzanne stood, took a last sip of coffee, and placed
her straw hat firmly upon her mass of curls. "Go find out
who wrote to you. Leave some extra francs for your suitor,
the waiter." She grinned. "Au revoir for le moment."

With a swish of her skirt, she started down the street toward her sister's dress and stitchery shop on Boulevard Saint-Germain, a business she and her sister Honoré owned together. Bridget admired Suzanne and her sisters for their fortitude, their ability to pull catastrophe and misfortune out of the fire and rebuild their lives from nothing after the war. They were "modern women," admired by some, rebuked by others.

Hated by some…men like Jack Blackwell.

Bridget knew how fortunate she was to have someone like Suzanne, a friend here in Paris, someone who knew the city, who'd helped her find an apartment on the Left Bank not far from the bookstore. It was Suzanne, too, who'd persuaded Bridget to walk into Shakespeare and Company, introduce herself to Sylvia Beach, and offer to volunteer in the store in exchange for a place to write. From that moment all unfolded as though meant to be and without flaw.

Strolling along Rue des Écoles, and stroll she did, Bridget felt the time had come to open the letter back in the drawer of her desk at the bookstore. Bridget had considered what might be next for her, and each time she walked these streets, each time she entered Shakespeare and Company and was greeted by Sylvia or the authors she collected there, Bridget felt a sense of belonging.

Maybe Paris could be where she'd put down roots. In the meantime, she'd read the letter.

BRIDGET LISTENED, AS SHE SAT AT HER DESK, TO THE murmur of the few people still browsing, some finding a corner where curling into a chair was encouraged. Some of the people who frequented Shakespeare and Company read till they nodded off and then placed the book back on the shelf for another day. This bookstore was a haven for readers and writers. A sanctuary for Bridget. On this late afternoon, Sylvia had left her assistant Myrasine in charge, with Bridget taking care of library check-ins. Closing time was three hours away.

The letter lay on Bridget's desk, waiting. With one last sigh, she picked up the one that had arrived a week ago, the one she'd stuffed away in a drawer. Curious now because she recognized neither the address nor the script, she began to undo the flap of the envelope, carefully holding the tissue-thin paper lined with red and blue. The postal stamp on the front gave no clue. Bridget was playing a game with herself, taking her time, anticipating—good news or bad? The first line caused her to sit up, feet flat on the floor.

Sunday, August 5, 1923

Dear Bridget,

I'm not sure if you remember me, Elva from the muni-tions factory outside the city. We worked together there for a while before you shipped off to the Mon-treal factory.

If you're wondering who gave me your present address, it was Sophie. She's kept Irene and me abreast of where you are. She wanted us to know your where-abouts in case something happened to her and in case someone needed to contact you.

Thus, I have news about Sophie—first let me say she's all right or will be.

Bridget stopped reading, her scalp prickling with fear. As she read on, she hoped, like the stories she wrote, whatever dark thing had happened was going, at the end, to be all right.

I don't know how much you know about what she's been doing since the factories closed. Her work as a female supervisor in a munition factory was quite out of the ordinary, and as well, being an artist, she recorded some wartime activities of women working in munitions. There were other women artists who gained prominence depicting the war on the home front; Sophie never did, and that was intentional on her part. She's always wanted to remain anonymous, for reasons only she knows.

I'm telling you all this because two months ago, Sophie was attacked by a man as she was leaving the building where she works as a columnist for a city newspaper.

The police have been involved. I want to assure you that she is recovering. She stayed with Irene, our Irish friend, for a week or so but now is home and insists she's fine. She's talking with the police; however, saying very little to Irene about who or why.

The investigation is ongoing. However, there seems to be little evidence of who would want to do such a thing. We wondered, Irene and I, if she might have written a column that offended someone. She has written articles about recognizing the art of Armenians, a subject that could create controversy among some populations. You and I know, Bridget, that Sophie is fearless and not afraid to speak her mind.

Bridget realized she was holding the onionskin paper between her fingers so tightly her knuckles were pale.

Sophie, vigilant about Bridget's safety and keeping her away from Jack's tentacles, had herself been harmed. Her hands felt cold and clammy. A horrific idea began to form—a sour taste in the back of her throat, the same sour taste she'd had for years whenever the memory of Jack Blackwell arose. Was he searching out Sophie, and, if he was, what had reignited his madness? For the first time since arriving in France, Bridget felt vulnerable. She remembered the chilling words in George's letter: *He's a man obsessed.*

A seed, an unconscious knowing, crept across the skin on her neck. What if she hadn't escaped with her life that night? What if he hadn't fallen down the stairs? Would he have come back? What if Sophie knew more than she was revealing? Was Sophie holding some secret about him? If she was…why?

Questions whirled as Bridget went back to the letter. But when she picked it up to read on, Myrasine called from the front room of the store.

"Bridget, could you take the front desk for half an hour or so? I need to slip out."

Another time, Myrasine's request would have excited Bridget—being trusted to take over the store, not knowing who or which author might wander in—but, this moment, reading Elva's letter felt more urgent than the store.

Before she could decline, Myrasine poked her head into the back room. "You're a dear. If anyone arrives, you know where all the new fiction is, don't you, and if you have a question that you can't answer, just ask the customer to find a comfortable place, and I'll be back. Oh, be sure Teddy and the cat don't slip out. And if Mr. Joyce comes by, put Teddy in the back room…Mr. Joyce is not fond of dogs. Loves cats." And she was gone.

It was now early evening, and both the bookshop and the library were quiet. Left in charge, Bridget folded the letter, stuffed it into her sweater pocket, and walked out to the front room of the store. All was quiet. A man sat cross-legged on the floor in front of tall shelves, his body taking up the aisle, books around him piled one on top of another, each with a bookmark extending from the pages.

Bridget knew he was probably going to put those books back on the shelf, bookmarks still in the pages, but Sylvia told all who worked in the store that, if the book wasn't damaged, to let readers read however they chose. Some, like Sylvia's friend Ernest Hemingway, faithfully bought the book.

Now, she stood at a table in the large front area, shelves of books rising behind her like a protective wall. Bridget smoothed the letter onto the surface of the counter as though she wanted to magically wipe away the news. When she looked down at it, the words glared up at her: *Sophie was attacked.*

The rest of Elva's letter gave no more clues about what had happened outside the newspaper building nor what the police had discovered. Only that Sophie was badly bruised around her arms and shoulders where the attacker had tried to grab her. Obviously, Bridget thought, the attacker didn't know about Sophie's toughness. She'd watched the woman when the husband of one of the workers in the munitions factory blundered in drunk to try to pull his wife away from her station. He was a sorry sight after Sophie rushed up behind him, took his arm, and bent it up his back. Letting that image of Sophie rest, Bridget took a long breath and read the rest of the letter.

Sophie's said very little to me or to Irene about what happened, but we are all suspicious that the attack may have something to do with your stepfather. I don't want to put any ideas in your head. One thing I do know, you'll hear from Sophie.

Bridget flung her head back and looked over at the shelf where Sylvia placed Bridget's mail. Because the bookshop was a home away from home, some of Bridget's mail landed on that shelf. And there it was, another letter.

With a scramble she jostled her way from behind the counter, stepped over the books lying in a pile by the door leading into the back room, slid by the table of new fiction, and grabbed at the letter. The handwriting that addressed Bridget at Shakespeare and Company, 12 Rue de l'Odeon was Sophie's—a bit shaky, but Sophie's. Bridget tore at the envelope, scanned the words across the page, and sank to the floor.

Myrasine arrived to find her there on the floor, back against the bookshelf, head in her hands. Bridget was weeping.

Chapter Thirty-One

Myrasine Mocha, a young Greek girl who'd been a member of the bookshop's library, had offered to assist Sylvia in all the workings and complications of running the shop. One of her strengths especially valued by Sylvia was Myrasine's understanding of the needs of customers, which were many and varied. Like Suzanne, she had a family of sisters, and the presence of Bridget there on the floor weeping among the bookcases reminded Myrasine of caring and soothing when heartache descended, whatever the cause.

"Ah, Brigitte, whatever is the problem?" Myrasine knelt beside her. Spotting the letter, she asked, "Do you have the bad news from home?"

Crumpled in a ball, head to her knees, her arms wrapped to her shoulders, Bridget nodded yes. A customer started to walk along the aisle and backed away when he saw the two women, one crying, the other kneeling beside her. It seemed an intimate scene, one needing a private moment.

As the man disappeared down another aisle, Myrasine offered her hand to Bridget. "Would you come upstairs with me? I'll make us a café. Is there someone I might call to come be with you? You needn't worry about leaving, I'll lock the door soon, and you can stay if you want. Sylvia and Adrienne will be back later."

Bridget, grateful that Myrasine asked no questions, stood and brushed the dust from her trousers, giving herself a moment to breathe in the news from Sophie once again. Grateful, too, for the offer of time here in the shop.

When she climbed the stairs and walked into the apartment above the store, Bridget found a large cup of steaming coffee on the table in the small kitchen, a warmed croissant beside it. "Myrasine, you are so kind. I feel I owe you an explanation for my behavior."

Pouring a coffee, Myrasine offered a chair. "You needn't worry at all. We have young writers from America and Canada who are sometimes homesick for family. No need to explain."

"Ah, were it as simple as that."

A sip of the extra strong coffee seemed to clear a place in Bridget's brain, or so she'd say later when she told Suzanne the story. She reached into her jacket pocket and pulled out the letter she'd stuffed there.

"This letter is from a woman who has befriended me and protected me. She is the reason I'm in Paris, meeting people like you, Myrasine, people like Sylvia."

Myrasine sat waiting. "You want to read the letter? I will listen."

"Yes. And when I've read it to you, I wonder if I might make an international call on the telephone in the shop. I will gladly pay the cost."

"Of course."

Bridget smoothed the crumpled page across the linen cloth, sat forward with arms resting on the table, and read aloud.

August 1923

My Dearest Bridget,

Many thanks for the beautiful silver locket you sent to me from Paris. I'm sure I've never had anything quite so lovely or exotic. The best surprise was opening it and seeing your face smiling out at me. I shall wear it proudly.

Your gift arrived at just the right time. My life took a downturn, which I'll explain here in this letter. It was as though you knew I needed something good to counter a very unsettling event. I understand that Elva has already written to you and told you about my wretched experience. I purposefully asked her not to tell you too much because I wanted to try to unravel some tangled incidents. Maybe writing to you will help me figure out what happened.

Last June I went to an opening for a novice artist at a new gallery in the city. While I was there, I thought I'd take a wander through the gallery to look at some other paintings I haven't seen for a while, some painted by artists who were in classes with your mother and me, some just now gaining recognition. I was about to leave when I spotted two beautiful paintings along a wall by themselves in one of the smaller rooms. One a still life of sunflowers bursting from an intricately designed blue and white pitcher, the other a young girl sitting among lilac bushes reading. Bridget, I swear that young girl is you, and that these pictures were painted by your mother. In fact, the sunflower painting was one we wanted to take to the showing she was to have all those years ago at the society. The one Jack canceled!

Bridget looked over Myrasine, who'd been listening intently, leaning forward, her elbows on the counter, chin resting on folded hands. "My mother was a beautiful artist," Bridget started to say, paused, and with some heat added, "and my stepfather couldn't handle how gifted she was and shut her down. Literally."

"That's the man Jack she's referring to?"

"Yes."

"Keep reading, Bridget. I didn't know you had such an interesting family. You've never talked about family."

"Um, probably because I don't think of my stepfather as family anymore, if I ever did."

The air went dead for a few seconds, like a balloon deflating.

"Bridget?"

"Just got lost in old memories for a moment…I'll get back to the letter." She returned to Sophie's words on the page.

Here's the part that took my breath away…when I walked over to have a closer look, I got chills. Each of the paintings was signed "Jack Blackwell." He'd painted his name over Clara's signed signature. When I talked to the curator (I know him because I've written articles about the showings there), he was incredulous. First, he said no one would dare falsify a signature on a painting in his gallery. But then, he remembered an older man had come to him, saying he was representing a client who wanted to show his paintings—he said his client had once been a member of the Society of Artists and wanted to share some of his paintings from those days. Why the curator didn't check out your stepfather's status with the society, I don't know. When the older man returned, he brought the two paintings with him, those painted by Clara. They were immediately accepted.

I believe this man who came to the gallery, probably a forger himself, was hired by Jack, to pretend to represent him and his paintings.

"Mon Dieu! This is extraordinaire! Why didn't your friend...Sophie...let you know sooner?"

"Myrasine, there's more. Wait, listen to this."

So, I did a foolish thing. With the OK of the curator, because he didn't want to be held responsible for swindling the public, I wrote an article about falsifying signatures in the art world and credited the curator with the discovery of Jack's forged signatures. I specifically mentioned your mother's paintings as "examples" of clever signature falsification.

It was foolish, because I know from experience the kind of man Jack is, and the day after the paper came out, I was attacked outside the newspaper building. Luckily one of my colleagues was on his way out and saw me go down.

I won't go into more detail except to say, I'll be OK. But, it's all been hushed up—the police are saying the paintings have been taken away, it was "unfortunate" for me that some-one tried to "rob" me leaving work. I think Jack has power beyond what you and I have thought. He shut this story down. Unquestionably.

"Bridget. You said you wanted to use the international phone." Myrasine stood up, startling Bridget who looked over to her.

"What's going on? Are you leaving?" She wondered at Myrasine's sudden decision to stand.

"Non, of course not. Read no more. This is very serious. Go, call your friend. Tell her to get on a ship and come here. Come to France."

Bridget was stunned by Myrasine's abrupt reaction. Who was Sophie to her?

"I don't know if she'll come."

Bridget sat for a few moments taking it all in: Jack's ruthlessness bordering on insanity, and the horrible realization that he could be an accessory to an attempted murder.

Based on everything she'd experienced and what she knew about him, he was almost certainly the man who'd ordered the attack on Sophie.

"This is not a time to hesitate. Go, Bridget, call her, call her now."

A sense of unreality entered Bridget's body, the same feeling she'd had on that night when Jack had attacked her and tried to strangle her. Bridget stood up. Myrasine walked over to a telephone that sat on a desk. She picked up the receiver and asked for the operator. "Long distance, please. Canada."

An international call lasting less than ten minutes convinced Sophie to give herself what she'd historically created for Bridget—an escape route. By the beginning of October, she'd booked a passage on the Empress of France sailing from Quebec to Liverpool. Six days and nine and a half hours after leaving Quebec, she arrived in Liverpool, where she caught the train to Dover, crossed the channel on the ferry, and arrived at the Gare du Nord in Paris.

"You're here! Sophie, you're here!" Bridget called, letting the joyous girl within free to run down the platform, holding her floppy-brimmed, flowered hat with one hand and waving with the other.

"Of course, I'm here. How else can we take care of one another if we're not within sight?" Sophie, who was known for the art of muted expression, dropped her embroidered canvas bag, opened her arms, and engulfed her friend, Clara's daughter, in a long embrace.

Four days later, Sophie, Bridget, and Suzanne sat under the large awnings of the Café de Flore. Sounds of Paris surrounded them like an orchestra preparing for a concert.

Suzanne and Bridget were attuned to the city, the buzz of scooters cruising past, the hum of people's voices talking, murmuring, occasionally bursting forth passionately, arms waving. Nearby, at the edge of the terrace, a man was reading from a book of poetry, two women and another man leaning in to listen. Sophie sat, eyes closed, seemingly in a trance.

"Are you all right, Sophie?" Bridget touched her arm, not wanting to startle her.

"Ah, I'm at ease, Bridget, possibly more than I've been for many weeks."

"This city will do that for you, if you let it," Suzanne said, taking a spoonful of peach dessert. "It'll soothe you with food and wine and possibly love."

Bridget smiled over at her friend.

"Non, mon amie…nothing to tell. Only that Paris is becoming Paris again since the war." Conversation drifted above the sonorous strains of a young cellist by the edge of the terrace. The warm, mellow notes gave the afternoon a lyrical quality, one that Bridget hesitated to break into.

"Sophie?"

"Hmm."

"Are you ready to talk about what happened?"

"Maybe we need to leave the lady alone for a while," Suzanne broke in, sensing a crack in the afternoon's serenity.

"No, I want to tell exactly what happened, because" Sophie looked to Bridget, "Jack is a dangerous and, I believe, a sick man. I was foolish to believe that I could expose him for who he is by writing that article. All I did was release the beast, that same one who attacked you, Bridget. He hates with a vengeance, one that is out of hand. He used your mother and then turned on her. Destroyed her dream because her success was too much, and when she died, I'm not sure if he felt any remorse."

No one spoke.

Sophie's words hung in the air like a sudden chill. Suzanne looked from Sophie to Bridget. "Did you know he is a sick man?"

"Yes, I knew. I knew because I saw what could happen when he was threatened."

Sophie watched Bridget's mouth tighten, her eyes darken. "Oh yes, I've seen him when people praised my mother's paintings, when he lied to buyers in the factory about my designs, saying they were his. And I've experienced his brutality, firsthand." Red splotches appeared on her cheeks; her fingers grasped the cup.

"Bridget, those days are over for you. He can't get to you anymore," Sophie said.

"How can you say that? Look what he's done to you. He tried to kill you."

"Bridget!" Suzanne swung her body to face her friend. "You're saying he's an assassin?"

Two women sitting at a table nearby stopped talking and glanced over. The war and its brutality hung in the air like a bad smell, and the word "assassin" could still cause panic. Scraping her chair away from the table, Sophie gathered her handbag and her gloves as she stood up. "We need to take our conversation away from other ears. Let's walk."

"Before we do that," Bridget looked up at Sophie, "tell me why you wrote that article when you knew there'd be a reprisal. Why, when you knew he might come back at you?"

Both Bridget and Suzanne sat, waiting for the answer.

Sophie dropped back down onto the chair, placed her hands flat on the table, and sighed. "Because I was angry about him still using and brutalizing your mother's talent. Because I want this to end. Because I want him to know he is powerless. Because…" and she paused, "I wanted to lure him out from his wolf's den." A look crossed Sophie's face, as though she'd gone to another place—one she remembered.

Suzanne, who'd lived through a war, responded. "It's like saying 'you can do your worst, Jack. I'll still be standing. Long after you fall.'" Her words reverberated truth. She knew how it felt to be still standing after her world had been shattered.

Bridget grabbed Suzanne's hand and raised her arm. "He hasn't stopped Sophie and he can't stop me. Finally, he's met his match." Looking to the sky, Bridget whispered: "Rest, Mama. Beautiful Clara."

Sophie smiled over at Bridget, her eyes shining. "The whole place is listening."

Bridget and Suzanne waved. Two women from the table nearby clapped their hands, grinned, and silently said, "Bravo."

Leaving the café, Suzanne and Bridget stopped on either side of Sophie and put their arms around her waist. "You are a hero," Bridget said.

"Not really. I'm just stubborn."

THE SEINE A FEW STREETS AWAY OFFERED THE MOVE-ment of brownish-gray water and the stillness of gray stones surrounding it. The river flowed. The lanterns began to flicker in the late afternoon. As the three women walked side by side, they let silence cover them—a cloak shared.

"I've had two stories published in a magazine," Bridget said. She spoke with quiet pleasure, glancing neither right nor left. "It's a small journal published at the bookstore."

"That's wonderful." Sophie stopped in midstroll. "Clara would be thrilled."

Her comment caught Bridget's breath. "Do you think, Sophie, Mama would be pleased?"

Suzanne shook her head. "Brigitte. I don't know your maman. But I know you and your stories…"

Before she could finish, Sophie interrupted, looked to Suzanne. "This is what Bridget's mother wanted, to come to Paris to paint, and now, here's her daughter. In Paris, being a writer. Bravo, Bridget, bravo."

With promises to show them her stories in the magazine, Bridget, Sophie, and Suzanne continued their stroll.

The shadow cast by Jack faded.

THE DAYS OF LATE AUTUMN DECORATED PARIS IN YELLOW, red, gold, and orange. Bridget gloried in the walks along the Seine with Sophie, the hours spent together in Shakespeare and Company, introducing her to Sylvia and to T.S. Eliot who'd published his poem *The Waste Land* just the year before. His "grouse poem," he'd called it.

"The moment you decided to come here, Bridget, was a brilliant one. I feel so sure that you're going to be fine on your own, maybe for a long time."

Eight days after she'd arrived, Sophie booked her passage back to Canada, confident that Bridget was going to be fine.

Sophie and Bridget said their goodbyes on the platform of the Gare du Nord, two women pushing against the inevitable. They'd talked about "the next time," but neither could say when that might be. Their conversation the night before had felt like it might be their last. Realization dawned. Words spoken held the essence of a final farewell.

"Promise me, please, there'll be no more trips back to see Meg." Sophie had lain on the small velour chesterfield in Bridget's studio, her head resting on the rounded arm.

Bridget stretched out on the floor, carpet softening the hard wood, pillow at her head, wool blanket covering her body. She lay, saying nothing to Sophie's plea, remembering only the bright-eyed energy of that girl, Meg, and that night in May lying beside her listening to the stories she'd invented. Pangs of regret, of grief, were buried deep within Bridget's body.

"I won't be going back, Sophie." She let the words fall. "Maybe ever."

The unspoken lay within her words, the possibility that she might never see her girl again. The truth she knew without hesitation: she needed to stay away, so Meg could be forever safe.

Part Five

I know, you never intended to be in this world.
But you're in it all the same.
So why not get started immediately.
I mean, belonging to it.
There is so much to admire, to weep over.
And to write music or poems about.

—MARY OLIVER

Chapter Thirty-Two

1924

THE 1920S IN FRANCE BEGAN WITH CELEBRATION AND
hope. Feelings of anticipation rode the waves of possibility
in Paris, and particularly at Shakespeare and Company. The
Great War had brought writers from America, who made
their temporary expatriate homes in the apartments and
small studios on the Left Bank.

Bridget found herself among those hope-to-be-writers,
the dreamers who frequented coffeehouses like Café de
Flore and Les Deux Magots.

The Americans she met were tired of Prohibition, cen-
soring, and a kind of puritanical air in their country, so a
mode of travel called Tourist Third Cabins brought aspiring artists and hopeful writers sailing into Le Havre on
their way to Paris. Bridget was a curiosity at first, a young
Canadian woman on her own, who arrived in Paris with her
friend Suzanne in 1919. But by 1924, Bridget had become
part of this community of writers and artists, where she
felt a sense of kinship, possibly for the first time in her life.

Bridget's disclosure to Sophie, "I won't be going back,"
meant something more to her than creating distance from
Canada. Bridget rejected the humiliation she'd experienced
living in Jack's household, allowing him to take credit for
her skill and talent at design. On a difficult day, the scarred
memory of his crazed attack sat in the back of her throat

like rancid food. Here in Paris, she was experiencing life's restoration, shame no longer filling her soul. Short stories published in small journals brought her acknowledgment from the writers who frequented Shakespeare and Company. They called her "the young Canadian author in the back room."

Her novel, which she'd begun writing when she arrived in France, was a fantasy—a story of a young girl disguised as a boy, who fought for the French Resistance group called La Dame Blanche during the Great War. Bridget wondered if her fictional character Ginot was how she imagined Meg— as a brave young Resistance fighter.

And, here in Paris, life carried a routine for Bridget; friendship with Suzanne and her sisters brought a sense of belonging she'd not experienced before. She wondered, is this how family feels? Is this what Meg has now?

But sometimes, during those moments when she thought of Meg, the ground caved and erased pleasure with Suzanne and her sisters. In those dark moments, nothing seemed real, nothing held purpose.

THE YEARS ACCUMULATED AND THE MEMORIES OF A distant place in Canada she once called home yellowed like old letters; she could barely remember the times she'd spent with George and Edna on the farm, barely remembered how it felt to birth her girl.

Occasional walks by the Seine and conversations with Suzanne lifted her spirits, unearthed hopes and possibilities helping her experience life right here, right now, in her adopted country. On this evening, after the celebrations of Bastille Day, the two friends strolled by the river, Suzanne's arm linked through Bridget's. They drew more than casual glances as the two of them sauntered along, silk chemise dresses hanging from their shoulders to just above their knees, cloche hats hiding their faces, creating an aura that spoke of mystery. Paying no attention to others, they walked arm in arm, deep in conversation.

"Would you keep writing your novel, Bridget, if you were to go back to Canada?" Suzanne asked. Her question was tentative and puzzling for Bridget.

"Why are you asking? You, more than anyone, know I'm never going back. Whatever happens here in this country, I will stay. This is my home. If my inheritance flows, as long as I keep writing and selling articles, I'll stay. I have no reason to go back."

Bridget's words were tinged with an edge of sharpness. "I'm beginning to feel you think I need to return." She stopped and faced Suzanne. "Is there something you want to tell me?"

Without hesitation, Suzanne turned to her friend. "No, no, I worry because sometimes you seem unhappy, très triste. As though you search for home." Bridget placed her hand over Suzanne's, a gesture of love for her friend, whose kindnesses were boundless. "You, Suzanne, have become my home—Paris is my city, France is my country. There's nothing, no one, for me back there in Canada." She dropped her hand and linked her arm through Suzanne's. "Come, let's keep walking."

"Non, Brigitte. Maybe that is why you are sad? There is someone back there for you in Canada. Someone who is a part of you."

Without warning, fireworks lifted over the river, the sky lit with color, the air crackled and thundered like the rapid fire of guns. Suzanne grasped Bridget's arm and buried her face in her shoulder. "Ah, my friend, bad memories? Oui? Here, come with me." Bridget placed a sheltering arm across Suzanne's shoulder and led her friend away from the river, away from the fireworks and the sounds of war.

For the moment, the conversation faded, and the two walked away from the river along Rue de Bonaparte toward Le Deux Magots, where coffee and a warm croissant awaited them, and possibly a brandy.

YEAR BY YEAR, THE TWENTIES DISSOLVED INTO THE NEW decade. The air began to smell of war again. France reeled from economic woes, some of which landed at Sylvia Beach's door at Shakespeare and Company. Some writers left to go to their home countries, some stayed, some found a new war to fight in Spain. Bridget mourned the death of the composer Maurice Ravel in 1937. Music, theater, and writing were her salvation when dark moments descended.

She found a new apartment on Boulevard Saint-Germain, two bedrooms on the first floor with a tiny garden, where she planted her sunflowers and urged a rose bush to blossom. Her life was simple: friends, the occasional concert, a walk by the Seine, and writing.

Absent from her life was any consideration of men or the love that others wrote about. Romances, affairs of the heart (which to Suzanne's sisters meant a French lover), held no place in her life. A sacred promise to herself, to the memory of Peter and what life had almost given her, fed her soul and her creative spirit. Stories rose from somewhere deep inside, inspired by the sweetness of an old sorrow and the courage of finding her heart's independence in her writing.

On other days, when sadness floated over her like a shoreline fog, she'd wrap herself in a thick wool shawl, brew strong French coffee, drag her writing desk to the window, face her typewriter toward the street, and lose herself in words and story. Those darker hours spent wrapped in her shawl, fingers to the keys, gave energy to her creative spirit and to the story of Ginot, her World War One fantasy hero.

Ginot was a young girl, part of a clandestine network in Belgium and northern France during the Great War, who appeared and disappeared among the Germans so deftly, she became known as a mythical creature. Rather like Bridget herself. And Meg.

Always the encourager, Suzanne thought the story compelling, particularly, she'd said, "For all the women like me, like my sisters, who lived through it." She'd looked away, letting her thoughts hang in the air. "Brigitte, you are our storyteller, you tell of who we were. Your story adds meaning to our lives."

Sophie, too—journalist, writer, art critic, and mentor from her distant place—encouraged Bridget to send out extracts of her novel to small journals. One magic day, a letter arrived from a monthly magazine printed and published in Toronto. It read:

Dear Miss Blackwell:

I am pleased to inform you that The Ontario Story-teller is keen to publish an excerpt from your forthcoming novel.

We would like to publish a chapter in our fall edition and, if receiving interest from our readers, possibly contract for another, or, as you had mentioned, a piece about a Canadian woman author in Paris.

Bridget read that first sentence, and for the first time in months, maybe years, whooped with joy. With confidence growing and encouragement surrounding her from Suzanne, Sophie and her writer friends at Shakespeare and Company, as the 1930s began to wane, Bridget realized she was close to the final draft of her novel.

Back in Ontario, Sophie was as proud of Bridget as Clara might have been despite one discordant note: Bridget's decision to take a pen name. It wasn't the fact that she'd assumed another name; it was the name she chose to use that troubled Sophie. Clara Nicholson. This was Bridget's way of memorializing her mother and intensifying the creative bond she experienced, a knowledge that somewhere within herself lay Clara's spirit.

Why that name, Bridget? Sophie wrote after she'd read Bridget's letter. *If Jack continues to use the strategies he's following to track you down, you might as well send up flares saying "Here I am!" Why that name?*

Bridget took three days to respond, the time it took to get over what she considered a reproach from her friend. Something in Sophie's comments irked her. "Why is she questioning what I'm doing? I'm the author." And just as she said the words aloud, she knew. Not only had Bridget broken from any sense of herself as victim, but she'd also assumed her own independence, no longer in need of protection. But Sophie, having the experience of being attacked by Jack's hoodlum, still feared for Bridget.

However, if Jack was still out there, lurking, Bridget was tired of living with the possibility he'd find her one day. *He's an old man, nom de Dieu.* Bridget's best expletives were in French, and they landed on the first page of her letter back to Sophie.

On the night of September 30, 1938, Bridget turned off her radio, pulled back the quilt, and prepared to climb into bed to read. The excitement around the British prime minister's visit to Munich had left her weary, that and a day of wondering if she might have to leave France. Already, friends at the bookshop were making plans to go back to America.

"Not me," she whispered to herself, and now after listening to the radio and hearing Prime Minister Chamberlain speak of "peace in our time," she pulled the quilt to her chin, like a child determined to keep the monster at bay. "I'll stay," she whispered, closed her eyes, and slept.

The next day, Paris woke to a clear October morning. Bridget was at her desk, coffee cup cradled in her hands. She felt the nourishment of contentment as she leaned back in her chair pillows. Another excerpt from her novel in the mail, the threat of a war dimming, a letter from George. A moment of guilt that she let George be the one to keep the threads between them open. Her letters to him, to her family, were scattered sometimes over months. But oh, how she delighted in the news of Meg's achievements—a high school English teacher, an accomplished pianist. "Mama, your granddaughter follows in your footsteps—she loves beauty, too," Bridget spoke aloud as though the spirit of Clara might hear her.

Edna and I are enjoying Meg's English students. They're rehearsing "Hamlet" and they come out here to the farm on weekends to practice. What a wonderful teacher she is. I think if I'd had an English teacher like her in high school, I may have been wooed by the Bard. She's done something remarkable, Bridge. I watch them out there on the porch delivering their lines—there isn't a one among them whose eyes aren't alight. And I'll be willing to say most had never heard of Shakespeare till Meg.

She held the letter between her fingers and treasured the thought of Meg, a young woman creating a love for Shakespeare in young women and young men, some who'd never heard of Shakespeare, just as George avowed.

Bridget remembered that young girl fifteen years ago, lying between her and George on the bed. Young Meg, unabashedly and wholeheartedly drawing George and Bridget into her stories, voicing the characters with an exuberance that stayed with Bridget for months. A night now that felt like a dream.

Bridget felt a rooted connection to that girl, one that was more than having birthed her; there was a thread, an invisible tie that conjoined the generations—Clara, Bridget herself, now Meg. The thread linked each with the pain Jack foisted upon them, a pain of which Meg knew nothing yet. Bridget sat with an image of her daughter, the teacher who could captivate the imaginations of young high school students, and knew there was something else, another thread, a resilient soul in herself and in her daughter. This thread spoke of possibility, of seeing one another once again. A knock at the door broke into her thoughts.

Looking out at the street, quiet in the new morning, she saw only the early risers, those on their way to open their shops and take their vegetables and fruit to market. Paris was peaceful on this morning.

"Who is it?" Bridget called out.

"It's me. Sophie."

Chapter Thirty-Three

October 1938

BRIDGET DROPPED HER CUP ONTO THE KITCHEN TABLE, darted to the door, and flung it open. Sophie, leather bag slung over her shoulder, a wicker suitcase at her feet, stood there, arms open. Hat askew.

Bridget hooted like a joyful child as she leapt into Sophie's embrace. "What in the world? What are you doing in Paris?"

"Well, my darling Bridget. You weren't answering my letters, so I decided to come find you. Now! May I come in? I've been traveling forever to get here."

There were times, though not often, when Bridget was at a loss for words. This was one of those times. She, the accomplished wordsmith, felt a rush of emotions. All of it—pure sensation, confusion, curiosity, gratitude, elation, relief, shock, and surprise—tumbled throughout her body, pummeling her heart, giving flush to her cheeks, and weakening her legs.

Bridget would try later that day to explain to Sophie what she'd been holding within since saying that last farewell to her, so many years ago. Fifteen, to be exact. But now words were superfluous; feeling the presence of her friend was sufficient. Sophie being Sophie took Bridget's arm and walked with her to that same velour sofa where they'd said their goodbyes. Sophie pulled Bridget down on the sofa, leaned back, her shoulder to Bridget's shoulder, and smiled.

"Bridget, take a breath. It's not as though I've magically appeared."

And for the first time in more than a few months, Bridget broke into laughter. "You know, Sophie," she said, "you and Suzanne are the only two people I know who can happily surprise me…well maybe the editor of *The Ontario Storyteller* runs a close third. Now, take off your shoes, sit back, and tell me. What's brought you to my door? And…" Bridget sat up, feet to the floor, "what do you mean you came to find me? I'm not lost, or am I?"

Before Sophie could attempt to answer, Bridget clapped her hands to her cheeks. "Jack's dead and you've come to give me the news."

Sophie grimaced. "No, Bridge." Bridget caught the nickname that her brother George had bestowed on her—and only George had ever called her that.

"Have you been talking to my brother, Sophie? Has he been in touch with you?" Bridget felt the possibility strangely comforting. But a shadow dimmed Sophie's eyes.

Bridget's hands rushed to her chest. "Oh, no, no. Oh God, no."

"Bridget, Bridget." Sophie reached for her hand. "No, no…George is all right."

"I knew something was wrong. I knew it. His letters have been all about Meg, about the farm. Nothing about him, about Edna."

"Stop. Bridget. He's all right. Listen to me. Take a breath. He's one of the reasons I'm here and yes, George and I have been talking to one another for a while now, but before we go there…."

"No, Sophie you can't just say 'he's all right' and leave me hanging." Bridget took her hand from Sophie's and stood up, tugged at the tie on her dressing gown, and shoved her hands into the pockets. "Why are you really here, Sophie?"

Sophie let her hands fall into her lap and sat, head bent. With a sigh that seemed to emerge from the soles of her feet, she looked up at Bridget. "George had an accident. Ran into a pole in his brand-new Chevy, or the police are calling it an accident…I didn't want to tell you in a letter…"

The air in the room suddenly felt oppressive—Bridget felt drumming in her ears—felt an empty place where her breath should have been. "Is he…?" Her words sounded like scratches in her throat.

"No, no. Bridget. He's going to be all right. But before you ask me more questions you need to sit down here beside me. George's accident, I believe, wasn't an accident."

"What are you saying? Not an accident? Sophie! For God's sake, tell me what's going on!" A seed of suspicion began to take form and Bridget threw her arms into the air, dropped onto the sofa, and turned full body to Sophie. "This is about Jack, isn't it? Damn him, will it never end?"

"I think I need…" Sophie interjected.

"Sophie, wait before you say anything else. Let me talk. I've listened to you all these years, but this must end. Whatever or whoever you think Jack is, or what he's capable of…"

"You've no idea what he's capable of," Sophie hissed.

"What?" Bridget snapped back. "I. Don't. Know? I can't believe you're saying that."

Neither woman moved. They sat silent, emotions teetering. Another moment filled the space between them. A voice broke into the dead air. Sophie's. "Forgive me. You do know. And so did your mother. That's why she asked me to protect you."

"Oh, God, what are..." Bridget, who'd kept her demons at bay for so many years, felt the crushing hold of suspicion.

She whispered: "My mother knew, didn't she? She knew how dangerous he was. She protected George and me, didn't she? Sophie, Jack was responsible for my mother's death, wasn't he? And George knew something—that's why he left home." Her words were sharp jagged points piercing the air. Sophie's second of silence was like a confirmation.

Bridget waited, knowing she was right.

Sophie walked to the window and stood, her back to the room. "We'll never know." Her voice was a whisper riding her breath. She spoke without turning. "But now, Bridget, I need a promise from you."

"What, Sophie, what?" Bridget moved to stand beside Sophie, took her hand, and faced her. "I have found life here. I have discovered my spirit. Whatever you might ask of me will change none of that. You've protected me and sent me out into life. Now maybe it's my turn to listen to the story you have to tell, because there is a story, isn't there?"

Sophie nodded. Bridget turned to walk away.

"Coffee and biscuits up on the roof garden. Bring a sweater." Bridget linked her arm through Sophie's.

SOPHIE FELT SHE'D BEEN TRANSPORTED WHEN BRIDGET opened the door onto the roof garden and beckoned her to come sit by a low wall. Cushioned chairs sat by the last of pink clematis vines, creamy white honeysuckle cascaded over and through trellises, small trees in tubs gave shade and privacy.

Bridget placed the tray of biscuits and the cups of dark French coffee on the small glass table by the wall. "Over here,

Sophie, come sit where you can look out at Notre Dame off in the distance."

"How did you ever find this?" Sophie asked, standing and gazing out at the beauty here above a busy Boulevard Saint-Germain. "One of the writers at Shakespeare was leaving to go back to the US and asked if I'd consider taking over her lease. She brought me up here when I came to see the apartment, and any hesitation I might have had dissolved."

"A place like this could be difficult to leave," Sophie murmured.

Bridget's reaction was immediate. "I'm not intending to leave. Ever." Hands and arms wrapped about her shoulders, face to the sky.

Sophie hesitated, then turned toward her friend. "Which is one of the reasons I'm here. Pour me a coffee, and we'll talk."

The story Sophie came to tell began well before she was born. It began with Jack and his entry into the world.

"Jack was born on July 14, 1865. His mother, Florence, experienced a difficult pregnancy, with several bouts of sickness and nausea. He came into the world squalling at the top of his lungs, which the doctor and his nurse believed a good sign for a healthy baby. His mother found his cries, which were frequent, disturbing. It might have been she was not meant for motherhood."

Bridget drew her legs up under herself and wrapped her shawl more tightly across her chest and shoulders. The October air, and the story, felt chilling.

Sophie continued, "Not long after Jack was born, less than a month, his mother began to show signs of what the doctors called puerperal insanity, a kind of deep melancholy. She'd push him away when the nurse brought him for feeding, she'd cry unexpectedly, and often left the dinner table weeping, causing Jack's father to become impatient with her and with his son. Mr. Blackwell, Jack's father, was a wealthy lumber baron who'd made his fortune in northwestern Ontario. He brought his wife at her request to the 'more civilized' parts in southwestern Ontario. This meant he traveled a lot going back to the north to oversee his extensive lumber industry. So, with Mr. Blackwell away more days than home, Florence began to sink into a deeper melancholy. Nurses came, left, sometimes two or three in a month. By the time Jack was a young boy he'd known no closeness or intimacy to anyone, except my mother who was his mother's maid. She tried to take care of him, but he was an angry boy, who'd lash out at her, sometimes physically. One time I remember, I was in the kitchen, Mom was getting a supper tray for Florence, Jack's mother. She asked him if he'd take it up to his mother because she had a sick headache." Sophie sighed and let a breath escape through her lips. "He took that tray with the bowl of chicken soup, a cup of tea, and warm bread, turned the whole thing over in front of my mother—soup everywhere, broken china sliding across the floor. And he yelled, 'That's what I think of her stupid sick headaches! Why doesn't she just die!' Kicked the door and ran out."

Finishing her story, Sophie leaned back in her chair, crossed her arms over her chest, and closed her eyes. "I can still see his face. It was twisted. Not an innocent boy's face at all. A taunting face of a monster."

Bridget reached toward Sophie. "You never told me any of this. Why?"

"Bridget. My mother and father left the house because they feared what he was capable of. There are other stories of what he tried to do to me. They asked me never to talk about what happened there. We depended on Mr. Blackwell's good word when we left, and he, being a powerful man, wanted no one to know that his wife was mentally unstable or that his son was bordering on madness. It wasn't till I went to study art in Toronto that Jack and I crossed paths again, and I met Clara. He didn't know who I was. And…since then I've kept track of him, mostly because of Clara…and because I promised to protect you."

Chapter Thirty-Four

Sophie's words dropped like sparks on Bridget's skin.

"Well, bon merde!"

"Did you just swear at me?"

"No! I just said, shit. Not at you, at what you've just told me."

Bridget was no longer sitting back. She'd moved to the edge of the chair and poured another full cup of coffee, which, being her third strong French brew, was about to send her blood pressure into orbit in concert with this horrendous news about her stepfather.

"How can you have known all this and never told me? Mama died in 1902—thirty-six years ago. I was ten years old. All these years, Sophie, how could you not have said something to someone?" Bridget shook her head back and forth. "Why now?"

"I'm going to be seventy. Seventy! And I've become tired holding the secrets of this man's wickedness. It's taken me this long to realize, I don't have to. I knew when I was a child what a beast he was. I've known all along."

"Is this why you've always protected me?" Bridget spoke, not knowing what to ask. "Is this why you've been so fearful all these years that he'd try to harm me, maybe even try to kill me?" The memory of that night, when Jack threw her across the floor, crawled up Bridget's spine. She shivered.

Sophie set the cup on the table and stood from her chair.

"Could we go back down to your apartment? I need to finish this story now that I've finally begun."

They settled themselves back in Bridget's apartment. Neither woman chose to speak. Bridget sat on a cushioned bench by the window, a view of Boulevard Saint-Germain at her back.

Sophie continued to describe what life had been like for her growing up in a household where Jack imposed his own brand of tyranny, checked by no one. Telling her story now was like lancing an infection.

"Was he cruel to you?" Bridget asked.

Sophie's face folded into incredulity. "Listen to me, Bridget. Jack was a cruel boy, a horrid young man, and has remained a vicious, monstrous human being." She pushed back the sleeve of her jacket and exposed her arm. On the underside was a fading scar rising from the skin, a scar that ran from her elbow to just above her wrist. She'd never mentioned it to Bridget, who had chosen not to ask. "This is the day he almost killed me. If my mother hadn't been in the house and heard my screams, I might have bled to death. He was in a fit of anger, not at me, but at my mother—she'd denied him something, I can't remember what, and I was the scapegoat. He grabbed me, swung me around, hung onto me, and proceeded to cut my arm with his Swiss Army knife."

Sophie spat each word and pulled her sleeve down over her arm. "I was a child. He was seventeen." Her jaw tightened, her lips a straight line. "That was the day my mother and father decided to leave." Bridget believed that if Jack were to walk into the room right then, Sophie would have lunged at him and strangled him. If Sophie hadn't, Bridget was sure she would.

"Oh, dear God, Sophie." Bridget reached for Sophie, who shook her head.

"No, Bridget, this story is not about sympathy for me, I had very little to do with the man after that till he appeared at the Society for Artists trying to get by as a painter." She sniggered. "The man was no painter. But then he got his clutches into Clara. I was horrified to see how much influence Jack had over my new friend. He had no idea who I was, and when I tried to tell her she wouldn't believe me."

"My mother was smarter than that," Bridget said.

"Bridget, evil can be very charming."

Silence put a period on Sophie's declaration. Bridget shook her head back and forth, her hands and fingers almost prayer-like against her lips. But the wail of a Paris siren broke into their stillness, causing Sophie to start up in her chair. "Bridget! What's going on in this city?"

Shaking her head, Bridget looked over at Sophie. "It's probably an ambulance. Why are you alarmed? Are you all right?" In that moment Bridget realized how agitated her friend had become. "Sophie, you and I have avoided this man for years and now he has to be in his seventies. How dangerous can he be now?"

Another wail. Another siren. Two ambulances rushed along Boulevard Saint-Germain, a police car following. Sophie ran to the apartment door and flung it open to the courtyard beyond.

"Sophie, what is it? It's a city. There are ambulances all the time." Bridget rose to go to her. "Come back in. Come here. Sit. Let me get you a tea."

Sophie turned back from the door, her face ashen, her eyes bright, not with tears but with fear. In all the years she'd known her, with all the frightening moments they'd shared in munition factories—explosions, gas poisoning, even deaths—Bridget couldn't remember seeing Sophie succumb to dread like this. Today, she was witnessing a woman, her hero, in the midst of panic.

Her own heart pounding, Bridget ran to her friend and, arm about her waist, led her to the sofa where she gently urged her to sit. She realized Sophie's hands were cold, yet her forehead was glistening with sweat.

"Sophie…are you all right…Can I get you some water?"

Without a glance up Sophie shook her head. "No, no, I'll be all right, just give me a moment." Sophie's early life experiences with Jack, every incident, lay beneath her skin, each horrific deed pushed away retained in a dark consciousness—yet she'd remained vigilant, knowing there could be a next time. The possibility he'd send someone after Bridget clouded her days, even though she knew an ocean separated her from his madness. An ocean, and years.

Sophie resumed her story.

"I watched my friend Clara slowly dying over time, all those years ago, and…" She paused, took a long breath, and let the words go. "It haunts me, Bridget, but I believe Jack wanted your mother dead. I really think she was poisoned… by him.…I believe that, without a doubt Jack gave arsenic to Clara, over weeks, causing her to die a long, painful death.… No one believed me or even let me suggest she was being poisoned. I wrote to Dr. Winslow, who'd been the last to see her, but he never replied."

Throughout Sophie's revelation, Bridget stared at her, letting her words penetrate, taking in the horror that Clara, her mother, had been murdered. Confirming what she'd already been thinking. Sophie was right. Jack could have murdered Clara.

"There's more. You need to hear me out. Please." Sophie took Bridget's hand.

"All right, Soph. I'm here."

"I knew how much Jack hated Clara's artistic successes, and how he coveted the huge inheritance left by your Aunt Vivian, riches he'd discovered when he contacted Clara's lawyer after her death. That lawyer succumbed to Jack's bullying threats and divulged the information about Clara's bequest. I'll never forgive his breach of faith. Jack would have been successful getting his hands on that money, except Clara in her wise way made clear stipulations that the estate would remain in trust for you and George until you reached legal age. He was angry and resentful, and I'm sure wants the two of you out of his way. I'm sure he wants the both of you dead, just as he did Clara. This is the reason I've stayed the course with you, Bridget. He's devious and sadistic. There was a time I thought that I could have a chance to avenge Clara. I went to the police in Westover years after she died."

Bridget sat forward. "What happened?"

"I went to plead my case and my suspicions about the nature of Clara's death. The chief of the Westover police was there, and two other young officers, one who took notes and who, when I think about it, listened carefully. But to no avail. Chief Anderson declared that I had no clear evidence for such an accusation. And too much time had intervened—his final statement told me everything I needed to know about how fruitless my case was. He said and I quote: 'Jack Blackwell is a fine upstanding member of this community, who has contributed much to its growth and prosperity.' And he ushered me from his office.

"But listen to this, Bridget." Sophie's eyes glittered. "The officer who listened so carefully to my deposition? The officer taking notes? He kept the records of that meeting I had with the chief there in Westover. There may still be a chance to create a case against Jack...even now."

"This is extraordinary, Sophie. You kept all this information to yourself all these years. You've protected me since I was a small child—I don't know whether to thank you or yell at you. But no. There'll be no yelling. You've given me my life over these years, when my life might have been damaged or I might have self-destructed."

A quiet entered the room, a silence pure with renewed connection between Bridget and Sophie. "I've not given up my pledge to Clara just yet." Sophie managed a weak smile.

"No. Absolutely not..." Bridget stopped in midsentence. Sophie gathered herself, straightened her shoulders, placed her hands on her knees, and let her words ride forth on a long exhale.

"Bridget, I don't know where or how he or his thugs will find you. What I know is that they will. I can't protect you as I have before because there's a war on its way. And Jack will use that in some nefarious way to his advantage."

The moment had a feel to it, a familiar feel, the day back at that first munitions factory when Bridget, Irene, and Sophie began to plan Bridget's exodus. The day she decided to go to George and to the farm.

Bridget took Sophie's hand and faced her. "Tell me exactly what scares you, Sophie. What makes you think I'm not going to be safe? And why is it your responsibility anymore if anything does happen to me?" Bridget was sure she knew the answers to her questions, but she continued to wait.

Sophie needed to say it aloud. Finally, in a voice small with regret, she said, "Because, I knew...I knew his power...and I let her down."

"OK, Sophie, say it. Who?"

"I let your mother, my friend Clara, down, and I could have saved her." With that, she let go and wept all the accumulated tears for Clara, for herself, and for Bridget.

Bridget felt an inner assurance that she was capable and could take on the course of her life, change roles with Sophie. She'd become the protector and care for Sophie throughout the next years, however they might look. Sometimes in our lives, Bridget thought, we need cathartic moments when we purge ourselves of our demons, so she offered to Sophie what she'd received from her; she gave Sophie her full presence. "I'm right here, Sophie, and I'll always be right here. We'll do this together. We'll find our way; you and I. Jack is no longer in our lives. He's gone, forever." Bridget wasn't sure if she believed her hopeful words, but they were a beginning of something new.

As the tears began to subside, an ambulance and the wail of a siren flew by the window. Sophie smiled. "Sounds like help is on the way."

And it was.

LATER THAT YEAR, ON NOVEMBER 9 AND 10 OF 1938, Nazis torched Jewish businesses and synagogues in Germany. The possibility of another war with Germany loomed.

As 1939 dawned, Bridget and Sophie realized they'd have to leave France. Both had decided that staying together this time seemed so much wiser. Sophie was determined to follow through on her promise to Clara, even though

Bridget had proven she was more than capable of taking care of herself. Even so, Sophie's presence brought something into Bridget's life she'd never really experienced. Sophie brought constancy and permanence.

March 15. Germany invaded Czechoslovakia, and both women readied themselves for what they knew had to be another escape, not only because of Jack's obsessive pursuit but because a war was about to crash in on them.

When Germany invaded France in June 1940, Bridget left her apartment on Boulevard Saint-Germain, and, in company with Sophie, retraced her path back to the village in Scotland where she'd been welcomed in so many years ago—back to another munitions factory established there, as another war descended.

Chapter Thirty-Five

June 1946

ORDINARY LIFE HAD RESUMED SINCE THAT MOMENT TWO years ago when Meg and George made a mutual promise to stay the course and find Bridget. Meg taught. George hired himself out to young farmers to help them get started—an enterprise that caused both Edna and Meg to smile, and renewed Meg's love and respect for him.

And so, Meg's painful hurt that George, and Edna, too, had betrayed her, faded and disappeared. In its place was a resolve: to follow clues in the found letters and to someday locate Meg's mother and George's sister.

The person they continued to rely on was Detective Bill McBride, who, steadfast and dogged, was a man determined to help the only family he'd ever known.

George expressed admiration for Bill's constancy as the search continued. "That young man is certainly in the right profession. He's tireless. A good friend to have." Meg nodded. She knew the search was as important to Bill as it was to her. Bill would not give up.

On a warm evening in June, Bill arrived at Meg's house looking as though he'd solved the last complicated cold case on the Milboro police books. He started talking the moment he walked into the kitchen. "I know where Bridget is, and I think Sophie's with her."

George and Edna now sat at the kitchen table, arriving

after Bill in his excitement had called and asked them to go out to Meg's house "pronto." George had no idea why or what possessed Bill to ask the two of them to be there right at the supper hour. Edna wasn't so enthusiastic, as she was a stickler for having supper on time each evening. The farmer's schedule was ingrained in her. Bill's request meant supper would have to wait, until she discovered that Meg, knowing Edna's need for routine, had made soup and biscuits.

Now, Meg leaned against the kitchen counter, ankles crossed, arms folded, and waited for Bill to explain why he'd insisted she, George, and Edna be there now. She was still dressed in the red suit she'd worn that afternoon for the high school graduation. Tomato soup simmered on the stove; fresh biscuits sat in the oven warmer. Meg knew her dad and Edna would be hungry, and whatever Bill had to say could be told over soup and biscuits.

George moved over by the window that looked out onto the vegetable garden Meg had planted since moving back into the house. His foot rested on a wooden stool. Beside the stool lay Argos, the black and white border collie Bill had brought to Meg when she moved back into the yellow house in '44, after her longtime retriever friend, Wyatt, had died a peaceful, old dog's death. Meg had immediately named him Argos after Odysseus's dog, in honor of their quest to find Bridget. When George moved by the window, Argos followed him and now lay sleeping at his feet, not concerned at all by the possibly stunning news Bill was bringing. Scrabbles, Meg's old feline confidante and friend, rested her head contentedly on the dog's paw. She, too, seemed without interest in her human's strange ways.

"You know where Bridget and Sophie are, or you think you know, Detective?" George managed a smile, holding back any expectations that this could be the time they'd set out to find Bridget. There'd been two years of false starts, telegrams left unanswered, letters returned with "no such person at this address" stamped on the envelope, and one major disappointment for Bill, a nonresponse from a detachment of the French prefecture just after the war ended. He chose to believe they were more engaged with finding collaborators in the population and among their own ranks than looking for missing mothers from Canada.

Eventually he'd decided to regroup, stopped trying to contact the French police, and set out upon another tactic. He used his own strategies, more intuitive than police procedure—and on his own time he followed up clues from her letters, places that Bridget mentioned, particularly Shakespeare and Company, a bookstore in Paris, which turned out to be another impasse when he discovered that the store had closed in 1941.

A name occurred every so often in Bridget's notes, a woman named Sylvia Beach, who'd been the owner of the bookstore. However, when he wrote to the address he had for the bookshop, hoping someone would forward it on, what he received was a "return to sender" stamp on the envelope of the letter he'd sent.

Meg, the realist sprinkled with optimism, urged him on. But each time a search ended at a dead end; he felt his attempts to find Bridget could be fruitless. He thought too that George could become a target for Jack, thinking of course that her brother would know where she was. But Bridget, probably with Sophie's advice, had kept herself well concealed, even from George. It occurred to Bill at one time that maybe Bridget didn't want to be found, a thought that only caused him to pause for a moment before he decided on his next attempt.

And then it happened.

It wasn't exceptional police sleuthing that uncovered what he'd tracked down; it was a lucky break, a conversation with his chief, when Bill, feeling discouraged, talked to him about strategies for finding missing persons. It was an exchange he couldn't have predicted, because Chief Roman Sanders, head of Milboro police, knew the name Bridget Blackwell.

With this bombshell news penetrating, and with what the chief chose to tell him next, Bill called George, asking him to go out to Meg's house with Edna, and then called Meg. "I think I have a lead, so stay there, don't go anywhere. I'm coming over." Meg still had the phone receiver in her hand when he hung up.

Bill arrived at Meg's house feeling like the water boy who accidentally found King Tut's tomb. He felt triumphant. He knew the whereabouts of Bridget and Sophie, and he was very sure he'd broken open an old cold case. The mystery of Clara's death. So, he called. Everybody. George and Edna. Meg.

There in the kitchen, George and Edna, keen to hear Bill's news, waited at the table as Meg, who seemed to be getting on with life in spite of Bill's possible breakthrough, served up soup and biscuits.

After an urging from George—"Meg, could we hear what Bill has to tell us…?"—and holding the chair for Meg, inviting her to sit, she dropped into her place, as though she might be expecting more disappointment.

She looked across the table at Bill, her eyes penetrating. "Are you sure, this time?"

Without a pause, Bill said with a triumphant grin: "Sure enough that I think we should get a passage to Scotland."

"Who's we? Who do you mean, 'we?'" George and Meg said in unison.

"Me, you, Meg, Edna." He smiled. "Harry can stay with his new love and take care of the houses. Yours and Meg's, while we're gone."

"Are you saying Bridget is in Scotland?" George rubbed the back of his neck. "And, you're sure?" A sigh escaped his lips. "You know, Bill, I've wondered sometimes if she's still alive."

"What do you mean, still alive?" Meg stared at her father, her eyebrows almost touching, her eyes dark. "What do you mean?"

"Damn, Meg, I don't want you to start thinking the worst." George looked like the proverbial boy caught in the act of emptying the cookie jar. "I don't believe that for one minute, but it's just that…I haven't heard from her for a while."

"Which is more reason to follow what Bill might know. And remember, Dad…there's been a war. You have a son to attest to that."

"I know, Meg. I worry about her…." For a moment George's usually bright eyes shadowed over and his shoulders drooped. "I worry…." His voice wandered away.

George was the first to admit to all that he was feeling.

"You know, Bill, I'm pretty sure you have something there, I'm just…" and he paused, turned to Meg, and facing her, put an arm across her shoulders. "I sometimes wish we hadn't found those damn letters. What if it's all been for nothing? Nothing will come of nothing."

For the first time since Bill's arrival, the air in the room lightened. Meg put a hand on top of George's, still on her shoulder. "Oh, listen, Bill, he's quoting King Lear. This is more serious than I thought." She smiled over at George and threw her arm around his neck.

Bill wasn't sure what to do right at that moment. He felt he was witnessing a moment between two people who wanted to believe what Bill was trying to say.

He saw two people taking care of each other: George who'd promised to care for Meg like a daughter, and Meg who loved George, her dad.

It was George's short "Ow!" that startled Meg. He drew away from her, his arm across his chest, his hand holding his neck and shoulder. "Oh, my gosh, Dad. Did I hurt you? Was I too rough?"

Rubbing his neck, George moved back and shook his head no. "Not to worry, every so often some old injury flares up. Maybe I just moved my neck the wrong way."

Bill tilted his head and, with a quizzical expression, asked: "When was that accident? Wasn't that a good eight years ago? Shouldn't that have healed? And, while we're talking about this, did they ever charge the guy who ran you off the road?" Throughout the moments that Bill quizzed, George attempted to hush him, shaking his head no. But too late.

"What accident? What guy? What injury?" Meg said, still facing George, suspicion coloring her words. Both Bill and George sighed; Bill because he realized he'd spoken out of turn, George because Meg was never to know about the accident or the circumstances.

Trying to deflect, George pointed to the dishes on the table. "Nothing to concern ourselves with now, OK? Let's have some more of those biscuits and get on with why we're here. Bill still needs to show us what he's got."

He turned to get up from his chair but stopped when Meg took his wrist in her hand. "There'll be no more biscuits till someone tells me what accident." She dropped her hand and folded her arms. She waited.

"Meg, truly…it happened eight years ago. It's done, over."

"Not for me." Meg's voice was a decibel louder.

Knowing Meg's tenacity when she needed answers, George sighed and sat back down at his chair by Meg. "If I promise to tell you the story, can we do it over dessert and get on with why we're here?" Now, it was George's voice expressing tension, maybe impatience.

Silence reigned until Meg spoke. "Dad? Before you begin. Where was I when all this happened?" George placed his biscuit on the edge of the plate and sighed. "OK. Here's the story. It was 1938. You'd left home, gone to finish teachers' college, and instead of coming back here to work at the local high school, you decided to stay there and teach at one of the big schools, you called them."

He paused, long enough for Meg to comment: "That's 'cause I needed to find a bigger world. You know that, Dad."

An old trickster entered the room—Meg still feeling she needed to justify not coming back home after she finished teacher training, the way most farm girls usually did, and George still wondering why she'd needed to spread her wings so broadly. Occasionally, in the privacy of his own thoughts, he saw Bridget in her, and that scared him.

"Dad. Let's not make this about me. Please. I need to know about this accident of yours." Her tone was edged with the sometimes-Meg testiness, causing George to sigh again and get on with what was unfolding here and now. The accident. He knew Meg wouldn't stop until she'd heard the complete story—how he was run off the road into a pole, how he'd almost gone through the windshield. Most notably, how suspicious he'd been later about who was responsible. As George finished telling his tale, Bill held his breath and waited. Edna, who'd been silent throughout it all, waited. In that moment, Meg and George could have been the only people in the room. Meg spoke. "And no one thought to tell me you'd been injured in a car accident?"

Bill watched Meg and George fencing, wondered if it was time to intervene, thought better of it, and waited.

"Meg." Something in George's tone, something in the way he turned to face her, telegraphed a choice he'd made. "I'm going to tell you something. It's about your mother, my sister, and all that she's gone through over the last almost thirty years. Some of it you already know, but the part I'll tell you tonight, you don't."

On that night, George unraveled the pieces of what he knew had happened to Bridget.

"Your mother lived with our stepfather many years longer than I did." Putting his head down, he folded his hands and leaned his chin on them.

He was a man remembering and regretting. "He is a man, Meg, with malice in his heart. I know that probably sounds old-fashioned to you, but it describes who he is."

Meg saw such misery in his face that she reached over and placed her hand over his. Without words the two sat, daughter absorbing her father's hurt. Edna, who knew George's story well, resisted her impulse to go to them. She waited for what would be said next.

George lifted his head, held onto Meg's hand, and looked straight into her face. "With all the suspicions I carry, for all the reasons I have..." He paused, inhaled one long breath, and continued, "I think...No. I know he poisoned my mother, your grandmother. He murdered her."

"Dad…Oh, God…Dad." Meg stood, slid her chair back, went to her father, and, there behind him while he sat tall on his chair, encircled his shoulders, and held on.

Bill sat quietly, taking in the pain, knowing that maybe he might have the way forward for everyone. Edna, feeling and knowing how much she loved this man, her husband, chose still to remain silent.

"My car accident might have been a deliberate act on Jack's part. I was on a road near Milboro, a road I know well, no other cars anywhere, out of the blue a car came up beside me and forced me off the road. I'm sure this was no accident. To this day I believe it was one of Jack's thugs."

"Why, why?" Meg shook her head side to side to side. "I don't understand. What kind of a man are we talking about?"

"This is not about a stable man, Meg. This is about evil. He was and probably still is a man with no heart, a man who destroyed my mother, your grandmother, and who is determined to destroy Bridget. Everyone he ever called family he has set out to sabotage, and that includes me." He paused and looked beyond the room, through the window, perhaps seeing his stepfather's face reflected in the glass.

"He's an old man now, who hates and wants to destroy Bridget and me," George said, his voice taut with repressed anger. "I believe that's why Bridget hasn't told me where she is. She's protecting me." George acknowledged for the first time that he too, could be in danger. Only the sound of his voice stirred the air in the kitchen. Meg sat immobile, repelled by his words, her arms crossed against her body as though she might shatter.

"Can I say something? Before we go any farther?" Meg and George turned to Bill, as though they'd realized he was still there. "You could be right, George. Why don't you ask her when you see her, because I think I may have some answers."

Before either Meg or George could charge into another story, Bill leaned down, opened his briefcase, and took a file from among the several contained there.

"If you'll…" He gestured to Meg and George to sit comfortably where they were. "If you'll sit, please, I have a lot to tell you. All you need to do for now is listen." He smiled and looked toward Meg, "Just listen. Okay?"

She nodded slowly, a wary glance toward George.

Bill shifted his shoulders, rustled his papers, arranged them in a tight pile, and began.

"Last week, at the end of the day, I started going back through some of Bridget's letters to see if I might have missed anything. It's been a while. When I first read them, I documented every letter, the date it was written, any address she'd given. Sometimes she didn't give an address. Your mom is a wonderful writer, Meg—she wrote about meeting a French woman, Suzanne. Seems she was the reason Bridget went to France at the end of the war."

Meg raised a hand and pointed at herself.

Both Bill and George laughed at the sight of Meg complying with Bill's rules. "You, in the red suit, you wanted to comment?" Bill grinned.

"Yeah, Bill. About Suzanne. We knew she was the reason she landed in France, but where is she now? That was years ago."

"I'm coming to that." He leaned forward, warming to his report and their attention. Arms on the table, hands flat on either side of the empty plate, Bill McBride the detective set out to tell his story.

"Here's the missing piece."

Chapter Thirty-Six

"I WAS AT THE POLICE STATION GOING THROUGH ALL THOSE papers, again—one, by one, by one. Nothing was giving clues that I needed, nothing told me where to find Bridget. The search got especially hard when the letters stopped and there was no communication for a while. I even wondered…" looking over at George, who knew what Bill was about to say, "if possibly she'd died." He waited. No one responded.

Meg spoke out with fierce intent. "She's not dead. Keep going."

"Okay." Bill went back to his papers, where he'd written notes. "That night, the chief stayed late in the station. I could see him at his desk. And the idea hit me: I'll go talk this case over with him. He's a clever sleuth and maybe I was missing something. The guys often go in to talk cases over with him because he's…"

"Bill," George interrupted. "The findings. What did you find?"

"Sorry, got sidetracked." The sound from Meg's nose sounded a bit like a snort as she uncrossed and recrossed her legs.

"All right. I told Chief Sanders that we, you, Meg especially, were looking for your mom who'd been gone since the 1920s, and we'd heard nothing during the war. You should have seen the look he gave me when I said how long it'd been—until I gave him the name 'Bridget Blackwell.' He put his hand up to stop me, and he said, 'Bridget Blackwell? Why do I remember that name?'"

George moved back, scraping his chair across the floor. He turned directly to Bill and leaned forward, his elbows on his knees. "Are you saying, Bill, that your chief knows about Bridget?"

A rustling over by the fireplace paused Bill's storytelling. Argos, hearing the tone in George's voice, was standing, shaking his body from the long nap he'd been enjoying and looking over at George, expecting further commands. Scrabbles stirred, stretched, and headed for her basket.

"Sorry, boy, we're okay," George assured Argos, and beckoned him to join them—an invitation he accepted, trotting to the table, crawling under, and lying down at Meg's feet. If she was upset, he'd be there, he seemed to be saying.

"Go on, Bill," George said.

"Back to the chief..." Bill continued. "Let's see, where was I? Oh, yeah. Chief seemed to recognize the name. He went to his file cabinet, thumbed through to the back of a drawer, and pulled out a folder. The name across the top was 'Bridget Blackwell.' Who'd have believed!" And Bill sat straighter in his chair. Without pausing, he opened the file, pushed aside the plate and cutlery, placed it on the table, and started to read:

"On September 4, 1923, I, Constable Roman Sanders..." Bill paused. "That's Chief Sanders to me." A stern look from Meg said, "Get on with it." He resumed. "I, Constable Roman Sanders, was a member of a team organized to investigate a cold case, or more accurately, to respond to a request to open a possible murder investigation, a request made by one Miss Sophie Watson. Chief Anderson of my detachment *in Westover, Ontario, requested that I, in company with a fellow constable, listen to Miss Watson's testimony, which involved an accusation against a Mr. Jack Blackwell, citizen and businessman in the town of Westover. Her accusation: intentional homicide involving his wife, one Clara Blackwell. The charge: poisoning by arsenic."*

Bill stopped reading. Meg stiffened in her chair and covered her mouth with her hand. George, silent, walked to the window, where he began rubbing the back of his neck, his other hand clenched into a fist. A guttural sound emerged from his throat, possibly a sob.

Meg ran to him. "Dad, Dad, listen to me. We're going to get through this, all of us." Holding her father's arm, afraid to let him go, she turned back to Bill. "What did the investigation reveal, Bill?"

In that moment, hearing that question, Bill seemed to deflate. His face bleak, he answered, "Meg, George—there was no investigation, not even a preliminary look into the allegations she made."

George swung around when he heard these words, almost toppling Meg.

"What?! What do you mean no investigation?!"

Bill inhaled, and with one long exhale, said, "As a police officer I find this a difficult call." He leaned back in his chair, folded his arms, and for a moment seemed to drift. Sitting forward, he spoke words that to him were distasteful. "The chief of the Westover detachment said, apparently, there wasn't sufficient evidence to carry out any further investigation. Sophie had been clear about her observations of Clara over time. She'd outlined the symptoms with an assurance of someone who'd done her research on poisonings. She also highlighted the fact that the doctor's report was ambiguous…"

Before Bill could launch into his next sentence, George's hand hit the table. Everyone jumped.

"Jack, goddamn him, allowed no autopsy!" Forty-four years after the death of his mother, a young boy buried inside George erupted. "Bridget and I watched her die, there in front of us, and he stood there. He just stood there!" His shoulders and his chest shook with such force that Meg and Bill believed he might be having an attack. Meg reached out and grasped his hand until he stopped shaking. The three sat for minutes, giving the space for years of unspoken grief to enter the room.

George's voice, hoarse with emotion, asked the question that hung in the air. "What now? What's the point?"

And Bill pulled out another paper from the file, held it, and pointed. "Here are the notes that Chief Sanders, then Constable Sanders, kept because he was disturbed by his then-chief's dismissal of what Sophie had brought forward. He was disturbed by what the chief said after Sophie left..."

"What?" Meg asked.

Bill read Sanders's notes aloud: *The chief said we, none of us, should repeat to anyone what had been said in this room, because Jack Blackwell* (and I quote the chief here) *"is an upstanding member of the Westover community. There is no reason, legal or moral, to take this any further." End of notes.*

"It's all horrible, but how does any of this help our search for my mother?"

"Constable Sanders kept other notes which he's given to me, notes that he hung onto after he left the force in Westover." Bill took a breath before he continued. "Constable Sanders resigned from that police service and moved to Milboro, where he joined the local police force, and was promoted through the ranks to chief. He's a man who cares deeply, and Sophie's story troubled him."

"Bill, I know you respect your chief, but I'm still not sure how…" Meg stood up and began to take dishes from the table over to the kitchen counter.

Her back to the table, she placed her hands on the counter and leaned in. "I'm not sure, but I think we've hit another blank wall." The voice of failure echoed.

George was first to go to Meg. He stood beside her, and, sounding close to despair, said, "I'm sure Bill has more to tell us, let's listen, please." Sighs accompanied Meg and George when they turned back to Bill.

"George is right, Meg." He pointed to the sheaf of papers. "This file has everything we need to find your mom. After Chief Sanders left the Westover police force, he took the information from the notes he'd kept. When Sophie was at the police station, she'd given him her address in the city, her phone number, and even her work number at the newspaper. And…Chief Sanders, who was troubled by the way Sophie was dismissed, remained in periodic contact with her over the years."

With those words, Bill picked up one of the papers and waved it over his head. "Meg and George, I have an address for Sophie…and," handing the paper to Meg, he added, "I've already contacted her. I know where she is!"

Meg whooped. And then smacked Bill on the shoulder. "It took you this long to tell us!"

"Accosting a police officer?" A sound breezed into the kitchen. Laughter.

"Wait. I have the…what do they call it?…the 'pièce de résistance.'" Laughter erupted again. Bill's French accent came through his nose, making him sound like the French actor Charles Boyer on a bad day. Bill waited as they settled into quiet again, then reached into his jacket inside pocket and presented an envelope to Meg.

"I had a letter back from Sophie. She's in a village in Scotland, with Bridget."

Chapter Thirty-Seven

1947

GEORGE, BILL, AND MEG STOOD ON THE PLATFORM OF Dumfries Town Station in Scotland, suitcases, one for each, sitting at their feet. Meg had a second bag over her shoulder, for she'd insisted on bringing Edna's woolen bag, the one she'd kept her knitting in for years.

When it was decided that Edna couldn't make the trip, Meg and her stubborn stare could not be moved. "If Edna isn't coming with us, then her favorite bag is." George sighed. Edna became pleasantly teary. Meg would always be her single-minded girl.

Edna, whose arthritis had finally placed her in a wheelchair, had sat at the Montreal docks, watching the ship carrying her daughter, her husband, and the detective Bill, sail down the St. Lawrence River out to the gulf. Harry stood at her side, his hand in hers. He knew how difficult this moment was for his mother—she'd lost a son to the 1918 war, and she may be losing a daughter to the mother who'd birthed her. Harry wondered if he, too, might be losing a sister. He surely hoped not. He loved that girl.

THE ADVENTURERS WHO'D SAILED AWAY ON THE EMPRESS of Britain across the Atlantic to Liverpool, taken a train to Glasgow, Scotland, and another train to the town of

Dumfries, now waited for the bus to the town of Kirkcud-bright where Sophie and Bridget would meet them. That was the plan.

Standing at Dumfries station, waiting for the bus to arrive, George wondered how Meg would be, seeing her mother, that woman she'd met once as Aunt Bridget. Meg had been seven years old. Now thirty-one, she was soon to meet the woman who'd left her not once, but twice.

"Is the bus late, Dad?" Meg paced a determined course out to the edge of the station platform and back.

"You're going to wear a rut in the wood, Meg, if you keep doing that. And no, the bus isn't late, it's about ten minutes away, I'd reckon," George answered, remembering that patience was not Meg's strong suit. As the time narrowed when Meg would be in her mother's company, George and even Bill found it difficult to read her state of mind. She'd not said a word since coming off the train from Glasgow; in the almost two hours on the train to Dumfries, Meg had been uncharacteristically quiet. Till now. "What if this is all a huge mistake?" Meg asked the air. She pivoted back to them, retracing her steps along the platform.

George waited till she stood face-to-face with him before he answered. "Meg. We're here because she wants to see you. We know that."

"Then why didn't she write? Why was Sophie the one who asked us to come?"

"We've been over this a thousand times." George was a father feeling strained and anxious for Meg. "If I know my sister at all, and it's been a long time since last I saw her, she'll be pretty apprehensive about seeing you."

Bill listened to their words and understood the depths and the qualities of Meg's fears. He wondered how he would feel if his mother appeared—the woman who'd walked away and out of his life. "Meg? I'd bet that George is right. I might even go as far as saying she's hitting the bathroom several times an hour waiting for you to arrive."

"That's not funny." Meg stopped in midstride and laughed. "Yeah, it is. Thanks, Bill."

In that moment, a bus's horn honked on the other side of the station, nearest the road. They scrambled to pick up their cases, George grumbling, "Why didn't the stationmaster tell us the bus'd be out on the road?"

Bill grabbed his case and Meg's and took off running to be sure the driver knew they were there. Meg was at his heels, but stopped, turned back, took her father's arm, and walked around the station, across the graveled parking lot over to the coach waiting out on the road.

To be sure, she looked up at the destination on the front of the bus and breathed the words, "Bridget. Mom? Here I come." Meg wasn't sure at all what she would call the woman she was about to meet.

MEG SAW THEM AS THE BUS PULLED UP TO ITS STOP AT the Harbour Square in Kirkcudbright Town—she saw Bridget, and a woman at her side who must be Sophie, standing next to a bright blue car.

Time stopped for an instant, freezing everyone in place: Meg stared out the window; George sat, his hand on her shoulder; Bill watched. Bridget began walking toward the bus, leaving Sophie at their car. Sophie, who'd said to Bridget, "Go on."

As Bridget approached, Meg looked out the bus window into a face, a smile she remembered—Aunt Bridget urging

Milree Latimer

the seven-year-old girl beside her on the bed, "Let's hear your story, Meg."

Twenty-four years ago.

George moved aside, letting Meg stand and walk to the front of the bus. Bill began to rise from his seat, but George shook his head and said quietly, "Not yet, let her go herself."

Bridget stood at the bottom of the bus stairs looking up at Meg as she alighted, one step taken, the next step taken, till she stood on the gravel road. Both women stood as though caught in time—letting the years drop away. Bridget asked with a smile, "Did you finish that story you told us all those years ago?"

"I just did, right now, this very moment." Something caught in Bridget's throat when Meg smiled in return—a relief and a recognition.

Meg's smile was Peter's.

Gradually, like characters taking their places in the story of Meg and Bridget, Sophie, George, and Bill moved in and around the two women who stood, hands clasped, until Bridget opened her arms and gathered her daughter in.

Chapter Thirty-Eight

LIFE BECAME DISCOVERING THE DETAILS THAT CONNECTED mother to daughter, daughter to mother. When Meg turned up her nose at broccoli, Bridget laughed. "See Sophie," she said, turning to her friend, "I told you; normal people don't eat broccoli."

George and Bill, there at the table, cheered Bridget on. Sophie threw up her hands in mock despair. "I've been outvoted, by the whole Blackwell family!"

Three days, story after story after story unfolding. Night after night. One question in particular needed asking, a question George needed answered. On the third morning he and Bridget met early to walk by the river Dee. To be together just brother and sister once again.

It was there, standing by the bank of the river, that he asked the question.

"Why did you never write or even send me a telegram to tell me where you were?"

Bridget, head down at first, turned and faced George. "I didn't want him to go after you, to find me. Because he will and he has."

"But he didn't, I never saw him again," George protested.

Bridget shook her head side to side. "Oh, George. Don't ask me how I know this, I'm sure he had his goons going through your mail, listening in on your phone calls. Sophie knows all about him, and now Bill does. He's a hell of a detective. I thank my daughter for him." She looked up at him, a fierceness brightening her eyes. "Have you forgotten your so-called car accident?"

George, startled at the momentary fervor in her tone, stepped back and looked at his sister with new eyes. "Oh my God, you were protecting me from him. You thought he would use me to get to you." He ran his fingers through his hair, dropped his head, and sighed. "And who was protecting you?" Bridget folded her hands under her chin and looked up at George. "Throughout all of it, I was sheltered. Sheltered by women who would not be daunted by his ruthlessness. And when I left that house, I saved my own life, just as you saved yours, George, when you left. It took me a while, but I followed your lead." George, at a loss for words, stood and gazed out over the river—the ancient and sturdy stone Tongland Bridge distant in his view. Bridget first to punctuate the moment, linked her arm through George's and pointed to the bridge. "Kind of like us, George. Sturdy, strong, and stubborn."

THROUGHOUT THEIR TIME TOGETHER, MEG AND BRIDGET sat on the front porch of the cottage where Sophie and Bridget had lived since arriving in Scotland in 1940; they sat and wove their lives, tapestry-like, for one another. Bridget and Meg walked often during those days, strolling through the village from one end to the other, wandering through the graveyard among the ruins of the Old Abbey. George, Bill, and Sophie drifted alongside, listening to them tell their stories. No one chose to ask questions, not wanting to interrupt the two women who were fashioning their lives there, on the spot, filling in unrealized memories.

Meg's ear for story was captured by Bridget, who told about her days creating shell fuses at the munitions factory run and staffed by women. Every so often the three, eavesdropping, heard Meg exclaim, "My mother was ahead of her time!"

Bridget, too, weaving the strands of life: "There were many of us, just ask Sophie. Oh, Meg, I wish you'd been able to meet my friends—Irene from Ireland. Suzanne, my friend from Paris." As Sophie listened to Bridget's telling, she heard the sad notes creep into her voice. Bridget had lost both friends. Irene, who'd gone back to Ireland in the 1930s, was wounded when the Germans bombed the South Circular Road area of Dublin in 1940. She'd died from complications a year later.

"It didn't help at all that the Germans said it was a navigational error," Bridget told Meg, who quietly took her mother's hand as they strolled out from the Old Abbey ruins.

"But then, what happened to Suzanne?" she asked. Sophie inhaled and held a breath, waiting to hear what Bridget might say about her friend.

"What I'm about to tell you, Meg, I only know because Suzanne's sister contacted me after the war." Bridget had faltered for a moment. When she spoke again, her voice was fogged in sadness, as though she'd received the news in only the last moments. "Suzanne was captured by the SS and executed in early 1944 before Paris was liberated. She was helping Allied pilots who'd been shot down, escape." As Bridget walked through the graveyard, she seemed to lose herself in the memories of her friends, sadness clouding her eyes. No one spoke.

It was Meg who murmured, "Such sadness."

Taking her mother's hand, the two women walked together in shared silence, until Bridget stopped, turned to Meg with a smile, and said: "Meg. Sadness lives in company with loving. Look at us."

Bridget's stories and Meg's desire to hear them could have paused there, but as though turning a page in her book of memories, she'd added: "Suzanne brought joy and gave place for my creative spirit to unfold. She brought me to Shakespeare and Company in Paris. Irene gave me heart when I needed courage to decide what to do next or where to go."

And, with an artful glance over at her brother, she continued, "I went with her blessing, and Sophie's, to your Uncle George, your dad's farm." She added in a whisper: "I gave birth to you there, on the farm. It was an extraordinary moment, wasn't it, George?"

Bridget turned again to look back at her brother, who grinned. "I don't remember, Bridge, I was out in the barn sitting on a bale of hay." This was the moment when Meg turned to Bridget, her face begging for the answer. "But who was my...?"

"It's beginning to get dark. I think we need to make our way back to the cottage, don't you, Sophie?" said Bridget, already walking toward the entrance.

As if on cue, Sophie stepped up beside Meg. "Let's you and I go on ahead, get tea ready for everyone, give George time with his sister, and Bill, too."

A gentle quiet descended over the Abbey ruins. Meg wondered if she'd said something to upset her mother but agreed with a mute nod and walked out onto the road with Sophie. George and Bill caught up with Bridget as she headed down the road away from the cottage.

"Did I say something? Do something?" Meg asked as she and Sophie made their way.

"Not at all, Meg, not at all. I think your mom needs some time to collect herself. It's been an intense time…for both of you. There's more to tell. Maybe she's taking a breath… before she sets off down that road."

Later that evening, peat briquettes glowing in the fireplace lent a warmth to the room where George lay across the chesterfield with ankles crossed and hands folded on his stomach. He looked like a man ready to doze, but he was watching Meg, who sat folded into the leather wing chair by the fire. She in turn sipped her scotch and waited. The two of them seemed to be holding a place that had been left in pause that afternoon out by the Abbey. No one had chosen to return to the earlier conversation. Sophie had busied, with Meg's help, to prepare the steak pie and potatoes for supper, while Bridget had excused herself for a short nap after returning with Bill and George.

Bridget came into the room after supper, pulled up her rocking chair, and sat down beside Meg. Everyone—Bill, Sophie, George, and Meg—waited.

To the surprise of all, Bridget grinned. "Meg, have I told you the story about meeting James Joyce?" The air lightened, for each knew that Bridget wanted to tell the rest of her life's tale on her own terms, in her own way. Her story of Meg's father, Peter, and her escape from her stepfather, would emerge in her timing and on her terms.

Thus, Bridget began, buoyed by their expectant faces. Clara Nicholson's storytelling daughter regaled them all with her experiences at Shakespeare and Company, working and living among authors, names that Meg delighted in hearing: Ernest Hemingway, T.S. Eliot, F. Scott Fitzgerald. She had read those authors, taught their poems and novels to her senior English classes. For Meg, though, as her mother recounted her writing days upstairs at 12 Rue de l'Odeon, the pièce de résistance, was her story of meeting James Joyce.

"You met James Joyce! Good God, Bridget. What was he like? James Joyce! *Ulysses*! I taught…"

A low rumbling laugh rolled across the room, where George, now sitting up, grinned. "Don't let Bridget get started. She's going to be quoting James Joyce and *Ulysses* soon."

"Dad! Don't tease. Let her tell her story."

"Not to worry, Meg. George can be a terrible tease, but then you've known that all your life, haven't you, Meg?"

"Don't we all know that," Meg smiled. The moment gave space and certainty to Meg that her dad, her Uncle George, was there as she rethreaded the truths of her life.

And Bridget, feeling her connections with Meg strengthen, experienced the soundness of George's care for her. At that moment, she saw and felt George and Sophie's gentle blessing: time to tell Meg about her father, Peter Radcliffe. And time to tell her own story of leaving her girl all those years ago.

The earthy scent of the turf fire lent a welcoming air of peace and warmth, lulling each into a quiet moment of reflection about some other place, some other time. Years ago.

George, eyes fluttering with the need to close, stood, walked to Meg, and kissed her on the cheek. "It's this old man's bedtime."

When he turned to Bridget, she placed her hand on his cheek. "You will never be an old man. You'll always be my big brother."

George, clearing his throat, straightened his shoulders and moved through the room out to the hallway where he paused and, without turning back, waved his hand in the air. "Good night, all. Meg, my girl, soon time to climb that wooden hill." It was then his voice cracked, and he disappeared up the stairs to the loft bedroom.

Meg looked to Bridget. They knew.

That had been George's way of announcing bedtime when his sister had been only a girl herself and he'd felt a need to be fatherlike for her. Now, he'd carried the tradition on with Meg.

As though George had given the word, Sophie and Bill stood from their chairs, and, with little ceremony and quiet good nights, they left. Sophie went to her room overlooking the garden, Bill to a small room off the kitchen. Only Bridget and Meg remained, neither making any move to leave.

Like the storyteller she was, Bridget sat back in her chair and stared into the fire for a moment, looking as though she might be forming words from the few ashes still glowing.

Meg waited, wanting to give spaciousness to Bridget, a clear landscape for the telling.

She had mined the pain of being left by her birth mother. A new story awaited.

George had decided not to speak of Jack and his anger as Meg grew up, but he'd needed her to know always that her mother, Bridget, had wanted to keep her far from harm's way. From Jack's villainy. And so, she'd left her where she'd be safe.

She left her with George and Edna.

Now, as the evening waned, the time had arrived. Bridget lifted her eyes from the ashes and turning her gaze onto her daughter told the story of her long journey back to her daughter and the wonder of Peter, the father whose life lay within Meg.

Two days later, George and Bill, packed and ready to leave for home, stood by the gate, ready for Sophie to take them back to the station.

Meg had chosen to stay another two weeks. "Bridget and I are going over to France. We're going to find my father's grave." Wondering how George might be, Meg took his hand. "We need to do this. Mom needs to go, and I need to go with her." Meg paused. "That's the first time I've called Bridget 'Mom.'"

George smiled. "This is exactly where you need to be. Then you'll be family. A complete family."

Today, goodbyes hung in the air.

Bill was standing off by himself. He'd been acting strangely since early morning when he'd left the house saying he was taking a last walk in the village.

"Bill, come say goodbye to Meg, you'll not see her for a while," George called over to him. Coming down the graveled path, Bill reached into his jacket pocket and pulled out what looked like a telegram. George's reaction spoke fear. "Is Edna all right?"

"Edna's fine, Harry's fine. That call I had last night. It was from the telegraph office. They wanted to deliver this message and I asked to go and fetch it myself."

Bridget stepped down from the porch and walked to the gate. "Bill, what is it?"

Sophie, who'd brought the car around, stood with her. Looking to Bridget in particular, he told them: "Jack has had a stroke, a serious stroke. He died yesterday."

Something in their collective worlds had been upended. They realized—the silent undercurrent of fear that had pervaded their lives was now gone. No one spoke.

Bridget waited a few moments, letting the news penetrate. Looking off into the distance, she asked, "Where was he when he died?" Bill, George, and Meg looked over at her, wondering, but Sophie knew what she was asking: Did he die alone? Bill knew this moment would require clear and final details, so he'd called his partner to check out Jack's death.

"His housekeeper found him in the hallway outside his bedroom. Looks like he was trying to get to the stairs but collapsed at the top. She wasn't sure how long he'd been there."

Sophie, Bridget, and George seemed to take a simultaneous breath. A collective sigh.

George turned to Bridget, who stood, arms folded, face impassive. He reached for her hand. "Now we are a family again," he said. Sophie closed her eyes and felt the air around them lighten.

Meg finally spoke. "It's over. He's gone. The story is finished. He no longer matters. He never was."

Meg, who'd never known the man, had shut the final door on his memory.

Chapter Thirty-Nine

SOPHIE STOOD BY THE IRON GATE OF THE CEMETERY AND watched as Bridget and Meg walked across the grass among the three rows of headstones. A circular wall built of rubble surrounded the tended graves. Each headstone told the story of the soldier who had fallen.

They walked separate from one another, heads down, looking, searching, until Bridget called out and beckoned: "Here he is, Meg. Here he is."

It took a moment for Meg. Taking a long breath, she walked over to her mother and stood by her. There, she bent down and placed flowers on Peter's grave, daisies she'd bought from the flower lady in the village nearby.

Neither of them spoke, giving breathing space to Bridget's memories of those three days, memories that felt like gossamer. Meg let the silence be a canvas for imagining this man who'd given her life, and that Peter smile.

Private Peter Radcliffe
Canadian Expeditionary Force Service 81179
Canadian Expeditionary Force Private, Infantry.
Born 1892
Died 1918
Remember me.

Sophie left her post at the gate and walked toward the

two women who stood, still and quiet, shoulder touching shoulder. Bridget was the first to move. She reached into her leather bag and brought out a small paper. Sophie saw Bridget smile as she turned to Meg and handed the paper to her daughter. "Here," she said. "I want you to have this. He'd want you to have this."

Sophie went to Bridget and placed a gentle hand on her back. She knew what the paper was. It was the poem that Peter had written for Bridget while he sat waiting for her there at Warren Hall. A poem about remembrance, a poem about hope. A poem about returning.

The circle was complete.

Home beckoned.

"Did you pack the brooch, Meg? I want to be sure you have it; you know it was your grandmother's." Bridget fussed, straightening Meg's collar.

"Mom, don't worry. I have the brooch, and I have your letter for Edna and George…and sweaters for everybody."

Bridget knew she was stretching out the moments until Meg would board the ship and sail away, back home to Canada. After their trip to France, they'd now arrived at yet another parting for the two of them—yet this one was different. Meg, going back to Canada, was returning to her life, to her new school, and to her family. She'd return, no longer feeling old restlessness, but instead holding a sense of belonging.

Bridget was returning to her village in Scotland, a place that had welcomed her in, not once but twice, a place where she'd become the pride of the village, their own local author.

Sophie, too, knew it was time for her to return home, back to Canada, return to her painting, return with a peaceful heart. She had kept her promise to Clara.

They had sought shelter, and found it, in each other.

Epilogue

1950

FORTY-EIGHT YEARS AGO, SOPHIE HAD STOOD IN CLARA Blackwell's studio, her face alight with the anticipation of introducing her friend to the art world. "A room in an art gallery, that's what I've arranged, Clara. Your own room where you'll show your paintings."

And, at the moment when everything had been arranged, paintings wrapped and ready to be transported, the dream died. There would be no showing, and there would never be another. Till now. Dreams can be resurrected.

On this day, forty-eight years later, Clara Blackwell's paintings graced the walls of a room in the Toronto Gallery: portraits and landscapes she'd created in her halcyon days, times when life held promises for her, a talented artist whose inspired energy generated beauty. Even though she'd been gone these many years, her spirit bathed the room in translucent colors, shining through the nuances of nature and the faces of her children.

Bridget stood alone in the middle of the room. She'd had one request of Meg when they'd arrived at the gallery that evening.

"Before anyone else comes, I want to be in here, myself. Do you mind?" So, there she stood, turning slowly, taking in each painting, and feeling the presence of her mother. Lost in the moment, she hadn't heard the footsteps approaching.

Then a familiar voice spoke close to her ear. "She was pretty extraordinary, wasn't she?" George whispered from behind her. A hand slipped into hers. Meg had come into the room with him and stood by her shoulder.

The quiet the three of them shared for those moments was broken by voices in the hallway outside the gallery room. One voice was familiar to each of them. Sophie.

"Thank you, Eric, for helping me to make this showing happen. I appreciate everything you've done. Your dad would be proud of you, following in his footsteps."

"Anything for you, Miss Watson, I know that Dad thought the world of you when you were his arts editor. I'll leave you to your friends now. Let me know if you need anything else from me."

Meg moved away from Bridget and George to greet Sophie at the entrance to the gallery room. She smiled as she watched Sophie come toward her, cane tapping on the floor, eyes shining. Meg wasn't sure whether they shone with brimming tears or sheer delight. Possibly both.

Giving Sophie a moment to breathe a long sigh, Meg reached for her hand. "You are remarkable. We've always known you have special talents, and now you've outdone yourself. How did you do this? How did you bring Gran's paintings back into the world?"

A voice spoke just behind Meg. Bridget had followed her to greet Sophie. Throwing her arms around her, Bridget buried her face in Sophie's shoulder. It had been almost three years since last being together. At the cemetery in France.

Bridget grasped Sophie's hand. "I think I know exactly how." When she turned toward Meg, George was standing there. Bridget laughed. "Now that we're all here, let me tell you the magic this lady can perform. She may be old, but she's not finished making miracles. Right, Sophie?

"Oh, but I had help." Sophie looked to Meg. "You have a very versatile and well-connected friend in Bill. And, by the way, where is he today?"

"He's on his way. He's got a case he must finish, but he'll be here. Said he wouldn't miss today for the world." Meg paused and bent her head to the side. "Are you saying he made this happen?"

Sophie smiled. "Your well-connected Detective Inspector Bill was the mastermind—let's say we colluded. I devised a plan; he made it work. So, miracles? Maybe. Finding the paintings, using his detective skills, that was Bill. Remember, he knows people, important people, everywhere. When I asked him last year if he'd help me create this miracle, this showing, he gathered all his ingenuity and all his contacts."

Meg was first to say it. "Did he search out what happened to the contents in Jack's house?"

Sophie's face lit into a mischievous grin. "Oh, and didn't he." Without a doubt she had the attention of everyone— George, Meg, Bridget, and four women who'd come into the gallery room, now gazing at Clara's paintings.

"Bill called in his best contacts, right to the lawyers who handled the sale of the house and disposal of the furnishing and fixtures. Jack had a will. Everything went back into the company. He'd left the lawyers to sell the furnishings, and that's where Bill entered the picture. In company with me, and a letter I had that Clara had signed all those years ago, her artwork became the property of her children. Bridget and George. I knew without a doubt that Jack would create a major legal battle, so the letter remained with me until the time arrived I could legally, with Bill's help, go into the house and gather them up. And we did, Bill and I."

Sophie smiled and looked around to Meg. "I didn't work miracles. I just did what Clara asked. I sheltered her family, with the assistance of one Detective Inspector William McBride. Clara was the miracle worker. She passed on the beauty she saw in the world and gave it to your mother, whose stories embody the grace of Clara's art. And now you, Meg, carry her spirit, and every young woman and man who walks into your classroom will experience her."

Bridget and George stood silently enfolded by Clara's peaceful spirit. Meg looked over at her mother and smiled. Bridget saw Peter's smile.

Their journey home was complete.

Acknowledgments

MY GOOD FORTUNE THROUGHOUT THE LAST TEN YEARS has been to live in the countryside of Central Oregon, where the Cascade Mountains, the valley of trees below my window, and the foothills in the distance have congregated to inspire me to tell my stories. I am grateful for this world of nature that is inextricably linked with my creative spirit.

I'm grateful to the urging of those who've encouraged me as I set out to tell this story of a generation of women who steadfastly and creatively lived their lives, trusting themselves and one another.

MY GRATITUDE:
To Barb Morris, wordsmith and keen-eyed editor, with whom I discovered this story's deeper centers; I was grateful every week, if not every day, for her editorial insights, her care, and her attention to making the story better. And her wit.

To Jaclyn Desforges, poet, novelist, and writing coach, who gave meaning to the words "creative advocate"—constancy is her middle name. She inspired me to push through to the unfamiliar, cheering me on with a trail of emails and zoom calls.

To Patricia Marshall and her remarkable team at Luminare Press, thank you for encouraging me on and for creating a book that shines.

To friends, who listened to pieces of a story not yet formed. When my own sense of where the characters were taking me wavered, they stayed the course as it unfolded. Thank you.

To Elizabeth McAuliffe, who's been telling me to write my stories since we started creating our own at that supper together in State College, Pennsylvania.

To Catherine Comuzzi, for bringing her wisdom to me throughout all those Saturday Zooms, and awakening insights as we shared our writer's paths.

To Genie McBurnett, for her encouragement over numerous cups of coffee and toast with cream cheese—feeding my body and my writer's soul.

To Annie Peace, who creates her stories out of her heart, lives thousands of miles away, and whose presence lights my life—my everyday life, and my writer's life

To Jennifer Baker, retired librarian, who inexplicably landed within my scope of vision, offering her extraordinary sense of storying, and convincing me that all of us, all of us, have stories worth telling.

And there are those who come into our lives unaware of the ever-reverberating echoes of their impact.

To Nolina, met by chance at a Pacific Northwest Writers' conference, thank you for following my path to story with such care and attention. I love your emails, the expected and the unexpected.

To Kathy Bowser, retired police lieutenant, who sat over coffee and gave me insights into what a cold case might look like. Amazing connections can grace the writer—Kathy is president of our Garden Club.

To Sue Campbell of Pages and Platforms, who has helped and continues to help me beyond measure to take my stories out into the reading world.

To my families. Here in Oregon: Tom; Bob, Jen, and Carter; John, Jenna, Claire, and Olivia. In Kingston, Ontario: Heather and Michael, Tyler and Graham. In Clarksburg,

Ontario: Kath, Bryan, and Theo. In Westport, Ontario: Phil and Julie, Trevor and Nikk. In Atlanta, Georgia: Janice, Steve; Alex in London; and Jack in Rhode Island. Thank you for encouraging the writer who lives in me.

To Jerry. You are my ever-present, ever-constant muse. You are the reason I gave my creative spirit wings—you brought me here to this place, Central Oregon.

And, yes, you are a very lovely man.

To those readers who have time and again said "you wrote a story about me"…thank you.

Author's notes

THE SHELTER OF EACH OTHER WAS INSPIRED BY A FRAMED picture of my grandmother that sits on the corner of the desk where I write.

This photo hung on the living room wall in the house where I lived as a child. I remember feeling a childlike unease when I'd gaze at the picture. I have only faint memories of Gran because she died when I was four years old.

The path back to her began with an exploration into my family history. I wanted to know about the stories that brought me to where I am, life stories that remind me of disappointments, lessons learned, joys of overcoming hardships. I discovered a woman, my grandmother, who lived, breathed, and, in ways I'm beginning to know, left a legacy of herself within me.

From the moment I put pen to paper (fingers on the keys), I wrote from an image I created as I thought about, read about, and remembered my grandmother—an image that gradually became Bridget Blackwell. Bridget soon stepped into her own skin and set out upon her life adventures. In the historical context of Bridget's life, I gave her real time and real places.

One of those places was Shakespeare and Company bookstore and lending library, originally opened by Sylvia Beach at 8 Rue Dupuytren and later moved to 12 Rue l'Odeon, an actual bookstore and lending library in Paris, she owned and ran from 1919 till 1941. Bridget Blackwell is a fictionalized character living and working in this bookstore. If you'd like to know more about that famous bookstore, I recommend Sylvia Beach's story. (Beach, Sylvia. 1991. *Shakespeare and Company*. Lincoln: University of Nebraska Press.)

In the same manner, using the freedom of fiction, I created a setting based on a munitions factory in a small southwest Scottish village, Tongland. This factory was created for and staffed by women in the middle and later years of the Great War 1914–1918.

The Shelter of Each Other gradually became the story of three generations of women who, in the course of their lives, carried their creative spirit forward, one to the other. In the context of life's adventures and with resourcefulness, they sheltered their intergenerational spirit.

Any mistakes or misrepresentations of historical places or eras are mine as the storyteller.